This book is dedicated to my friends,
particularly Angela and Jackie whose patience knows
no bounds.
And to my family who spurred me on to keep writing
with love and encouragement.
With special thanks to Detective Sergeant Sarah
Mackett (Rtd) whose in depth knowledge of the process
in investigating a murder on board ship has been
invaluable.
Finally, to my beloved Charles Harris for his technical
expertise and design.

Who's the Dummy Now!

Who's the Dummy Now!

Melanie Harris

Who's the Dummy Now!

PROLOGUE

Only the reading light in the stateroom was switched on. The balcony door was open, the wind gently moving the curtains. Cynthia liked to feel the cool breeze caressing her as she drifted off to sleep – it was so much nicer than the annoying hum of air conditioning.

The ship was making steady progress, cutting through the water at about twelve knots with hardly a sound. She knew this from the daily newsletter that was left on her bed.

Leaning over the balcony, she breathed in the fragrant air. Miles away in the distance she could see the twinkling lights of another cruise ship; otherwise it seemed the sea was just an expanse of nothingness.

She mulled over the day's events, taking delight in the knowledge that she was irritating everyone with her sparkling personality. They were just jealous, pure unadulterated envy. Her forte was bringing light, laughter and glamour to the party and if she saw a chance to 'catch a big fish' - even if he belonged to someone else, she grasped it with both hands.

Another of her attributes was holding on to her man of the moment. She worked very hard to capture his heart to ensure that he was mesmerised by her. A feat in itself, especially when there was so much temptation out there for him to stray. Why couldn't other women do the same? Naturally, her few close women friends were very precious to her, but one couldn't beat the admiration and company of a lover. It was the best feeling in the world.

She booked the cruise on this beautiful ship without a moment's hesitation and, once on board, felt an integral part of a warm group. She wouldn't tell them how much she enjoyed being bang in the middle of the goings-on in the Club. There was no doubt in her mind that their holiday experience would be enhanced by her company.

John had reluctantly gone to his room after his second nightcap and a quick fondle earlier in the evening. He was an ardent lover with great stamina and she had no intention of giving him up any time soon, but she knew she couldn't go on forever, flitting from one lover to another.

She felt lucky to have been married to the man of her dreams for so many years. He wouldn't fault her, despite her transgressions. She pondered on how much easier it would have been if her husband had died earlier when she was a few years younger, or later when the time for love had passed. Not that she wanted to be without him - she missed him terribly. A replacement must be found quickly while she could still pick the best of the bunch. He wanted her to be happy, not lonely.

The persistent knocking on the door disturbed Cynthia's thoughts. Perhaps John had left something behind or it was just another attempt to persuade her to allow him to stay the night. She came in from the balcony, sliding the patio door closed behind her to stop the through draft. Taking several long strides, she threw open the stateroom door. Upon seeing the person standing there she raised her eyebrows in surprise but smiled warmly anyway.

"Hello! What a surprise. I had no idea you were on the ship. Come on in. I didn't imagine for one moment that I would receive a late-night visitor making house calls." Cynthia laughed, standing aside to allow entry through the narrow doorway.

The familiar figure wearing a peaked sports cap walked into the room. "I couldn't sleep and thought I would pop by to say hello and bring us two glasses of champagne. Everyone else seems to have already turned in - the ship is deserted. I knew a night owl like *you* would still be up."

"I heard you don't drink champagne and prefer to drink wine or cocktails?" Cynthia said, noticing her visitor seemed overly friendly. She thought that was rather strange in view of the circumstances.

The visitor ignored the remark. "It has been an eventful day and I thought a couple of glasses of bubbly would be a fitting end to it."

"Indeed! We've all had an eventful day; except I've drunk quite a lot already. Come and sit down." Cynthia couldn't take her eyes off the incongruous outfit.

Her visitor looked a complete mess. Who wears a sports cap and baggy, unattractive clothes as evening attire? Someone should definitely have a word about it. Cynthia's mantra had always been that a person should make every effort to look good, particularly on a luxury cruise, for goodness' sake! It doesn't matter who you are or your financial circumstances - you have to look your very best!

The visitor noticed Cynthia's ill-concealed disgust and raised their glass "Shapeless is comforting – Cheers!"

Cynthia took a good gulp of champagne; she didn't notice her guest abstain.

"This is delicious. It must be the good stuff." Cynthia squinted to try and look at the label on the bottle. "I have to admit, I did get a bit upset today listening to my friend talking about my reputation as a man-eater. Imagine that! If it makes her happy to exaggerate, so be it – you see, she's not attractive to the opposite sex at all and I suppose deep down that must bother her. Did you hear about it?" Cynthia didn't wait for an answer. "Awful, isn't it and it's really not true - you know that don't you?" Cynthia was getting angry again just thinking about it.

The visitor looked at her for some time before

answering. "Isn't it?"

Cynthia was startled at that comment, decided it was a joke in rather poor taste and chuckled. "You know it isn't."

"Now how would I know that? Oh who cares, have some more champagne. I can't take it back. It will look awful rolling around the corridor carrying a half-empty bottle of champagne." The visitor topped up Cynthia's glass and hoped it wouldn't be too long before the crushed diazepam would take effect.

Cynthia was beginning to feel a little woozy and giggly. "No, it won't, it will look like you're having a bit of fun and I'm all for that, as you well know."

"I certainly do. Everyone thinks you're very good company, Cynthia. It's hardly surprising you're so popular. I'm sure the cruise would be terribly boring without you on it."

"I know", Cynthia said sleepily. "I wish I could say the same about you - only joking darling," she threw back her head and laughed. "Have you introduced yourself to everyone? Nice bunch aren't they! Some need a bit of a kick-start, but they come to life eventually."

The face was swimming in front of her. It looked evil, malevolent and very large. She shrugged the silly thought away. It must be the drink.

"Oh dear, I'm afraid I'm falling asleep." Cynthia lay down on the bed propped up by two plump cushions. "We'll have a bit of a chat and then would you mind letting yourself out? I don't think I can stand up."

The visitor waited a good few minutes until Cynthia started to snore softly before beginning to search the dressing table for a mobile phone, security key card and passport, finding all three with relative ease. They might come in handy. What a bonus! It just proved that Cynthia was an airhead and careless not to lock her things away in the safe. After all, one never knows who might come knocking and steal things in the dead of night.

The visitor tried to lift Cynthia off the bed. "We'll just walk across the corridor. Will you keep me company?"

"Where are we going? I want to sleep, I'm so tired and it's been such a busy day." Cynthia was slurring her words.

"We're just going into the laundry room. It's so close - just opposite your room and down a bit. We won't be long. We might see some interesting people along the way." The visitor was holding her up firmly by the arm.

"Really? Have you met anyone noteworthy? Did you leave your laundry there?" Cynthia was very confused.

"Yes, I have. I'll tell you all about it, you'll die laughing. Would you mind helping me retrieve it?" The visitor pushed open the door of the laundry room.

"Can't it wait for tomorrow? Freddy will find it for you, he's so helpful. Does Freddy look after your stateroom, too? How funny..." Cynthia giggled sleepily. "Oh look! Someone has left a wheelchair in the middle of the room. That will surely get in the way of any ironing?"

"What a bit of luck! You sit in it while I look for my laundry. That's right. Sit on that clean towel. Now, it should be hanging up somewhere." The visitor pretended to look around the room.

"I'll just sit down for a minute." The wheelchair was surprisingly comfortable. Cynthia could feel herself drifting off to asleep again.

The plan was coming together nicely. The visitor reached for the industrial iron perched on the counter. It was heavy and attached to the wall by a long cord. The visitor briefly pondered on why a modern ship with everything new and sparkling, didn't have an up to date, light weight steam iron before bringing it crashing down on Cynthia's head, twice, knocking her unconscious.

Wow! What should have been a shockingly traumatic act was surprisingly liberating. The visitor noticed blood already seeping from Cynthia's head wound and there was some spattered on the floor. Alarmed that persisting with this satisfying act whilst watching Cynthia's skull disintegrate would produce a blood bath, the visitor decided that this might not be the way forward.

Pulling the wire from the iron with superhuman strength, the visitor wrapped it around Cynthia's neck, leaned back and pulled. The wheelchair started to move backwards and the brake was quickly applied.

"You are a vile, evil woman." The visitor heard the words escape from between clenched teeth as the cord tightened and held around Cynthia's neck for what seemed an age. The words sounded louder because of the stillness of the night.

This glamorous, vain, self-obsessed woman wasn't looking so pretty now. Who knew that it could be so easy to snuff the life out of such a thorn in the side? A woman who taunted and played with people's feelings. To extinguish the life from this bloody pest and never have to worry about her poison again must be the right thing to do in anyone's book.

The plan to murder Cynthia developed at very short notice and, judging by the quick change of tack, was still in the process of formulation. It wasn't so much pre-meditated as opportunistic. Would that be viewed as mitigating circumstances in court? Probably not.

The visitor was breathless from the exertion and looked around anxiously checking for any signs of blood, noticing with satisfaction that most of it seemed to have been contained within the wheelchair. There was some blood on the floor which, smeared with a towel, looked like a small accident and a clumsy attempt to clean it up. That was the beauty of spilling blood on a ship - everything was unquestioningly cleaned and sanitised until it gleamed.

The iron with its cord was carefully unplugged, broken off from the gizmo that angrily hissed steam and wrapped in a plastic bag. It was concealed under the voluminous outfit, along with some other useful pieces of equipment. There was no sign of the violence that had just taken place. Cynthia was good and dead, there was no doubt about that.

The visitor exchanged the peaked cap for a blonde wig, styled in a similar way Cynthia wore her hair and put it on; making sure all the natural hair was tucked in. Another wig in a mousy brown was placed carefully over Cynthia's head to cover what was now a bloody mess with the sports cap placed on top. The effect was grotesque, and the visitor found that mildly amusing.

Opening the door to the laundry room and looking out, the corridor was still deserted as anticipated. The visitor pushed the wheelchair, with Cynthia holding two freshly ironed shirts on wire hangers hastily grabbed from the rail, towards the lift.

The lift doors opened at recreation level on the twelfth floor. There were a few people milling about, thankfully nobody familiar or curious. The visitor pushed the wheelchair around the deck, chatting gaily to the dead occupant for the benefit of the cameras perched high above and angled facing different sections of the deck. It was amazing how deserted the ship was at this time of night. Most guests were either sitting in the piano and cocktail lounges or having a nightcap on their balcony before turning in.

The wheelchair came to a stop close to the handrail and they both looked out to sea. The visitor pointed to a beautiful clear sky, admiring the twinkling stars that always look particularly lovely far away from dry land. With a little assistance, Cynthia pointed at the stars, too - her lifeless arm falling back down as the wheelchair was hurriedly pushed out of the way of the surveillance camera.

The visitor slowly walked towards the crazy golf pitch. It was unusual for any facility on the recreation deck not to be ready to be used and enjoyed by the guests. The Entertainments Director had given his assurance, over the loud speaker, that crazy golf will be bigger, better and more fun after some minor adjustments were made in a day or two. The announcement came at the same time as the visitor was formulating the plan to dispose of Cynthia's body should it be necessary which, until now, was a bit sketchy.

The section was slightly hidden from the public areas, taking up a large chunk of the deck and was well covered by a huge blanket of green AstroTurf. Under this, no doubt, would be a miniature castle, a mini waterfall, a fake grass mound and the recent addition of a lifeless, self-absorbed, immoral woman.

The visitor had earlier noticed with satisfaction that the security camera was angled to face a different direction, being temporarily employed to monitor another section of the ship.

Continuing the monologue, the visitor chatted away, struggling to lift up an area of the heavy green turf. Time was of the essence.

Tipping the wheelchair over was the hardest part of the plan - prizing a dead weight out of it was next. The visitor made a great show of fussing over Cynthia just in case a rogue monitor should pick up any activity, hugging her lifeless body as if to comfort her after a nasty fall, whilst simultaneously covering it over. To an onlooker, it would appear to be another fake grass mound under AstroTurf, just as it was supposed to.

The visitor quickly gathered up the towels and plastic sheet and made a big pile of it on the seat of the wheelchair, covering it up with Cynthia's dressing gown and tying the belt. Plonking the peaked sports cap on top completed the look and the chair was wheeled back to Cynthia's room. In the dim light, it might - just maybe, look like a person was sitting in it. It was risky, but it couldn't be helped.

The visitor raced down the corridor at great speed, bending over to talk to the mound of towels until the lift doors opened on Cynthia's stateroom floor. The visitor took it as a good omen that nobody was about. Once there, the plastic sheet was rinsed out in the bathroom. All that was left was for the visitor to dispose of the soiled towels and plastic as soon as possible. The steward was summoned and the door was left propped open.

"I'm very sorry to trouble you so late, Freddy"- a soft voice came from the bed in the dark, "but would you mind removing the wheelchair? I ordered it this evening and selfishly left it in the laundry room until it was needed. A friend of mine was feeling a little unsteady on her feet and I pushed her around the ship, but she's feeling much better and now I'm feeling a bit unwell. I'm so sorry about the bloodied towels and paraphernalia. It's very embarrassing - I've had an awful nosebleed."

The voice sounded awful - low and rasping. Not at all like the softly spoken tone the steward had become accustomed to hearing. The poor woman must be very sick. "No problem, Ms Cynthia, I'll take it away and return

9

it. The towels will go straight to the laundry. I hope you feel better tomorrow. Can I get you anything?"

"No thank you, Freddy. It's great to know you're here to look after me."

"Any time, Ms Cynthia." He grabbed hold of the handles and wheeled it swiftly away.

The visitor waited for some time. The blonde wig was removed and stuffed in the carrier bag along with the used champagne glasses and iron. The visitor opened the door wearing the peaked sports cap, making a big show of blowing kisses and saying good night to the guest in the stateroom, for the benefit of the overhead camera and walked slowly down the corridor where the peaked sports cap and voluminous garment was crumpled up and ditched through a door marked 'Staff Only'. Discarded items left in the rubbish all over the ship had a wonderful habit of mysteriously disappearing. After a few minutes, the visitor finally emerged through a different door on a lower floor and retired for a well-earned rest.

———

At 7.30am, *Holland Silhouette* docked at Livorno - located on the western coast of Tuscany on the Ligurian Sea. It is a working port servicing around thirty million tonnes of cargo annually. It conceals a very pretty old town with a smattering of historic buildings including an ancient fortress with an eleventh century medieval tower.

The queue of people waiting to disembark was small at that unearthly hour of the morning. Mainly those desperate to get on terra firma. Only one security officer was employed to check passengers' key cards and photo identification, without which they could not exit or enter the vessel. The ship would be sailing at 6.00pm that evening and everyone was expected to be back on board by that time.

The smiling blonde lady wearing sunglasses and a brightly coloured kaftan, handed over her identification. She was always so friendly, one of the few passengers that had a kind word to say while passing through. Dark glasses were supposed to be removed, but Ms. Cynthia was always so glamorous and the security guard thought that this early in the morning, without a full face of makeup, he might embarrass her by requesting their removal and he didn't want to delay her.

"Thank you, Ms. Cynthia, you have a nice day now."

"Yes, I most certainly will, thank you." The visitor walked down the gangway and into the town heading straight for a nearby café.

Ordering a large cappuccino at the bar, the visitor used the only bathroom available. The visitor looked in the mirror and was startled to see their reflection. This was getting to be rather confusing and becoming a bit of a headache, but not as much of a headache as the one bestowed on poor Cynthia.

The visitor sat down just as the waitress was bringing the coffee. "Yes, that's mine."

"Prego." The waitress giggled; relieved the coffee wouldn't be wasted.

The visitor sat back, admiring the pretty scene all around and sighed with relief, allowing the peace and tranquillity to work its magic.

After drinking the coffee, the visitor walked towards the old fortress and sat down on a little wall high up overlooking the sea, placing the plastic bag containing the heavy steam iron, the bloodied cord tied up into a knot, the champagne glass, Cynthia's mobile phone and passport close to the edge. With any luck, the missing phone and passport will throw a spanner in the works when evidence collecting by the security team and buy some time.

The waves were lapping the old stone wall below and the visitor began to read personal messages and emails on an iPad vibrating frantically. Appearing to be totally absorbed, the contents of the carrier bag were pushed off the wall and into the sea with a well-placed shove of the elbow. What wouldn't be washed clean by the water would most likely be stolen. The visitor stood up and walked closer to the old fortress to take pictures.

After a couple of hours of exploring, lunching, and shopping, the visitor walked the short distance back to the ship. It was a great relief not to have to wait for a crowded tour bus or pay an extortionate taxi fare.

Strolling unhurriedly up the gangway towards the entrance to the ship, the visitor produced the required key card and photo identification, placing two carrier bags containing souvenirs on the conveyor belt for scanning - purchases were screened very carefully and rightly so. The security guard looked satisfied and the visitor proceeded to leave. An alarm notification suddenly rang from his computer.

"Excuse me, may I have another look at your identification please," the security guard called out to the visitor, looking concerned.

The visitor's heart missed a beat and beads of sweat started to appear. "Absolutely! - what's the problem?"

He scanned the identification again, turning it back to front to ensure that it wasn't compromised. "No problem, Ms Cynthia. The computer can be very sensitive."

The visitor entered the Gentleman's Cloakroom, deposited the blonde wig in the dustbin, making sure it was covered up with paper hand towels, removed the kaftan, put on the last of the fake hairpieces and emerged, casually walking in the direction of the lift.

CHAPTER ONE

Miranda Soames wanted everything to stop, just for a moment, to reflect on her achievements. They had been hard-fought. The pressure of work and the constant stress of always having to 'get it right' was pulling her down. She had been feeling this way, it seemed, forever and it didn't look like things were going to change any time soon.

She closed her eyes and tried hard to remember the sequence of events.

School expected great things of her. Sometimes greater than she felt it was possible to give. Nevertheless, her grades were just about high enough not to have to throw her school reports, torn into shreds, into the large bins outside the school gates, together with the beautifully calligraphed copies belonging to so many of her friends.

Her applications to universities had to be checked and double checked as if her entire life depended on the result. Actually, that was part of the problem – her entire life *did* depend on it.

She had applied to many of the top Public Relations and Advertising Companies for hard to come by internships. Her particularly interest focused on those willing to employ a department of ill-prepared, fresh-faced graduates with little or no idea of what the real world expects of them.

How does one person stand out from another candidate also answering timed questions in a video interview? Sitting in their bedroom at home, top half dressed to impress and bottom for lounging around, trying to look groomed and confident. She didn't know the answer, but whatever it was, she succeeded.

She was now sitting at her desk on the twenty-third floor of an amazing building, its glass construction twinkling in the morning sun, looking at the marvellous view of London without noticing the slightly grubby window. She never tired of the scene laid out before her which changed hue according to the unpredictable weather.

She felt fortunate that she had occupied this quiet corner of the office for some time. The cherry on the cake would be to hear a kind word, a bit of praise, a modicum of encouragement such as "well done, Miranda - you've proved to be a real asset to the company." Not that she toiled only for that, but it would have been appreciated. There couldn't be any doubt that her clients were spending large sums of money just on her say-so.

She continued to stare out of the window. Perhaps the time was right to cut down the hours she was working, maybe to the length of a normal working day, so she could have a life outside of the office. She was always the last to leave and her commitment was being taken for granted. Was it unreasonable to have reached that stage so soon in her career?

She couldn't think straight. She could see a large number of client files stored on the computer, clients whose demands changed by the minute depending on so many factors, most of which were beyond her control and she felt overwhelmed.

She wanted, more than anything in the world, time to be a good friend, a lovely girlfriend and proficient at something else other than her work. Her conversation was boring the pants off even her. Her mind was wandering and as it was still only mid-morning, this was definitely not a good sign.

———

...The vision of the woman wearing a slinky black Givenchy dress was vivid; one could almost smell the

bergamot in her perfume. Her black Louboutin evening shoes exposing their trademark red soles with every step.

Her long red hair, cascading in curls down her back, complimented a black fur stole casually draped around her milky white shoulders. Her makeup was heavily applied to conceal the deep furrows of a worried frown.

Waiters carrying silver trays heavily laden with cocktails and whisky tumblers criss-crossed the room. Chandeliers twinkled above; the woman noticed the odd bulb here and there had blown, giving the impression of sad neglect. She frowned, thinking they should have been changed before the evening guests arrived.

She had been sitting at the gaming table all evening, hypnotically focussing on the clicking sound of the playing cards being shuffled and dealt. Her casino tokens on the right, stacked and colour coded – a cocktail on the left, regularly topped up. The game had not gone well, Lady Luck was not on her side and the stack of playing chips had diminished.

Oblivious to everything around her, the windowless room bathed in a soft yellow glow of artificial lighting contributed to her feeling of timelessness. She got up from the table, tipped the croupier generously and cashed in her few remaining chips. Outside, she squinted in the dawn light and breathed the early morning fragrance.

She tripped down the steps and grabbed the hand rail just in time to steady herself but dropping her jewelled evening bag on the floor in the process. The contents spilled out and spread across the highly polished granite. The doorman fast approached and helped her to gather it all up.

"Good night madam. Can I call you a taxi to take you home?" The only expression on his face was concern.

"No thank you, the walk will do me good." The look on

her face was embarrassment.

"Very good madam, see you tomorrow..."

Miranda shuddered at the thought. What a horrible image of herself! That would never happen, *could* never happen, but it does to some people.

Her imagination was running riot for no good reason. It surely wouldn't come to that after all, a game of bridge was not usually associated with the slippery descent into gambling addiction - it was more to avoid the 'slipper' descent into dementia, so ancient were most of the players who favour the game or so she thought.

Henry had assured her on many occasions that her view of the game was outdated. No longer was it the game of the blue rinse brigade, the elderly and the lonely. It was now considered a very millennial past-time.

Were these thoughts just an escape from the reality that was really on her mind? The difficult task of having to make yet another mammoth decision that would affect the rest of her life.

Darling Henry - He was such a lovely, supportive boyfriend. What would she do without him – she would hate to find out. There was no doubt he was her soul mate - so why was she wriggling on the end of the hook? Why was she reluctant to make their relationship permanent? Henry made her feel safe. Was that the problem, she wondered? She couldn't confide in her friends; it sounded too ridiculous. On paper, he was perfect – or as near to it as possible.

Miranda had previously dated the dark and dangerous, the frivolous and irresponsible and the mean and moody. Henry was an easy-going lovely man who didn't mind showing his feelings; he didn't consider it weak and wasn't worried he would be exploited because of it. Henry believed that if they were right for each other it was important to be natural together. He also played a very good game of bridge.

They had drifted together over the drinks table at a party. Most of the wine had already been consumed and all that was left were half filled assorted bottles of alcohol and some jugs of fruit juices.

Henry saw her looking miserably at the motley assortment of drinks and, without hesitation, suggested she try one of his latest cocktail innovations which actually didn't exist but made a very good pick-up line in situations such as this. He busily started pouring the contents of all the bottles into a jug and mixed it up with a clean fork that was nestling in a napkin with a knife and spoon.

"Are you sure you know what you're doing? You do know you have a responsibility to make the recipient of your cocktail immediately feel upbeat and in the party mood."

"Absolutely. I consider it my duty. This cocktail is called 'fall into my arms.' I haven't had much success with it, but I live in hope. Is it working?"

She smiled up at him, liking him immediately. "Not yet, but it's got potential."

There followed a whirl of romantic dinners, beautiful music and numerous visits to museums and galleries and it wasn't long before Miranda found it difficult to imagine her life without him.

She decided it was time to look for a hobby outside of her usual interests. An amusing diversion. She was open-minded as long as it didn't involve getting hot and sweaty, spending a fortune on lycra with the ever present 'run faster' stripe running up the side of both legs, or requiring back and joint surgery.

Her job in advertising involved spending most of her

time thinking of clever things to say and do for her clients.
- sometimes sociable, but always stressful. She really
needed to find an outlet that was completely different. A
nice, quiet, competitive game of contract bridge was just
what she needed to take her mind off making any
important personal decisions.

"If you ask me, I'd say you were worrying over
nothing."

"I haven't told you what it is yet." Miranda looked over
at her colleague, Jane, sitting behind the desk opposite
hers frantically searching through her drawers for a fresh
piece of chewing gum.

"Why are you shuddering? It's June, for goodness'
sake. Has someone walked over your grave? You don't
happen to have anything to chew, do you?"

"Only my nails. I have just had the most horrible image
briefly occupy my thoughts. It was too ridiculous to
repeat."

"I assume – no - I know you're going to tell me, so just
spit it out." Jane couldn't really give a fig about the
feelings of another person apart from herself, but she
liked to sound concerned. Most people believed it was
genuine.

"Do you think I have an addictive personality? I mean,
if I learn to play poker just for fun, could I become
addicted and end up losing everything?" Miranda knew
her friend would be honest.

"Let's face it, you haven't got that much to lose. You're
not going to learn to play poker, are you? You would
make a terrible poker player."

"Why would you say that?" Miranda felt she should be
offended by that remark.

"Everything you've been thinking for the last fifteen
minutes has been written all over your face. Is that the

mark of a good poker player?" Jane had been watching Miranda struggling with her demon and lose.

"I was thinking about learning to play bridge, it's the same sort of thing."

"No, Miranda, it's not the same at all." Jane scoffed. "Good looking, glamorous people play poker. They sit in a smoke-filled room, drinking whisky and eyeing up sexy waiters and waitresses. Some spend other people's money. I have been reliably informed that sexy people do not play bridge."

It was giving Jane enormous pleasure to burst Miranda's bubble and she continued in this vein.

"I've never seen a single sequin, cocktail or handsome croupier leave a bridge club, but maybe that's just me being very unobservant. So, if you were playing poker with high-flyers, I would say you were more likely to become addicted, if only to the vodka martinis - shaken not stirred." She was the only one laughing at her joke - "but if you're going to play bridge, I doubt the Horlicks would have the same effect."

Already bored with the topic, she peered at her screen, trying to concentrate on her work, but curious to know what all this was about. "Actually, all these games are played online these days. You can sit in your dressing gown in your front room and play them all."

Jane hadn't forgotten the day Miranda arrived in the office, noticing with horror that she was dressed in an expensive, tight-fitting airforce blue skirt suit topped off with a small navy leather brief case. Jane looked down at her own tight black skirt with a dodgy zip and a cardigan that had seen better days and sighed. Maybe it was time to make more of an effort with her work wardrobe.

Sharing an office with Miranda was tough going. It made scrolling down to read her personal phone messages very difficult. On the face of it, Jane thought she was a thoroughly nice, classy girl, but a bit buttoned up and far too serious for the buxom, man-eating, fun loving Jane.

They had been out for lunch together a few times and, despite resistance, Jane enjoyed hearing about Miranda's social life with her friends, although they did sound as if, with a bit of encouragement, they could get down and dirty with the best of them.

Jane was part of a close-knit family and they were bursting with pride about how well she had done to get a job in such a prestigious company, Miranda seemed to take it for granted that she should be there - nothing less would do. Jane thought that was rather sad. She really was fond of her work mate, but envy was getting in the way of a closer friendship.

Just because Miranda went to university and probably graduated with flying colours, doesn't mean she can do a better job and it also shouldn't be the reason Jane had been passed over for promotion. She laid the blame for that squarely in Miranda's lap. It would have never occurred to her that her failure to be promoted had nothing to do with Miranda, but more about Jane's lack of commitment to her job.

This was the first time she had been consulted about Miranda's private life. It was usually something boring to do with work.

Jane's views washed over Miranda. "Bridge is coming back into fashion, big time. It's definitely a skill worth learning. I might just give it a go." Strangely, Miranda felt better after having had this discussion out in the open.

Jane looked at her. "I could understand your concern if you asked me about skiing or white-water rafting, even abseiling down the north face of the Eiger might cause me to stop what I'm doing and ponder this issue with you, but bridge? Tell me this is a wind-up?

Jane's idea of fun was hanging out with her friends, booking raucous holidays, the memories of which, when she returned home, were vague. That was the sort of thing worth boasting about in the office.

Miranda's phone rang and she was relieved that the conversation would be a lengthy one with a client who rarely listens. Miranda will be repeating herself, extending the time significantly. When the call ended, Jane will have definitely lost interest in the topic.

———

So, what do you need to tackle a game of bridge? Miranda studied the booklet on the train on the way home.

Four People.

A square table.

Two standard packs of playing cards (remove the jokers).

A pencil and a piece of paper on which to keep score.

A robustness to deal with the obnoxious players who forget it's only a game and are hideously competitive.

Snacks.

She knew what you didn't need and that was a crowd of people laughing at the very suggestion, although Henry thought it was a brilliant idea.

"You really should learn to play bridge. It's a marvellous game. You'll love it and it will challenge you." Henry was most excited at the prospect of a bridge partner he could mould. Challenges made her want to curl up in a ball.

"If you can play bridge, a musical instrument and speak a foreign language, all three will help fight off dementia." She wasn't sure where she read this, but there must be a reason why it was playing on her mind. The quote was lying dormant, waiting for a vulnerable moment. She could already play a musical instrument and order several dishes of food in a number of languages, so she was pretty much sorted in the keeping alert stakes.

Miranda didn't think there was any great talent required to playing card games, unless your living depended on winning - in which case every turn of the card needed a mathematical prediction, calculating the odds of either you or your opponent winning the hand in any situation. Oh, for God's sake, now she was quoting Henry.

As far as she was concerned, it's something you do when you've run out of ideas or if the weather's cold and miserable and you can't go out. Snap, Pairs, Gin Rummy, these were kid's games played in the Doctor's waiting room or on a long journey. Nevertheless, there must be something appealing about it or bridge clubs wouldn't be popping up all over London and her friends wouldn't be pushing her into it.

———

Harvey Stein had a very successful business. His bridge school spanned the first floor, above a bakery, a butcher and a hardware shop in Hendon Central. It threatened to expand over the double unit of a hairdressing salon if the landlord offered him acceptable terms. He ran morning, afternoon and evening classes and gave private lessons in between.

Who would have thought that Harvey could make a success of anything? Certainly not his family and many of his friends. They were eating their words now.

The place was packed to the rafters every day and every evening. It had become quite an institution. If you wanted to learn to play bridge, there was only one place to go – Harvey's Bridge Tutorial.

Life hadn't been easy for poor old Harvey. He left school at sixteen with no interest in pursuing any further education and this didn't surprise anyone. Shortly after a brief sojourn in the menswear business, starting at the bottom in one of the big high street chain stores, he chucked it in and moved on to other lowly dead-end jobs, soon falling into debt and begging his parents to ball him out. It was a pity because he showed promise and, had he stuck it out for more than five minutes, he might have been quickly promoted.

When Harvey could no longer find anyone prepared to lend him money to pay off his debts, he decided he had two choices. One was to develop his considerable skills at working out the odds of card playing at the poker table and hope for the best or learn to play the complex game of contract bridge and be taken seriously. Fortunately for him, for once in his life, he made the right choice.

During a particularly long period of unemployment, he taught himself the rules of the game, found himself some exceptionally good bridge players to help him hone his skills; opened up his bridge school giving his mentors jobs and never looked back.

———

Miranda climbed the stairs, alone. The last time she had climbed a dark and dingy flight of stairs was in her ballroom dancing lesson days.

She remembered carrying with her a pair of silver dancing shoes in a suede bag. A quick change and she was spun around the room in a routine for the quickstep, tango, and waltz under a mirror ball giving off a sickly pink glow.

She had to admit the close proximity of a selection of

usually perspiring partners was off-putting. A firm hand, sometimes a fist at the base of her back forcing her up close, feeling the hot breath of a complete stranger in her face and an inappropriate reaction elsewhere persuaded her to pursue an alternative past-time.

She was confident it would be easier to find a less sweaty partner at the bridge table and at least her toes would be safe. Thank goodness she forgot to mention all of this to Jane.

"Are you a beginner, intermediate or advanced?" Harvey asked Miranda as she stepped gingerly through the main door.

"I'm afraid I'm a beginner", she whispered nervously, looking around at the sea of green baize on the small square tables already occupied. People were staring at the cards in their hands, lost in the complex rules of the game; others were there just for fun and to prove to themselves and to others that they could concentrate long enough to learn a serious card game.

"Don't be afraid of that, my dear, everyone has to start at the beginning. In fact, some people have been playing for years and haven't got any further," he said, laughing at his own joke. Harvey Stein did that a lot.

"Come and sit here. These three lovely ladies need a fourth hand and you're all beginners so it should be fun."

The three ladies looked at Miranda as if she would make a tasty little morsel should she make a mistake. Miranda wished Jane had been right about old fogies playing Bridge. These women were glamorous and competitive. She sat down at the table, holding her coffee and placed her handbag on the small side table provided.

"Don't put it there. The table is for refreshments only." Sandra stared down her nose at Miranda and waited for a grovelling response.

Miranda sighed, already irritated. Not a good start. Harvey's voice boomed across the room.

"Okay everyone; can I have some quiet please? Settle down now. Can you all count up to twelve?" He was just warming up.

The crowd in the room giggled. Miranda's heart dropped. She didn't respond very well to this kind of teaching method.

"Then we're almost there," he continued. "Please DO NOT open the bidding with less than twelve points.

"Now, arrange your cards in suit order and then in chronological order, pictures first. As some of you may already know, Ace is four points, King is three points, Queen is two points and Jack is one point. Don't forget to count the extra point for a singleton, which is only one card in a suit, a doubleton which is two and five of a suit."

Miranda thought so far so good. She hoped it wouldn't get much more complicated because she was already teetering on the brink of confusion. She arranged her Ace, King and Queen ahead of their respective suits in her hand in a pretty fan shape and admired her handiwork.

"I would remind you all, for the umpteenth time, to please remember that this is a partnership game. Listen to what your partner is telling you, in bridge language, about the shape of their hand. If you're not sure, you can check your crib sheets. Please don't go merrily bidding any old thing without first thinking about how many points you have between you. There are very strict rules and they are all written down."

Cynthia, her partner for the evening, looked very smug, sitting there with a pink velour track suite with her midriff showing, matching gel nails and platform trainers. She was obviously sitting on a powerhouse of points. She raised her hand to call Harvey over to the table.

"What do I say now, Harvey," she said whiningly.

"Think, Cynthia. How many points do you have in your hand?"

Her lips moved as she counted the cards. "Twelve, but it's a nice hand and I think I should open the bidding."

"You have twelve points and a balanced hand, so you have to open. If you don't have a five-card suit, what do you think you should say?"

"One No Trump", she blurted out loudly, as if she had worked out a complicated mathematical equation.

"Well done", Harvey mumbled as he made his way over to the other side of the room.

Miranda didn't know how much more of this she could take. She looked at her watch. She had been there for precisely thirty minutes. Only another two hours to go.

"What do I do now?" Miranda looked over at her partner. She may as well make the women feel important. She could see that was the way to get on her good side.

"Jacqueline? Are you going to say anything?" Cynthia asked her opponent on her left with the charm of a sledgehammer.

"Yes", Jacqueline said proudly, "I'm going to say no bid. I've got rubbish cards." She laughed and winked at Miranda.

"Okay Miranda, you can say something", Cynthia said grandly.

Jacqueline and Miranda glanced at each other, both slightly irritated.

Harvey chose that moment to breeze by and stopped behind Miranda, putting his hands heavily on her shoulders and attempting a massage causing her to wince with the sharp pain.

"What do you think you should say in response, Miranda?"

She wanted to say that her response was to tell him to leave her shoulders alone.

"According to the crib sheet I printed off from your website, Harvey, I should say three no trumps."

"Good girl, Miranda. I can see we'll have you playing in competitions before you can say grand slam."

Cynthia pursed her lips.

"And I suspect you will be passing this hand out, too." He looked disinterestedly at Jacqueline's partner, Sandra. Looking cross- eyed after attempting to turn her hand into something worth shouting about, she spat "I'm afraid I'm going to have to say no bid."

"Surprise, Surprise! Right, Cynthia, it's your contract. This is your chance to shine. Go for it. Sandra, you lead and Miranda, you have to lay your cards down, laying your best suit on the right, alternate colours. Good luck ladies, you *should* make your contract."

Jacqueline threw down a card into the middle of the table. It was a ten of spades.

Miranda laid down her cards as she was 'dummy'. Whoever thought of such an awful name? It was bad enough that the game encouraged you to feel like one with people looking at you as if you were.

She looked around the room to see if anyone was having a better time of it. Judging by the tense expressions, it didn't look like it.

Cynthia was playing out the hand as she had called no trump first. The self-satisfied expression on her face was slipping.

"Thank you partner," she said disingenuously. Obviously, it must be part of bridge etiquette to thank your partner, even if you were doomed to fail.

The cards were placed in the centre of the table and to begin with Cynthia was making her tricks, possessively scooping them up each time she threw down her winning card and placing the little pile in front of her rather like 'snap', only not as much fun. However, she quickly ran out of winning cards in her hand and couldn't get back to the 'dummy' hand on the table to get some more and it all went horribly wrong.

"Oh damn, I haven't made the contract. How many did I go off?" Cynthia was peeved and looked around the table for someone to blame.

"You're two off, I'm afraid", Sandra voice boomed unnecessarily.

"Where did I go wrong?" Cynthia was hurting.

"I think you need to try to keep a winning card in each suit in your hand, instead of playing all your winners first. That way, you make extra tricks," Miranda said obligingly.

"Harvey? Could I borrow you again for a minute?"

"Yes, of course."

Cynthia explained the hands that had been played out which had been long forgotten by everyone else at the table. Life goes on, it's only a game.

"You need to keep a winning card in each suit in your hand instead of playing all your winners first. That way, you make extra tricks and extra points." Harvey quickly walked off.

She glared at Miranda who was celebrating her superior knowledge by dunking another gingernut biscuit into her coffee.

———

Miranda joined some other people at the bar. Set out was a variety of herbal teas and coffee. Sadly, there was not a drop of vodka or martini in sight. She poured herself another cup of coffee.

"How are you all doing? Has Omar Sharif got anything to worry about?" Miranda said, referring to the well-known actor's alleged champion bridge playing and trying to be amusing. The subject had come up on a TV programme she had seen about his life some years ago. Who knew it would come in so handy?

"I don't think dear old Omar need worry about me, mainly because he's been dead for about 10 years", a good-looking man with thick dark wavy hair, wearing a leather jacket and faded jeans said, smiling appreciatively at Miranda and trying to hide his surprise that she was young, pretty *and* a bridge player. They didn't always go together.

"We've all played for some time, but we've forgotten some of the rules so we like to come for a refresher course every now and again." The man looked impressed by his own banter.

"I thought the game was supposed to improve the memory. I sense there is serious misrepresentation going on here", Miranda said.

"My name is John and these are the lovely ladies with whom I play bridge".

Miranda smiled and introduced herself to the crowd at the bar.

"I see you're playing with sexy Cynthia. That should be a barrel of laughs", he said guffawing. Miranda laughed too.

She stared at the women who made no attempt to step forward to be introduced. Instead, they simpered into their coffee cups and stared hungrily at John and the biscuits.

"I know what you're thinking, he's a dangerous flirt," An attractive blonde broke free and approached Miranda, "but he's very friendly and polite. It's rather nice to have someone make the blood course through your veins. Have you been learning for long?"

"I can see that and, of course, he must also be the referee should things get out of hand at the table." They both laughed. "I can safely say I am a novice at the game," Miranda said.

"You'll soon get the hang of it, although I've been playing for many years and it all still baffles me."

Miranda was starting to get nervous. "Why are people learning a game that they're unlikely to master?"

"I think the company and the sarcastic, bordering on insulting banter at the table make for a fun evening all round," The blonde smiled. Miranda agreed.

"Okay everyone, back to your table please. The first half has been spent tackling bids and rebids, now we must concentrate on conventions." Harvey turned to his white board and started scribbling.

Chapter Two

Miranda had been going to Harvey Stein's Bridge Tutorial for over a year and she had to admit the game was addictive.   Nobody was interested enough to ask her how she was progressing and most of her friends had totally forgotten she was learning. This suited her very well.

Rarely was she asked to join friendly games or tournaments, which saved her from having to explain that she wasn't, as yet, ready for such an honour.

The place never failed to be jammed packed with wannabe bridge players and the noise was deafening. Poor Harvey had a terrible job trying to control the room so that his serious players could concentrate on the game.

He and his wife weaved tirelessly among the tightly packed tables, answering the same questions over and over again, uncomplainingly.

She looked forward to her games and was satisfied to notice that very often her previous mistakes had been ironed out. She thought she must be learning something after all this time, but it was difficult to tell. She rarely played a hand where she didn't feel she could have done better, bid differently and played more skilfully.

Harvey and his team were on call with good advice, but she had made her decision, enough was enough.

Miranda wanted to play and practice somewhere different. She felt the time was right to go it alone and be challenged; to take all she had learned and throw it into the arena. The only way she was going to learn the game was to ride into Dodge City, firing four playing suits.

Dodge City had morphed into the Four Suits Bridge Club. They hosted a busy game from a room in a club just off the A1.

Nick Lombardo started the club, assisted by his able

team of supervisors. Winner of hundreds of major tournaments all over the country, his CV was impressive and Miranda felt she was in good hands.

An authoritative figure, Nick didn't stand for any nonsense. If he had covered a bridge bidding convention in one of his lessons, he expected it to be understood and used immediately and proficiently.

She parked in the carpark of the members' club, close to the entrance.

"Are you playing golf today?" a rugged looking man loading up a swanky golf trolley shouted over to her as the alarm set itself on her locked car. He noticed the cute little red head getting out of her car, matching black suede thigh length boots and handbag and long hair blowing in the breeze. It didn't take a genius to work out that golf was *not* on her agenda and he felt obliged to mention it.

"I'm here to play bridge." Miranda hobbled along the tarmac holding the base of her back for effect. She knew she had parked in the wrong section but couldn't be bothered to move her car.

Miranda walked towards him and adopted her most persuasive tone. "It looks and feels like it's going to rain. You don't mind if I park here, do you? It's a bit safer than the dark, muddy area further down the track." She glanced over at the area reserved for bridge members.

He attempted to summon up and dust off the remnants of some charm and stuttered incoherently. "This area is mainly for golf members and their guests, but I suppose an exception can be made, just for today." He tried to smile, although he was a bit put out by her audacity.

"Oh I'm terribly sorry. I'm new," she said, adopting the flirtatious look so popular among her cohorts. "If I park too far away, I might forget the rules of the game on my way to the club house."

Rugged man laughed and threw his golf bag on to his shoulder, hoping his wincing went unnoticed. It seemed rather churlish to insist she return to her car and move it. "No problem, break a leg."

Miranda smiled. "I will resist the temptation to say, "and the same to you."

———

The room was a shared space and used by a golf club, the Four Suits Bridge Club and anyone wishing to hire a public area for whatever reason. As a result, it was often decorated with balloons from the previous nights' celebrations. These adornments did not detract from its sad, depressing state. It was in desperate need of a lick of paint and a new carpet, or better still an upgrade of a more modern, light wooden floor.

Too hot in the summer and too cold in the winter, the room must either have a very confused air conditioning unit or be controlled by a tight-fisted club manager.

Chinese lanterns would sometimes waft across the ceiling, blowing in the breeze into a christening balloon, which in turn nudged shoulders with a wedding banner. Miranda was sure that bets were taken as to which would give up the ghost and drop to earth, only to be kicked under the table out of the way.

Miranda found a table by a window, in the corner near a radiator. She had everything covered; means of escape, privacy from critical eyes and warmth. She was just about to sit down when a voice shouted from across the room.

"No, don't sit there!" One of the supervisors called out. "We have to fill the tables to make sure everyone has a game or we'll have loads of half-filled tables. Have you come on your own?"

"Yes I have. Will that be a problem?"

"No problem at all. Sit at this table here and I'll find you a partner. Lots of people come on their own. Are you a beginner?"

"I like to consider myself to be intermediate."

He laughed. "I am just asking so that I can put you at the right table."

Miranda looked around the room. Most people had regular partners and she could tell they had been coming to the club for some time. She noticed people were very loyal to their bridge club and felt guilty. Nobody looked up from the table. They were all too engrossed in establishing their own particular bridge convention.

Miranda thought she should turn around and race back to Harvey Stein's and beg his forgiveness for even thinking about defecting.

"I know how you feel", the supervisor whispered next to her, "but don't worry, I have found you three very nice people to play with. You may have played with them before."

Miranda recognised the three people he had chosen for her table. She now wished she had kept her own counsel about changing clubs. She touched his arm and looked grateful. "It will be a comfort to me to know you're in the room, somewhere."

"Good morning. May I have a diet coke, please." Miranda said brightly to the lady behind the bar.

The woman continued to fumble and fiddle noisily under the bar before answering, "We don't serve any alcohol or cold drinks here."

"Oh, where should I go?"

"You have to go to the other bar, through those doors. Here, we only have tea, coffee, and water. It's there on the table. Help yourself."

"May I help myself to a biscuit?" Miranda asked. A plate of biscuits was laid out on the bar, but she thought she had better just check with the dragon first. Dragon stared at Miranda, at the plate of biscuits and then at Miranda again and nodded.

"Have you ordered your lunch?" Nick asked her pleasantly. "If you go through the door towards the other bar, you can order lunch and cold drinks. There's a charge, of course. We stop at twelve thirty for an hour's break, you'll need it."

Miranda joined the long queue to order lunch. There were sandwiches, salads and filled jacket potatoes on offer on the menu.

"Do you make Ryvita sandwiches?" The lady in front of Miranda asked.

"For you, my lady, I can do anything. That will be £6.50." The steward said in broken English.

"For two slices of Ryvita with something on the top?" she asked incredulously.

"Yes, my lady. That is the price. Take it or leave it."

She looked behind her furtively at the ever-increasing length of the queue to order lunch and decided now was not the best time to argue about the price. She handed over a twenty-pound note, muttering loudly about daylight robbery and waited for the change.

"Yes, my lady?" The steward was relieved to see that Miranda was the last customer.

"I'll just have a baked potato with tuna please, light on the mayo."

"The mayonnaise is £1.00 extra whether it's light, heavy or anything else", he said irritably.

With all the lunch tickets tucked safely away in wallets and handbags, the game began in earnest.

A brief hush descended on the room whilst people

gathered their preferred partners, shuffled cards, and prepared bridge score cards.

Money was slipped into pouches to pay for the three-hour session and was collected by the supervisors. Miranda's heart dropped as she saw a familiar figure walk towards her.

"I think he's impotent." Cynthia whispered in Miranda's ear, not so very subtly, nodding in a man's direction. She was referring to the poor hapless chap standing in front of them looking embarrassed and pretending not to care and suddenly changed the subject. "So you decided to jump ship, too?"

Miranda smiled. Cynthia was now wearing a deep, plunging neckline that had no right to make an appearance during daylight hours. She was only in her mid-forties, but every part of her face had varying levels of enhancement.

Miranda was torn between staring at her unnaturally long eyelashes or her cleavage. It was obvious Cynthia was just teasing and meant no offence by the unkind, tactless remark, although it would be a miracle if none was taken.

"Do you mean he can't have sex? Will that affect his bridge game?" Miranda wasn't sure what else she was expected to say.

"She's right, you know", he nodded. "Impotence is quite common in reasonably young men. It's a bit of an epidemic at the moment." He looked longingly at Cynthia - distant memories of hot steamy nights evident in his eyes. Miranda wasn't certain whether those memories included Cynthia.

"I'm sure she's not right. Perhaps you just require more mental stimulation before it gets physical. Bed-hopping doesn't suit everyone." He reached for Miranda's hand and squeezed it, walking away towards his table wondering whether she could be right.

"Oh, stop it! You are funny". Cynthia was going to be Miranda's bridge partner, again. Miranda braced herself for the mayhem that no doubt would follow.

"So you see, he's admitted he's impotent and here you are, looking at me as though it was all my fault." Cynthia insisted as she shuffled the pack of cards and started dealing.

"How did you get on to the subject of his libido and why must you announce it publicly?" Miranda tried to smile. She tried not to make judgements about Cynthia.

"Oh, he doesn't mind. He finds it amusing. We were chatting about finding companions, you know, to have dinner with and weekends away and he offered the information willingly." Cynthia said. Miranda doubted that very much.

"Perhaps it was a subtle message in case you were getting any ideas?" Miranda thought that was quite probable.

"Oh good Lord, he knows I don't need to put it out there. I'm fighting them off." Cynthia's voice was raised for effect.

"That must be a nice problem to have. How are you going to choose one from the crowd, I mean, what will make one man stand out from another?"

Cynthia didn't need to consider the question. "The usual three things, you know – money, looks and physique. Making me laugh is definitely next on the list."

Noticing that she was perfectly serious and unlikely to negotiate on any of these points, Miranda said "That's not unreasonable at all. You're very easy to please."

They sat down at the bridge table and another two ladies joined them. Miranda was horrified to see the dreaded Sandra take a seat at the table, but happy that Jacqueline was joining them. There was a few seconds of strained chit-chat before the game started. It was Cynthia's turn to open the bidding. She stroked her chin.

"Err, hmm, I'm not sure what to bid. Eric? Can you help me?"

Eric jogged over to the table and looked at her cards.

"I would open with this suit and follow it up with that one, if necessary", he said pointing twice at her hand.

"You don't think I should bid that?" Cynthia argued.

Eric was one of several patient supervisors regularly summoned to help everyone play the game competently.

"No, because if you bid that, you'll find yourself playing in the wrong contract and judging by your partner's hand, you will very likely lose the game." He was referring to the points in both her hand and Miranda's hand.

"Great, thanks Eric. Don't go too far, I might need you again." Cynthia looked up at the handsome Eric and fluttered her eyelashes. It was completely lost on him.

The two opponents passed out the hand and Miranda, deciding they should switch to the stronger spades suit in her hand, prepared to play the game out.

Cynthia laid her cards down on the table. She was the dummy hand and had nothing to do except watch the game being played by her partner. She drummed her fingernails on the table.

Miranda wondered what was breaking her concentration and her eyes rested on the culprit. In between the drumming she was chatting loudly to the opponents about her latest fling with a Mongolian throat singer.

"Do you mind?" Miranda sighed. "I'm still at the stage where I need to think."

"Sorry, darling", Cynthia said apologetically, struggling to sit still and stay silent.

Miranda stared at the cards in her hand, then at the dummy hand on the table and again at the cards in her hand. Most people work out where they will make their tricks first before the play kicks off. Miranda played her winning cards and took a gamble on the rest, hoping for the best.

"How many have I made? I'm too scared to count my tricks", Miranda sat back exhausted.

"You made it, four spades and one over. Well done!" Cynthia was jubilant.

CHAPTER THREE

Miranda told Henry she was enjoying learning to play bridge and, for the most part, that was true. He didn't seem to have the same issues with his bridge partners that Miranda seemed to have. His game was more serious, less sociable and always predictable. He liked it that way.

Her experience, however, was quite different. Juggling a bridge game with becoming an agony aunt was distracting, but interesting.

Miranda tried very hard not to get drawn into the lives of her bridge friends and often wondered if it was part of the course. She was determined to keep going before attempting to play with Henry and she was feeling very positive that it wouldn't be too long.

"May I have a tuna sandwich with some slices of cucumber, please?" Miranda asked the Godfather politely on her next visit to the club.

She had started calling the steward 'the Godfather' after noticing him over several weeks, taking the lunch orders.

He sat at a low table outside the kitchen door with a cash machine from which he dispensed change, dressed in black trousers, a white shirt and a black waistcoat. He had a joke and a quip for his favourites and gave the silent treatment to those he considered to be unworthy. In other words, those who dared argue with him about the price of his food or tried to meddle with the selection on the menu. It felt almost as if one should bow down low and kiss his ring as a loyal subject and be grateful for anything that turned up from his kitchen.

"That will be £5.50 my lady", he said.

"But it says £4.50 on the menu."

"Cucumber is £1.00 extra." He looked at Miranda over the top of his spectacles and she felt her blood run cold.

"Of course it is", she replied.

The three players picked up their lunch, freshly made, from the refreshment area and brought it back to their bridge table to eat.

"You should have made that contract", Sandra said, irritated. She was referring to the last hand played which Miranda had found particularly difficult. Jacqueline and Cynthia buried their heads in cling film.

"I agree", Miranda replied, wanting to burst into tears. Why did she put herself through this torture?

Miranda often found herself at a table where Sandra was her opponent and she dreaded it. Most people at the club felt the same way about her. As a result, she was often seen wandering around without a partner of her own, trying to muscle in on a game.

"I noticed you've made that mistake a few times now, Miranda. You're not counting the trumps. You really should draw out all the trumps." Sandra thought Miranda should be grateful to have this pointed out.

Miranda was longing to tell her where to stick her trumps, but when you're wrong, you're wrong.

"You should be pleased, you won the game," Miranda said.

"It's like taking candy from a baby," Sandra replied, making her way to the coffee machine.

She was infuriating, but Miranda knew she should feel sorry for the woman.

"You wait until I'm a better player", Miranda screamed inwardly, hoping her eyes were burning a hole in Sandra's back. "Then you'll need something stronger than coffee."

It was rumoured that Sandra had been married twice and both her husbands had divorced her. Miranda didn't need to ask why.

Apparently, her second husband tried to take her for every penny she had and the experience had turned her into a shrew. Miranda doubted that one could become a shrew quite so easily.

A women who battles with their children and is positively poisonous to their partners must have a problem. According to Sandra, it was all their fault.

They should, without question, welcome her constructive verbal abuse and be willing to do her bidding around the clock. There was no point being too sensitive over her helpful comments about their domestic arrangements and child rearing. She had almost single-handedly done a sterling job with hers.

Unsurprisingly, she was hardly ever invited over and rarely saw her grandchildren. It was evident that they didn't respect her opinion or value her contribution. She wasn't going to beg.

Miranda knew what it was like to have a fractured relationship with a parent and felt sad that Sandra couldn't see how unreasonable she was being.

The woman was lonely, that was very obvious. Playing bridge was a good start, but hardly scratched the surface.

Gradually, Miranda won Sandra over and felt able to offer her some comfort. "You'll meet someone else", Miranda said, trying to sound kindly, looking into Sandra's unsmiling face whilst biting into her tuna sandwich. She secretly thought that was very unlikely given that she was so horrible to everyone. Sandra was a very bitter woman.

"I don't want to meet anyone. Look around you. Can you see anyone decent here?"

"I suppose their wives and girlfriends think they're pretty decent", Miranda offered unhelpfully.

"When you've had two of the best, third time

definitely won't be lucky." Sandra must have a very short memory. She was obviously having a bad day. A sure sign of this was that she had brought a meagre lunch from home. On a relatively good day, she would have tucked into a hot baked potato with melted cheese and beans which would have to double up as supper. Miranda could gauge her quite well by now.

"Look, Sandra, I don't mean to be horrible, but with that attitude it's hardly surprising you're riding solo."

"What do you mean by that?" Sandra chomped on a piece of melon and was about to go in for the kill. Miranda was ready for her and spoke softly so other tables couldn't hear their conversation.

"Come on, Sandra, you have to admit you haven't exactly got a bright and optimistic outlook on life and I think it would be better if you started counting your blessings." Miranda challenged her. She wasn't going to cower under her opponent's gaze. Sandra was a bully and people were wary of her, but it was obvious she felt a sort of strange attachment to Miranda.

"I think I'm a very positive person. Why would you think otherwise?" Sandra was genuinely surprised at Miranda's outburst. It may be time to revise her opinion of the girl.

"You're not judging people on their own merits; you tar them all with the same brush – men and women alike. When you're feeling low, everyone has to suffer. In the short time we've been friends, you haven't had one nice thing to say about anyone in this room. People have made a big effort to chat to you and I have witnessed men coming up to talk to you. They might have wanted to ask you out for dinner.

"Do me a favour! Ask me out for dinner?" she scoffed under her breath. "Do you expect that of this motley crew? I hardly think so and if they did, they'd get a piece of my mind."

Miranda turned away but made one last parting shot. "My point exactly."

———

Sandra put her hand up and looked wildly around.

"Mirage, could you come and help me please?"

"My name is Niraj, but I can see how you could make that mistake." He had long passed being offended. The table of players roared with laughter at the subtle put-down, all except Sandra.

She pretended she didn't hear. "What do you suggest I bid to my partner's one no trump?"

"Do you play transfers?" Niraj asked her kindly.

"With you standing behind me I do." Sandra laughed.

"How do you ask if she has spades?" He had more patience than was natural or deserved.

"Two diamonds?" Sandra looked up pleadingly.

"No! You pick the suit below the one you want her to bid."

"Two hearts." Sandra sounded as if she'd won the bridge trophy.

"Well done! Off you go."

Niraj walked around the table to look at Miranda's hand.

"You've got this. You don't need my help." He smiled and walked away.

———

"Settle down everyone, that includes you four ladies intentionally not listening to me in the corner. I would like to make an announcement." When Nick Lombardo wanted to speak, absolute silence must reign. The club was his own personal fiefdom and everyone needed to understand that.

"You've all heard of a booze cruise and a jazz cruise, well, I'm proposing to take you all on a bridge cruise for a week. Will anyone who is interested please come up and put your name down so that I can calculate the numbers? The more of you who are interested, the better the price will be." Nick stood tall and waited for the stampede. Silence!

He sighed deeply and decided to change tack and sound more up-beat.

"I will be printing leaflets with the details, but I'm happy to talk about the initial plans. We will be leaving from Southampton on Holland Silhouette which I'm sure you all know is a Dutch ship, sometime in April. I know its short notice, but that's how I've managed to keep the price down. We will be sailing to the Western Mediterranean, stopping at various ports – A Taste of Italy."

"How many people do you envisage taking you up on the offer?" Sandra asked.

"Realistically, it would need about a hundred people to make it cost effective." Nick smiled airily, but Sandra thought she could smell desperation.

Miranda didn't think a hundred people would go on a bridge cruise, but assumed Nick was pushing the numbers up anyway.

Surprised that the members were not biting his hand off to sign up, Nick thought he had better try to sell it a bit harder.

"I would like to just add that there will be a coach going from here to Southampton for anyone who doesn't wish to drive down themselves. It's going to be a wonderful cruise and obviously the standard of bridge will be amazing. I guarantee you won't want to get off the ship and explore. It will be a week of sun, a lot of sea and no sand." Nick hoped this would get a laugh. It didn't.

———

Miranda telephoned Henry as soon as she got home. He was such a great guy. He always supported her in everything she wanted to do and she did the same for him.

The cerebral side of their relationship certainly kept her on her toes. She enjoyed the banter and humour. Accustomed to hiding his feelings, probably a legacy from boarding school, Henry could sometimes be difficult to read. He was not by nature spontaneous, but with Miranda he was passionate and gentle and made her feel very special. Every thought and deed was carefully measured, except when he felt very strongly about something or not in control and then the safety catch was unlocked and all hell let loose. In that respect they were very alike.

He had proved himself to be a loyal and loving partner, supporting her in her fight against perceived injustices, quietly comforting her when she got it terribly wrong and she loved him even more for it.

She picked her moment carefully. "The bridge club is going on tour, Henry. Come with me – it'll be great fun."

They had been dating for some time now and she knew he was ready to make it official and get engaged, but Miranda wanted to wait a bit longer. She had to be sure and as yet; she wasn't. Any commitment needed serious consideration, particularly choosing a life partner. They were having a wonderful time together, both owning their own flats and entertaining friends separately and together. It was fun. Things would change and she needed to make sure she was ready for it.

"I'm really busy at work for the next few weeks, Miranda; I just can't take any time off at the moment."

Miranda couldn't decide whether to be relieved or disappointed. She didn't think it would be his scene, but she had to invite him along.

She had played the game with him a few times, setting up four sets of cards, trying to work out each hand and it was a very stressful experience. He would raise his eyes to heaven and sigh heavily if he thought she had made the wrong bid or played the wrong card. He refused to believe that was borderline cheating, as was crossing and uncrossing his legs violently under the table, and she was afraid if he persisted, he would get them disqualified from a game. The shame of it would be just too much to bear.

A lawyer in a medium size city firm, he was not only clever, but also decent, honourable and totally incorruptible. He had advised Miranda very wisely on several legal issues in the past and she was totally in awe of him.

"It's absolutely fine, you go and enjoy it." He told her, laughing to himself at the thought of the trip. He thought that being cooped up in a floating hotel with nowhere to hide from the obsessive bridge players might not be as much fun as Miranda hoped.

"I know what you're thinking, Henry, but if it all gets too much, I can always find solace in the cocktails."

At the bridge club, Miranda spoke to Nick quietly.

"How much bridge will I be expected to play?"

"As much or as little as you wish, it's entirely up to you." Nick replied, sympathetically. "If you're having fun in port, why not enjoy it? I'm hoping that there will be plenty of people on the trip to fill in when others want to go sightseeing and there are usually bridge players among the guests on board, not in our group, who like to join in a game after a hard day pondering on their next meal."

"It sounds like it could be a lot of fun."

"It most certainly will be."

———

A large crowd gathered in the club foyer and the chatter was deafening.

"I know you're all very excited and you should be, but could you please make sure you hear my call to get on the coach at the appointed time. I don't want to leave anyone behind."

Nick Lombardo was a flamboyant man, but he excelled himself with his cruise wear. He wanted to stand out and be noticed on board ship, but did he also need to be noticed by all the other ships sailing on the Mediterranean?

The Godfather came rushing over. "Lovely Ladies and Gentlemen, I have prepared some small individual picnics for the journey, if anyone wants to buy one."

He never missed an opportunity to make money and, obviously mourning for the loss of income while the bridge club was on a jolly, weaved his way through the waiting crowd offering brown paper bags.

"I have cheese and pickle, smoked salmon and egg mayonnaise sandwiches on brown bread for you to choose from and a couple of other little goodies in the bag too." However hard he tried; he couldn't make it appear to be good value.

Miranda wasn't interested in his overpriced food as the holiday was going to be an eating marathon anyway, but she had to ask. "How much are the picnic bags please?"

"£13.75 and an extra £2.00 for a bottle of water," the Godfather said with a straight face, as if it was a perfectly reasonable price for a picnic bag containing a sandwich, a mini muffin and a bag of crisps.

The queue for the picnic bags snaked round into the bar area. Honestly, as far as Miranda was concerned, these people deserved to be robbed – fools and their money were easily parted.

Henry had offered to drive her to Southampton, but Miranda thought she would feel tearful to leave him behind. It was better to just get on the coach. He did, however, insist on taking her to the bridge club car park to watch her be herded onto the coach with the others. He thought it might reinforce his decision not to join her. However, notwithstanding the strange mix of people, Henry was still a little sorry he wasn't part of it.

The coach driver flung open the large luggage space under the chassis and quickly walked away to have a cigarette, hoping he wouldn't be called upon to assist with lugging the cases and the first argument soon began.

"Don't put your heavy suitcase on my bag please, you'll break all my cosmetics." Sandra was in her usual mood. Unlike the rest of the group jumping around with excitement, her mood remained unchanged at the prospect of the approaching holiday.

"It may as well be *my* suitcase, instead of the seventy others about to be loaded." John gave her a filthy look. He was most disappointed to see that old crow on the trip. He had managed to avoid her on the bridge circuit for months.

He couldn't resist teasing her. "I've got an idea! Shall I crawl in and sort the bags out so that yours is left untouched?"

Sandra's face lit up at the thought of such a gesture. "Would you?"

John roared with laughter. "April Fool", he shouted childishly and stormed off, shaking his head. Ridiculous woman.

Sandra walked away, muttering obscenities under her breath.

"Oh God, is she always like this? Stay away from her otherwise she'll ruin your holiday." Henry gave Sandra what he thought was a withering look, a warning that he'll be expecting a daily report on her behaviour and it had better be good.

"You seem like a friendly chap." Sandra liked the look of the serious young man. "Are you coming on the trip?" She said with her best grimace. Henry shook his head.

Noticing the exchange, Miranda whispered, "If that was meant to be an evil stare, perhaps next time you should smile. That would really rattle her." She laughed and put her arms around him.

"Sadly, he's not. He has a lot of work to do," Miranda answered for him.

"No time for cruising, sadly." Henry added, at this stage not feeling very sad at all.

Henry was going to try to make his escape and nodded towards Sandra. "I'm going to leave it to you to take care of my girl while I'm slaving over a hot desk." Miranda pinched his arm. She had warned him not to say that.

"At least I know they'll be no chance of anyone else sniffing around you with her by your side," he whispered to Miranda, a bit too loudly.

"Oh, I will. I'm sure we'll be partners for most of the cruise." Sandra was in for a big surprise.

Cynthia pulled up in her little convertible with the roof down and glided into a parking space. She got out of the car and opened the boot, leaving the car and her suitcase to walk straight over to Miranda and Henry.

"Isn't it exciting? Who is this lovely man?" she gushed. "Have we met?"

"No, I think I would remember," Henry said, smiling.

"Oh, isn't he charming? – 'you would remember' – how nice!"

"Henry is my boyfriend." Miranda said proudly.

"Why aren't you coming on the cruise, Henry – if only to keep your eye on your gorgeous girlfriend? Don't worry; I'll make sure she doesn't get into mischief." Cynthia giggled and winked simultaneously.

"I know she will be in safe hands with you, being the shy, timid person you seem to be," Henry said quietly.

"What? Oh hilarious, you're joking, aren't you?"

"I never joke." Henry said with a straight face.

From the corner of her eye Miranda noticed John reaching into the boot of Cynthia's car, extracting her suitcase, wheeling it deftly to the coach and placing it reverently inside the luggage area. Cynthia followed her gaze.

"I have my own personal valet, don't you know," she whispered, highly amused.

Miranda wondered how Cynthia managed it. She remembered John from her Harvey Stein days – he was very popular there, too. It was heartening to recognise someone else amongst a sea of strangers.

"His wife is all tied up with home stuff and the kids – she's not a bridge player, thankfully." Cynthia mused. "He seems happy to have some company and I know him quite well from the club." She looked at Miranda nervously, hoping she didn't suspect any impropriety. Miranda didn't suspect it; she was certain of it.

Miranda looked around. The cruise had attracted a whole crowd of people she had never met before.

"I can see there's quite a few singles eyeing each other up," Henry observed. He had an interesting habit of reading her mind.

"Yes, there seems to be. That's good anyway; we can

quietly go mad together." Miranda hoped she wouldn't go stir crazy stuck on the ship without Henry's very stimulating company.

"I wish I was coming with you now," he said miserably.

"No, you really don't, Henry. Don't be disingenuous – I know you can't think of anything worse. If it gets too boring without me, fly out to one of the ports en-route and finish off the holiday with me – there's plenty of room in the cabin." The more Miranda thought about it, the more she thought it was a marvellous idea.

"Do you mean it, really?" He hadn't thought of that and wasn't sure if it was possible. He might make enquiries about it, but if he did, it would be a surprise."

"Yes. Why not? I'm sure you can jump on board whenever you like."

Henry didn't answer.

"Okay everyone, listen up. It's time to pack up and load up. Can you form an orderly queue and start getting on the coach please?" Nick was waiting, holding a clip board.

Miranda suddenly felt a bit lost and looked at Henry panic stricken. "Phone the office and tell them you've been abducted by your gorgeous girlfriend", she shouted, as Cynthia ushered her towards the coach "Perhaps I'll ask John to gently wheel you to the luggage area and stow you away – you can see he's very good at that."

"Oh well, think how many entertaining stories you'll have to tell me when you get back." Henry smiled lovingly at her.

"*If* I get back. I might be arrested for murder. I love you, Henry, see you soon."

He didn't answer, but she knew he felt the same. She waved, looking somewhat forlorn. Cynthia blew Henry kisses; needless to say he didn't reciprocate.

"If they break into a sing-song on the way down, I'm getting off the coach," Miranda thought to herself, luckily, everyone was too busy looking for restaurant deals on the internet. She sat back with her eyes closed and relaxed.

———

"There are three speciality restaurants on board this ship. Which do you fancy? They dress up a bit more in those restaurants." Cynthia was studying the menus with great concentration.

"The French restaurant looks nice and so does the Asian fusion." Miranda had looked at the menus and intended to give them a try.

"It seems a bit wasteful as we've already paid for our meals in the main restaurant. I don't think lack of good food will be an issue." Miranda was reluctant to wear the trousers with the elasticated waist she had put in her suitcase, just in case.

"The all-inclusive restaurant will get a bit monotonous after a while, so the odd dinner elsewhere won't hurt. If you sign up when you arrive you get a discount."

Cynthia was still focusing on the food. She thought how nice it was that everything was paid for in advance and she wouldn't have to expect someone else to foot the bill for a change. Sometimes, the effort to get a date to pay for dinner was too much. The age of chivalry, when the man never allowed a woman to pay for herself, was long gone.

Miranda wouldn't be heading to the restaurants as soon as she arrived. She would be checking out her stateroom, the bars, and sunbathing topless on her balcony. What luxury! She was very glad she had chosen not to share a room. It would have been more cost effective but completely ruined her holiday.

The coach pulled into a service station for a

refreshment stop and a walk around to stretch the legs and half the coach emptied out. Everyone hurriedly scattered around, taking over the few tables and chairs outside to eat their picnic. Miranda remained in her seat and called Henry.

"Are you there yet?" He thought the time was going to drag while she was away.

"No, we've stopped for lunch. We've been on the road for at least an hour, Henry; the poor dears must be starving," she whispered, giggling.

The driver flicked his cigarette into the air, climbed into the coach, sat down and hooted. The coach filled up again and they continued their journey down the motorway.

"It sounds like someone is in trouble." A voice from the back could be easily heard as most of the passengers had stopped chatting and fallen asleep. The sirens were heard first, followed by two police cars motioning for the coach driver to pull onto the hard shoulder, one behind and one pulling up alongside the driver.

The coach veered slowly off the road and came to a gentle stop. The driver opened the doors and three police officers questioned him quietly.

"Can I help you, officer? My name is Nick Lombardo and I am the organiser of this tour." He stood up and blocked the gangway until he was able to ascertain the problem.

"Do you have Mr. Sylvester on the coach?" The first officer was looking over Nick's shoulder as he spoke.

"Yes, we have Mr. *and* Mrs. Sylvester."

"I'm afraid I'm going to need to escort him off of the coach and take him in for questioning."

"What has he done wrong? It must be very serious if you've stopped us on the motorway and if it's not, I won't be happy."

"We're not in the habit of stopping coach trips on the motorway for fun, Sir. Could you show me where he is sitting?"

"Would you please let me have a word with him first before you march up and down the gangway alarming everyone? I don't mean to be rude, but this is a bridge holiday and I would rather not have any unnecessary drama."

"If you could tell him that we would like him to step off the coach that would be most helpful."

"Yes, of course, give me a minute."

Mr and Mrs Sylvester had both fallen into a light sleep, with Roger's head resting on the window and they required a gentle nudge to wake up.

"Roger, I'm afraid I'm going to have to ask you to come to the front. There are three police officers who want to speak to you." Nick leaned in and tried to be discreet, but the whole coach could hear, and everyone was staring.

"Really, how exciting! Why?" Roger looked at his wife, who thought Nick was joking.

"If you wanted our attention, Nick, you've certainly got it now," she laughed.

"I'm being serious – never more so. Come on, Roger, they want to have a word. I'm sure it will be all sorted in five minutes, but could you get on with it because we have a schedule to keep." Nick was sure it was just a formality.

"What can this be about?" Mrs. Sylvester asked her husband as he squeezed past her.

"Probably the non-payment of a parking ticket issued twenty years ago, knowing them. They never let anything drop." Roger looked a bit peeved.

"I had better come with you for moral support," she

said, looking at him nervously.

"No, don't do that, I'll be fine. It won't take long to sort whatever it is out."

One officer was waiting next to the driver and the other two were off the coach at the bottom of the steps.

"Would you mind getting off the coach, Sir?" It wasn't really a question.

"What's the problem, officer?"

"I'll tell you when you get off the coach. I'm sure you would like some privacy."

Roger climbed down, his hand trembling on the handrail. "Am I in trouble?"

"I'm afraid you are, Sir. We're with the Fraud Squad," the officer showed Roger his identification "and we would like to take you to the station and ask you some questions that need some answers."

"We're going on holiday. I don't know anything about any fraud; can this wait until I get back next week?"

"I'm afraid it can't. There have been some very serious allegations made against you; we need to deal with it now. Your holiday is cancelled, I'm afraid."

"Can I have a moment to sort my wife out? This is very inconvenient."

"I'll take you back on board, Sir; if you can be quick, I would appreciate it. We don't want to hold everyone up longer than necessary." The officer escorted him back onto the coach, tightly holding his arm.

"As I predicted, it's just a silly misunderstanding." Roger could feel tightness in his chest. "Go on without me and I'll meet you on the ship. We've got plenty of time before departure; I'll grab a taxi and follow on." Roger tried to look as if this were just a minor irritation, but his wife could see it was a lot more serious than that. People don't get hauled off coaches unless it's pretty serious.

"What's happening, Roger? Let me come with you."

"There's really no point, darling, I'll be in and out in a flash. They'll call me a taxi from the police station, and I'll come straight on. Hang on to the luggage. I'm sure Nick and his staff will help you settle in until I get back." Roger looked pleadingly at Nick.

"Yes, of course we will. Don't worry about your wife, Roger, concentrate on sorting everything out." Nick sighed; he really didn't need any added responsibility.

Roger walked heavily back down the gangway, got off the coach and was hustled into the back of the police car, lights still flashing and sirens screeching as it sped away.

The driver closed the doors, pulled away and bombed down the motorway, trying to make up the time. He had another trip to do later in the afternoon and couldn't risk being late.

"Before anyone else asks me, I don't know anything and I'm sure we'll be seeing Roger on the ship this evening for dinner and our first round of bridge." Nick's voice boomed from the front.

"You don't know what you're missing. OMG," Miranda texted Henry, using the messaging abbreviation. "There's been a police sting operation. Roger Sylvester has been arrested," Miranda typed frantically, fingers and thumbs flying over her smartphone.

"Who's Roger Sylvester?" Henry messaged back.

"He's Jacqueline's husband, you know, one of my gang of lovely bridge ladies and they were sitting three rows behind me on the coach, minding their own business. The police hauled him off and there I was, thinking that this trip was going to be on the dull side."

Henry didn't know Jacqueline Sylvester and didn't want to admit that his eyes glazed over when the bridge ladies were mentioned.

"Do you think he's a cold-bloodied murderer?" Henry was trying to process all the reasons he thought it was likely to be, discarding them all as highly unlikely.

"He hasn't murdered his wife if that's what you're getting at; she's still on the coach praying he makes it back before the ship sails, I should think."

"Don't get involved." Henry warned.

"What do you think *that* was all about?" Cynthia mumbled quietly next to her.

Miranda stuffed her phone in her pocket. "I'm not sure whether I want to know, but I'm not going to ignore the poor woman." Miranda got up and sat next to Jacqueline.

"I haven't come over to pry, but if you want to chat to kill some time while you're waiting for your husband to come back, that's fine with me – just let me know. I'm sitting three rows in front."

"I'm on my own, too. I'd be happy to sit next to you and help you ponder on the events of this morning. You must be in shock." Sandra bulldozed her way into the conversation.

"That's very nice of you both, thank you so much. I'm just trying to get hold of Abby, my daughter, to tell her what's happened. I've sent her a few messages and I'm waiting for a reply." Miranda got up and went back to her seat.

"Well? Did she say anything?" Cynthia asked her as she sat down.

"As a matter of fact she did. She said to tell that woman sitting next to you to mind her own business."

"She did not, you liar! You're so funny."

"It's fraud and that was probably the fraud squad" The text from Henry bleeped loudly as his message came in.

"How do you know that?" Miranda answered.

"The case is on the internet and has apparently been

going on for some time."

"Poor Jacqueline. I feel sorry for her – It looks like she'll be on her own." Miranda tried to text message away from prying eyes.

"I think your friend will probably be advised to go straight home; this trip will be a bridge too far."

Miranda laughed. "That's not funny, Henry."

Holland Silhouette was docked in port. 122,000 tonnes of metal, glass and chrome looming in the distance, blinding the passengers with its sparkle and shine. It sat defiantly in the biggest berth Southampton had to offer, putting any vessel that sailed alongside to shame.

Miranda could see it as the coach followed the signs to the cruise terminal and felt a lump in her throat. What a feat of engineering! She felt the same way when she had driven across the bridge into Manhattan, visited the Temple of Karnak and climbed the Acropolis.

"Let's stay together until we get into the hall and check in. All your bags will be taken and brought to your staterooms so don't run around searching for them and, finally, remember there will be a lifeboat drill later on so check your muster stations. The details will be in your stateroom." Nick was trying to stay one step ahead.

She waited until everyone had got off the bus and didn't want to be herded. It was essential to make time to enjoy the whole experience. She fumbled in her handbag to find her phone and sent a text message.

"It's a beautiful ship, Henry, very intimidating in its size. I'm sending you a picture so you can imagine you're on board with me. More to follow later." She didn't want to hang around waiting for a reply.

"Are you coming, Miranda, or spending the week

driving around in the coach?" Nick was checking everyone was off and was surprised to see Miranda still on board.

"I'm taking it all in," she said, staring ahead of her in wonderment.

He smiled. "I know, it's magical, isn't it? Come on! Let's get on the ship and start having a good time."

After an easy check in and some minimal form filling, Miranda walked through a set of doors, down a long corridor and up the gangway to board the ship. All the way along, she was greeted by the smiling, welcoming staff from *Holland Silhouette*. Any misgivings about the trip were left behind.

'All roads lead to Rome.' That was Miranda's first thought as she tried to find her stateroom. Every deck looked exactly the same. There were only four things to remember and they were proving impossible – Port, Starboard, Aft and Forward. If she could master those, she might stop trying to unlock someone else's cabin and frighten the occupants half to death.

"May I help you, Madam? What number is your stateroom?" A young steward literally appeared from nowhere, as if by magic.

"Oh thank goodness, I've only been on board five minutes and I'm completely lost."

"No Madam, you are not lost. No problem. You are on deck eight, port side, this is deck six."

"Thank you very much." Miranda tried to find the lift.

"Madam?" The steward called out, not that way."

"Oh goodness, will I ever find my way around this ship?" Miranda wailed.

"Just before it's time to get off." When she looked back, the Steward had vanished into thin air and all she could hear was his chuckle.

She recognised her bright orange suitcase outside her

stateroom, patiently waiting to be unpacked.

"Good afternoon, Ms Soames." Another steward, obviously a member of the same magic circle as his colleague from deck 6, morphed in front of her. "Let me help you with your bag. My name is Freddy and I will be looking after you on this voyage."

"Please call me Miranda," she said, taking two long strides to the window and fumbled with the lock to open the sliding door leading onto the balcony.

"Thank you, Ms Soames." He immediately came over and assisted her to unlock the balcony door and then hurrying to open her wardrobe, reaching up high to produce her lifejacket. "Call to the muster station will be very soon. It's in the theatre on Deck 5."

"Oh yes, of course. Thank you."

"If you need anything, anything at all, please use the phone and dial number 6. I will come to you straight away." He backed out of the room, smiling and waving.

Miranda forgot to ask about the contents of the minibar. She opened the door and looked out – the corridor was empty. Freddy had vanished. She really wished they wouldn't keep doing that.

Here she was in her stateroom on a luxury liner, all alone – well not exactly alone – she was with a group of charming people willing to be friends with her – The only thing niggling was whether they were willing to be friendly with each other. This trip could turn out to be more interesting than she thought.

The soft knocking at her door was hardly audible. She didn't hear it at first, concentrating on flicking through the channels on the TV, advertising everything available to purchase on board at vastly inflated prices.

"I know you're in there, do let me in. I've got a surprise for you."

Miranda was intrigued and climbed off the bed on which she was resting, just in her underwear. Slipping on a bathrobe she opened the door. John was dressed in a T-shirt and shorts that were far too small for a man of over six feet tall. He was holding a bottle of champagne in one hand, and a couple of glasses in another. Miranda watched his face drop with disappointment.

"She's a few doors down, John. Sorry to be such a let-down." Miranda was fighting not to laugh. He was looking for Cynthia and by the look of it, rather urgently.

He marched into her room. "You could never be a let-down, Miranda. While I'm here, may I look at the view from your balcony – I'm on the other side." He pushed his way in. "Yes, well, it's not very nice now, but it will be. Southampton has always been a busy port." He was looking at the cranes waiting to load and unload their cargo. "It will be gorgeous when we're out at sea. I'm one floor up; you must come in for a gin and tonic, I've got some in the fridge."

"Do you know what time we're all meeting up?" Miranda was feeling lonely. She also had some in the fridge; in fact, the selection of alcohol lined up and standing to attention was looking more tempting every minute. It won't be there long at this rate. Miranda's eyes glazed as the imagined scene playing out before her.

...The room was completely dark, and she couldn't feel any motion. She felt disorientated as she slowly climbed out of bed and opened the curtains. Her hair was dishevelled, and she had been in her nightgown for days. The sea was a murky grey, reflecting the colour of the dark clouds which had suddenly descended, threatening to burst. Apart from endless water, there was nothing on the horizon; land seemed a long way off. The seagulls took advantage of the ship's slow progress, swooping around

looking for something interesting to plunder.

She opened the minibar and extracted a bottle of champagne. The cork popped out and disappeared behind the dressing table. She took the glass and the bottle out onto the balcony and continued to watch, alone, sipping until the bottle was empty. She had been in her cabin for three days, the only visitor being the steward to clean the stateroom and replenish the bottles of champagne and the ice bucket. Muffled conversation and a loud bang on the door broke through her alcoholic stupor.

"Ms Soames, could you open the door please? It's the Captain speaking..."

There she goes again. It was futile imagining high drama. One would have to dig very deep to even discover low drama. Nothing was going to turn a sedate Mediterranean bridge cruise into anything more exciting. The sooner the bridge arguments started, the better.

John looked at her strangely. "I think we're meeting in the martini bar for drinks at about seven." He was in a hurry to find Cynthia while he was still in the mood but turned around at the door and looked at Miranda. "You're welcome to join us for dinner whenever you wish, if you don't find more exciting people to hang out with."

"That's lovely of you, thank you. Now off you go before she changes her mind."

John fancied Cynthia like mad. He loved his wife dearly, but she was busy with their children and encouraged him to take up bridge to get him out from under her feet. She thought they had a happy and fulfilled marriage and she was right, most of the time. Agreeing to let her husband go on the odd bridge holiday was not a problem. In fact, she found the idea very amusing.

"Don't be surprised to see me on one of your bridge jollies, John", she joked. "I might just appear when you least expect."

John put his arms around her and cuddled her. He knew she would rather go away with her girlfriends and drink wine all day.

"And you would be most welcome, my darling," he said, complacently.

The game and the club had opened a very welcome door, creating a new interest for him and he suddenly began to look forward to some spare time. Playing with different people and also getting involved in the social aspect, rather than worrying about having too much free time on his hands, was a great boon.

He had built up a large, successful business and owned a vast warehouse selling plumbing and general building accessories and he made sure he had plenty of trained staff on the shop floor to keep the business ahead of its competitors. He had worked like a dog for years and had earned a reputation for being excellent value, selling good quality goods. However, it had all come at a price, as it often does. He had neglected his relationship with his wife and children, never finding time to go on holiday or spending quality time at home and the family had grown up without him noticing. He had earned some time off to have fun.

When Cynthia agreed to be his partner, he couldn't believe his luck. This vivacious, attractive blonde was going to be a regular feature in his life, and it was all above board and kosher.

He understood her need to flitter from one man to another. He was comfortable with watching her giggle and flirt her way around the room. She was, after all, a single lady with much to offer. She would eventually settle down at the bridge table, stroke his arm and smile lovingly at him and the game would commence in earnest with Cynthia heaping praise on him after every contract he made.

He couldn't remember when, exactly, her flirting became an issue or when he began to be seriously bothered by it, probably at around the time he was ready to take their relationship to the next level.

The cruise was his chance to put their relationship firmly on the map. A quasi-honeymoon with all the trappings and none of the commitment and it was looking promising – very promising indeed.

———

"Are you about to tell me that you're on your way to Southampton and you'll be here in the next ten minutes? You'll need to be, we're sailing soon", Miranda texted Henry.

"I'm afraid not, I'm on my way to the coffee machine and will be in my next meeting in ten minutes, but that's no good to you, is it. Fed up already?"

"Not really, Cynthia has had her first gentleman caller, via my cabin – completely by accident, you understand."

"You had an accidental gentleman caller? Am I expected to believe that?"

"It could be the most exciting thing to happen to me all week."

"Have you been exploring?" Henry would have been sprinting up and down the decks, looking in every nook and cranny by now.

"I'm just enjoying my stateroom at the moment. Doesn't that word conjure up an image of the presidential suite rather than a smallish cabin with a cubicle size bathroom?"

He laughed. "What's that awful noise in the background?"

"Time for muster station drill or whatever they call it.

More from me later, over and out."

Miranda hadn't noticed, until she put her phone back in her handbag and looked in the mirror, that she had been crying. She was already feeling homesick and *Holland Silhouette* hadn't yet set sail. Perhaps she should have gone with Henry on a big holiday – life experiences should be shared. He should be lying next to her on the comfy super-king-size bed – both clinking their champagne glasses and looking forward to their adventure.

She had arranged this trip on purpose believing that if she missed Henry, he must be the man for her, the Mr. Right she had been looking for to spend the rest of her life with. Perhaps Henry was also testing his feelings for her. What if he was using this time to see if life was unbearable without her? What if it wasn't?

This could be the biggest mistake of her life.

CHAPTER FOUR

Jacqueline Sylvester was a plain but striking woman. She had dark, thick, curly hair styled by a top hairdresser. Her pale skin was surprisingly devoid of wrinkles and her eyes danced with humour. Tall and stylish, a shapely figure could be seen under her fitted jersey dress.

Alone in her cabin, she lay on the bed and thought about everything that had happened. Her memory took her back to the days when she first met and married Roger.

She worked for her husband part time in his family's china and glass hire company, supplying the catering trade with high quality products for large corporate and private events. Roger's father had started the business many years before and had employed her as book keeper and office manager. She knew the business back to front and upside down.

It was her first job straight from school and, over the years, she had witnessed many family dramas, including the breakdown of Roger's first marriage. They hand-picked his wife for him as she was a beautiful, sweet natured girl from a well-to-do family and wouldn't interfere with the family dynamics.

Jacqueline was heartbroken when Roger got engaged. She secretly harboured an enormous crush on him. He was handsome and charming; a real cheeky chappy, but not terribly bright. Luckily for him, his father had built up a small empire and was willing to employ his wayward son.

Roger would wander into the office late, sit at his desk with the door open and chat away on the telephone to his many girlfriends, spending his time making social arrangements in preference to doing any work. So deft was he at flirtatious conversation, he would simultaneously look over at Jacqueline and wink, sometimes blowing her a kiss. She would rush into the kitchen and make him a coffee, ensuring he had two of his favourite biscuits.

Watching from his office, Roger's father would sigh and walk over to Jacqueline's desk.

"He's such an idiot, Jacqueline, what am I to do with him?"

"He's not an idiot, he's just a loveable rogue," she would reply, flushing pink and smiling at Roger.

Roger's father nodded towards his son. "I'm bloody lucky I have you to make sure the orders are correct and go out on time *and*, more importantly, to take the cash. God help us if he was in charge." He walked into his son's office and closed the door, but their conversation soon became heated and could be easily heard.

"That girl is far too good for you. She's been on the phone to your mother again this morning, crying her eyes out." Roger's father was visibly upset.

"Crying her eyes out? Why? I haven't done anything to upset her. She was perfectly alright when I spoke to her this morning." Roger looked at his nails, wondering if he had time for a quick manicure.

"How would you know if she was perfectly alright this morning, you never notice her?" He had inadvertently created a monster.

"She would have told me, oh wait, no! - She would rather tell you and mum than have a meaningful conversation with me."

Things soon settled down and Roger must have made more of an effort with his fiancé, because early on a Saturday morning, a cream envelope with embossed writing dropped heavily onto the mat and Jacqueline's mother, suspecting what it was, called her daughter downstairs and handed her the letter. Jacqueline ripped it open and read the invitation to the wedding of the year.

"I wouldn't get too upset about it, darling, it won't last." It broke her heart to see her daughter hurting.

"Yes, it will. They'll stick it out even though they're completely wrong for each other. It's all about suitability. Let's face it, I'm just not good enough." Jacqueline had resigned herself to that fact long ago.

"We'll see. Meanwhile, I want you to buy a gorgeous dress and look amazing. Let him see what he's missed." Her mother knew her daughter would look stunning.

Jacqueline had her fair share of boyfriends and was active on the dating scene. What she lacked in looks she made up for in personality. Witty, clever and funny, she somehow managed to manipulate her date to take her to the most fashionable venues. From the most exclusive restaurants to the best shows in town, they all pushed the boat out to impress her even when money was tight, but her heart just wasn't in it. She hankered after the 'bad boy' son of her boss and that was that.

She may not be considered text book pretty, but she dieted hard and her figure was svelte with long, shapely legs, a perfectly round bottom and a small waist. A whole week's wages had been spent on her gown. The wedding was a black-tie affair in a smart London hotel and she was determined to look like a winner.

"Hey, how are you doing?" Roger walked into her office and closed the door - an unusual occurrence in itself as her door was never closed. She liked to know what was going on in the office and the rest of the staff liked her to know what was happening, too. She was a fair person across the board. If she heard anything that was inappropriate or unfair, she would step in and referee, putting everyone back on track.

"I'm great and you must be feeling quite excited now? Have you got your penguin suit?" She was referring to a dinner suit for his wedding. "What's with the long face?"

"I'm too young to die." Roger stared at her unsmilingly.

"It'll be fine, it's just pre-wedding nerves. You've got yourself a beautiful girl who adores you." Jacqueline cleared everything away that was in front of her. She wanted Roger to know that she had plenty of time and was listening.

"Is this it? Is my life as I know it over? No more laughs, adventures, scrapes…"

"The life as *you* know it is over, but a lovely new one is just beginning and let's face it, Roger, you couldn't go on chasing every bit of skirt around London forever. Eventually, somebody was going to come up from behind and overtake you." Jacqueline almost felt sorry for him.

"What do people mean when they talk about a partner in crime?" Roger was sitting in the little tub chair facing her with his feet up on the corner of her desk.

"I suppose they mean a kindred spirit, you know, like Bonnie and Clyde, Anthony and Cleopatra, Abbott and Costello…"

"Or it could be like Cain and Abel, Punch and Judy?"

"Yes, it could be, but it won't be."

"Do you think I'm doing the right thing? Be honest."

"No, I don't! I think you're making the biggest mistake of your entire life and you're going to die of boredom, well before you die of old age or any medical ailment…" was what she wanted to say, but instead she reached over the desk and took his hand in hers.

"I am a single woman, still searching for the man of my dreams. Why the hell are you asking me for advice on matrimony?" She hoped she had sidestepped the question.

"I'll ask you again; do you think I'm doing the right thing?" Roger knew her so well.

"Call her tonight and tell her you're very sorry, but you won't be attending your wedding as you will have run off with Jacqueline, the bookkeeper and office manager." She threw back her head and laughed.

"That's all I wanted to know." Roger got up from the chair, winked, blew her a kiss and walked out of her office.

———

"You look wonderful, have a lovely evening." Jacqueline's mother was watching her only child get ready to attend the wedding of the year. The event had occupied their thoughts for months and she was relieved that the day would soon be over and Jacqueline could get back to normality. "Daddy will be waiting outside to pick you up at midnight."

Jacqueline refused to allow anything to spoil the evening. Wishing she could swap places with the bride was a complete waste of time and anyway, she knew Roger wasn't in love with the woman he was about to marry. He was marrying out of duty and marriages like that rarely lasted the test of time. She would be waiting.

Roger's parents had put her on a wonderful table with nine of his closest friends. Good food and conversation flowed throughout the evening and the music topped it all off. Jacqueline danced the night away and as she glanced over at the top table; she could see Roger looking at her with a resigned expression on his face. He caught her eye and waved. She could have given her phone number out several times and no doubt there would have been a succession of wonderful dates, invitations to family events and maybe even the eventual suggestion to 'meet the parents', but what was the point? None of them were Roger.

As it turned out, her prediction came true sooner than anyone thought possible. The first few months of Roger's marriage seemed to go smoothly. They both returned from a beautiful honeymoon looking tanned and rested and moved into a lovely house in a leafy suburb. They had a wide circle of friends and entertained lavishly. Roger's father had the look of a man who had, yet again, clinched another successful deal. Jacqueline noticed that Roger was drinking heavily and often came to work looking bleary eyed and tired.

"Is everything alright?" Jacqueline would ask lightly; she didn't want Roger to think she was prying into his personal life. "I can do some extra bits this afternoon if you would like to go home and have a rest."

"No, I don't want to go home. If I fall asleep at my desk, so be it." It was unusual for Roger to be serious, not to make a silly joke or quip, so Jacqueline just nodded and kept her head down for the rest of the day. She knew when he wanted to talk.

It soon became apparent that Roger was leading a double life. He had become two people. The person speaking harshly to his wife, who called him more often at the office than usual, berating him for yet another crime committed and the second person who whispered softly in conversation, gently bantering with the person on the phone and looking amused and relaxed. Another clue was the absences from the office, growing in number and lengthening in time.

"I don't know what to do or say." Roger's father burst into Jacqueline's office well before his son had arrived at work. "His mother is beside herself; she seems to be getting the brunt of it. There are only so many times you can listen to how rotten your son is."

"I'm not sure there's anything you *can* do." She wouldn't have given an opinion anyway. Words have a habit of backfiring. Jacqueline felt very sorry for Mr. Sylvester, but she wished he wouldn't involve her in their family dispute.

———

"You look particularly chirpy this morning", Jacqueline said, amused at how Roger had bounded into the office, late and unapologetic.

"I have a lot to be chirpy about." He threw himself into her tub chair and waited to be questioned.

"Oh?" Jacqueline raised her eyebrows, knowing who would speak first."

Roger couldn't wait to be asked, he blurted it out. "I've met someone. Actually, I know her very well. She's married to a friend of mine."

"Nice! A very good friend *you've* turned out to be." Jacqueline was horrified.

"It's not like that. She's very unhappy."

"A good friend would listen, make sympathetic noises and try and help her see the positive side of her relationship. Let me guess! You're telling her to cheat on her husband, sneak around behind his back and have an affair with you. All of which will make her feel *much* better?" Jacqueline couldn't keep the irritation out of her voice.

"I didn't suggest it, nor did I force her. It just happened." Roger looked very smug and at that moment, Jacqueline wanted to hit him.

"What happens when your affair is discovered? Are you prepared to face the consequences?" For the first time ever, Jacqueline was very glad she wasn't married to Roger.

"I'll cross that bridge when I come to it."

———

"It says an awful lot about a man who could betray his new wife", Jacqueline's mother shook her head in disgust. "I knew he was feckless and daft, but I didn't think he would stoop so low and behave like that."

"Neither did I." Jacqueline agreed.

"I know you've been hankering after Roger for years, but this could be happening to you. How would *you* feel?" Her mother was very happy it wasn't happening to her daughter.

"I'd feel awful, but not as badly as Roger would feel after I got my hands on him."

"You would have to know about it first and usually the wife is the last person to find out, as you can see by this example." Her mother was quite right and Jacqueline shuddered.

"There's no question that dad and I would like to see you settle down and find a partner, no! I'll re-phrase that - a soul mate and have a parcel of kids so we can babysit, but the thought of you marrying someone like Roger would be our idea of hell."

———

"She's dumped me!" Roger burst into her office, expecting surprise.

"Who has? Your long-suffering wife?" It popped out before Jacqueline could stop it.

"No such luck. I'm talking about my bit on the side."

"I don't know how you can be so brazen about it and just come out with that. Where's your conscience?"

"You don't seem to understand, Jacqueline. She was my lifeline! I can't stand not to have anything to look forward to and, at present, my future seems very bleak."

"From where I'm sitting, it seems your wife's future is

even more bleak."

"I can't leave her; my parents will disown me. She has to desert me."

"How likely is that?" Jacqueline had never met such a wimp.

"If I make her life miserable enough she might."

"I can't listen to this anymore, Roger. It's cruel and I don't want to be party to it."

"You *have* to listen to me. I have nobody else to talk to. I can't trust my friends; I certainly can't confide in my family, there's only you, Jacs." He only ever used that nickname once before and that was many years before when he needed to borrow some money, no questions asked. In his defence he had paid her back, eventually.

"People get divorced, Roger, it happens. If things are getting so bad at home, move out and start divorce proceedings. It's got to be more dignified than creeping around behind her back." Jacqueline was rapidly losing respect for him.

"Creeping around behind her back is the safest option. Trust me, I know."

Roger took Jacqueline's advice and stopped confiding in her, but she knew things were no better because the intimate telephone calls and poor time keeping continued so she assumed the 'bit on the side' had been replaced with a new one.

———

"He's really screwed up now." Mr. Sylvester literally fell into Jacqueline's office. She thought he was about to have a heart attack and die right in front of her.

"What's happened?" As if she didn't already know.

"He's been having an affair, sleeping around, unfaithful from the very beginning." It was a whispered shout. Roger's father didn't want the already fully aware office to hear his shame.

"Are you sure you're not mistaken?" Jacqueline got up from her desk and guided him to her tub chair.

"You know, don't you? I can tell you already know."

"Yes, I do. I'm sorry. I tried to encourage him to behave honourably."

"She's been on the phone, her parents have called, closely followed by our family solicitor. What am I to do?"

"It's not your problem, it's his – theirs. They have to sort it out between them without parental interference - they're adults. I hope you don't mind me saying."

"Of course I don't mind, but his mother and I can't just sit and watch."

"Yes, you can. As uncomfortable and upsetting as that may be, you have no choice."

"He blames us, you know, for all of this - as if his mother and I frogmarched him up the aisle."

Jacqueline was *so* close to saying *"well actually that's exactly what you did. The signs were there from the beginning…",* but instead she said, "I'm going to make you a nice cup of tea and give you some biscuits from my secret stash."

What followed was the most acrimonious divorce of the century and Jacqueline started to close her office door. She could feel herself getting stressed at work, the atmosphere was heavy and depressing and she was losing some of her good staff who weren't prepared to put up with the working conditions. Gradually, things returned to some semblance of normality. Roger's personal life and work started to become two separate entities.

———

Mr. Sylvester was working late. He was usually out of the office and on his way home by 4.30pm. The routine worked like clockwork. She could set her watch by it, but

Jacqueline noticed that he was in no hurry to leave.

The rest of the office staff had left for the day and Jacqueline was doing her rounds, making sure everything was in order and papers were safely filed away, the desks ready for the cleaners who would let themselves in early in the morning.

"I'm going home now, Mr. Sylvester, are you coming out with me?"

"I've been waiting to talk to you, Jacqueline and I had to be sure everyone had gone home and we were alone here."

"That sounds creepy." She smiled at him.

"He says he's in love with you. He wants to marry you and always has." Mr. Sylvester looked the picture of misery.

"Who said that?"

"Roger! He told his mother and me that if he had married you, he wouldn't be getting divorced now and that he should never have allowed himself to be persuaded to marry anyone else. He said I should have seen the chemistry between you and encouraged the match and not insisted he marry some vapid, pale creature who obviously was going to bore him."

It was Jacqueline's turn to fall into one of Mr. Sylvester's guest tub chairs in *his* office.

"I don't believe it. He's having you on."

"No, he's perfectly serious. I know my son and he's telling the truth. Did you know he felt that way about you?"

"I had absolutely no idea. I'm very fond of Roger, as you well know and we have a special connection. He knows he can talk to me about anything. He has never behaved inappropriately or given me any reason to think he was in love with me. I haven't encouraged him. You do know that don't you?"

"Do you love him, Jacqueline?"

She looked at the man she regarded as her second father, a man who has been kind and fair towards her, recognising her talent and her hard work and generously rewarding her for it and nodded. "Yes, I have always loved him, despite all his faults," she said smiling, trying to lighten the atmosphere.

"What can I say?" He asked her gently.

"Nothing if you wish. We can pretend we haven't had this conversation. I hope you're not going to sack me or ask me to resign. I love my job."

"Sack you? Resign? That's a fine way to treat my new daughter-in-law." He got up from his desk. "May I have permission to take liberties with a member of my staff and soon to be newest addition to our family and hug you?"

———

He didn't know what put the idea into his head, but he was being backed into a corner and needed an excuse, fast. Accusations were flying around like bullets and he needed a reason for his diabolical behaviour and confessing to a secret longing for Jacqueline seemed the obvious solution.

"So, you never loved me? Why did you go through with it and let my parents pay a fortune inviting *your* friends and huge family to a lavish wedding they can ill-afford?" His wife was looking at Roger in amazement, disgust and loathing.

Roger thought that was as very reasonable question, unfortunately he didn't have the answer.

"I do love you, of course I do, but I just can't help my behaviour." He was happy to take the blame, say anything as long as he could walk away from his marriage, "although I didn't ask your parents to get into debt by paying for our wedding."

"You didn't, but your parents expected it. The whole thing was for show and now we all look stupid." His wife was cringing with the shame. The first of her friends to get married, she was enormously proud to be marrying such a good looking, successful man and be the envy of everyone who knew her. It serves her right for being so vain.

Roger sat next to her on the sofa and took her hand. She snatched it away. "We don't look stupid. Isn't it better that we call it a day now rather than live miserably together for the rest of our lives? I'm not happy and you're not, either - what's the point?"

"You never gave it a chance, Roger. As soon as you realised you had to grow up and be responsible, you freaked out. We were going to have our own little unit, start a family and have a lovely life. Why would you throw all that away?" His parents thought that was a very good question and wanted to know the answer.

Roger had always been spoiled. He was good looking; popular and great company and people enjoyed being around him, unfortunately he lacked intelligence, a conscience and a heart. Everyone was dispensable; there was no need for loyalty.

He was sent to one of the top boarding schools in the country and proceeded to waste his father's money getting poor grades and bad reports. His parents realised that to waste further money on his education would be pointless, so joining the family business was the only option open to him.

He was happy for his father to make all the decisions at work and had absolutely no desire to take over and put his own stamp on the business. Leaving the running of it to other people suited him very well. It gave him the means to pop in and out as and when he felt like it and when he did grace the office with his presence; he was greeted by Jacqueline's smiling face. She was always good for a laugh, a nice strong cup of tea and decent biscuits. Smart and discreet, he felt safe to confide in her about almost anything. She was the only person in the world unafraid to tell him what a wimp, rogue and general ass he could be and the only one he allowed to say it.

That's why he thought of his fool proof plan. The reason he couldn't settle down in his marriage was because he loved someone else, not just a 'five-minute wonder' relationship, but someone he had known for most of his adult life and had grown to love and respect. He had to think of something that would carry some weight and *"sorry Dad, but I haven't finished playing the field and hate being tied down"* would not be an acceptable reason in his parent's opinion. It was a light bulb moment.

"I had no idea you felt that way about Jacqueline, why didn't you tell me?" His father looked at his son in astonishment.

"I didn't think you would approve. I mean, let's face it, you're a terrible snob, Jacqueline is just a working girl. You would have said she wasn't good enough for me, wouldn't you?"

"Not good enough for you? What a thing to say to me! She's too damned good for you and if she's taken in by this garbage and falls for you, you'll be bloody lucky."

His father was right. It was a bit far-fetched to think he would be madly in love with the office girl, but if it meant it would stop being gossip fodder, so be it.

———

Jaqueline was with her parents, sitting in the living

room in front of the fire. All three watching the flames licking the last of the logs in the grate.

"We're not happy, Jacqueline." That was evident by their raised voices as her parents began to pace around the room. "We're very much against you marrying him, but you're a big girl and obviously accustomed to making your own decisions, be they right or wrong. This, however, would be the biggest mistake of your life."

"Let's look at this sensibly, without prejudice on your part," Jacqueline was sitting down watching her parents over-react. "Roger married a woman he knew he didn't love in order to please his parents. He couldn't say "no" to them, even though he knew he should. Isn't that a point in his favour?" Jacqueline felt very calm in the knowledge that, at last, the man of her dreams was in her life and there to stay.

"Of course it isn't. Only a lily-livered coward would go through with a marriage to a woman he didn't care for, hoodwink his parents and hers and dupe an innocent girl into believing he was in love with her. She was evidently beguiled by his charm and what she supposed was glamour instead of the reality that he was a fraudster." Her parents weren't having any of it.

"Have you ever known a divorce that wasn't acrimonious? They are two perfectly nice people who turn into the most horrible people in the world when they're together." Jacqueline explained patiently.

"No, we have not, but this situation is completely different because Roger was never 'perfectly nice'. He must have always been horrible to have let things drag on for as long as they did. He had an agenda, no question about it."

"And what agenda would he have had?" Jacqueline was bemused. She would like to know.

"He probably thought he could stick with it. His wife, by all accounts, is quiet, timid and shy and he thought he could get away with anything and take up where he left off as a single man. Unfortunately for him, the worm turned and she proved not to be so timid after all."

"Well I can't argue with that. It sounds about right, but he's dealing with me now and I won't be such a pushover." Jacqueline was smiling, but her parents thought she was being very naïve.

"If he can behave like that with one wife, what makes you think he won't with another?"

"Because I won't go quietly, and he knows that very well."

———

The waiter reached over and removed the vintage champagne from the ice-bucket. They were sitting in Roger's favourite restaurant, celebrating their forthcoming engagement and looked the picture of a couple totally besotted with each other.

They lifted their glasses up, ready for a toast before Jacqueline said, "I don't have any doubts that you're the man for me, but I know plenty of people who have."

"Who cares what other people think? I've never been bothered as you well know." Roger put his glass down, took her hand and kissed it then reached over and kissed her on the lips. "It's so lovely to be with a woman I don't have to impress or pretend to be something I'm not. You know me, warts and all and you still love and want me." Roger had never been more sincere.

"I'd rather have you without the warts, if you don't mind, but yes, I'm a firm believer in taking a person for who they are and not try to change them, but I expect you to do the same. Are you sure this is what you want? I know it's what I want and have done since I first saw you."

"I was so busy messing around with women just so that I would have some juicy tittle-tattle to tell you every day, an excuse to come rushing into your office and make you laugh. Even seeing your raised eyebrows in shock was entertaining. I didn't stop to think about the real reason why I was itching to see *you*. I didn't care about those women one bit. It seems I've wasted an awful lot of time, but then I'm very good at that."

"I think we're going to be very happy, darling." Jacqueline squeezed his hand."

"I agree, and *never* bored."

———

Their wedding was a very intimate affair, so different from Roger's first marriage in every way.

Roger felt part of this one, interested in every aspect of it right down to the choice of fillings for the canapés. He felt safe with Jacqueline - not to the extent that he could take her for granted, but content in the knowledge that they would have a wonderful and exciting life. She would see to that.

Only close friends and immediate family were invited, and the atmosphere was perfect. Jacqueline's parents insisted on paying for the wedding, refusing to accept any contribution from Roger's family. That way, *they* called the shots and invited who *they* wanted. There would be no spectators, just the people whom they knew would be genuinely happy to come and celebrate.

When they returned from their honeymoon, Jacqueline knew immediately that two would soon be three and proceeded to prepare for the arrival of their much-wanted child with great excitement.

Jacqueline took a long hot shower and prepared for

dinner, after which she intended to take a book and sit on her balcony to read. Hopefully, there will be nothing to worry about and her beloved will come back on-board ship soon.

CHAPTER FIVE

"Don't eat a banana in front of Michelle, she doesn't like it." Miranda turned around and was startled to hear the instruction fired at her from a complete stranger, quite rudely she thought. She turned to Michelle and put her banana back in her bag.

"I'm so sorry; are you allergic to bananas?"

"No, I just don't like the look of them, they repulse me." Michelle looked expectantly at Miranda.

Miranda reached into her bag, extracting the banana once again and peeled it. If she pandered to everyone's eating phobias, she might die of starvation. "Please feel free to look away; it won't take long to eat."

Michelle got up and walked to the other side of the room, tutting and whispering in disgust.

The little group had just come back from a glorious tour of a small Italian market town and were spending the afternoon resting on sunbeds around the swimming pool.

The ship had docked in the early hours of the morning and by the time Miranda had woken and had her usual breakfast on her balcony, the gangway had been latched on and people were disembarking ready for a full day of activity.

The horses and carriages were waiting in the square to take the tourists for a fifteen-minute ride around the town. Miranda ran up to the driver before the others could stop her and chatted in fluent hand signals.

"It's a hundred euros for a lovely romantic trip around the town." Miranda shouted.

"Well you can go without me," Sandra shouted back.

"We all have to go for it to be economical." Miranda never let a high price stop her.

Sandra walked up to the driver, spoke in a low voice and they all watched the blood drain from his face.

"I've got him down to fifty euros – that's more like it, but it's still a fortune," she said, climbing in and sitting down, facing forward.

"What did you say to him? He didn't look very happy", Miranda asked.

"I just reminded him that the police don't take kindly, in any country, to the natives robbing the tourists and that I just passed one on my way over."

"Oh, that's a shame, he probably won't take us to the nice parts now", Cynthia said. "I feel sick facing backwards."

"*You* should have gone up and worked your magic on him – then *you* could have had the first pick of the seats." Sandra looked victorious.

The driver took them on a lovely slow trot around town, through the narrow, winding medieval streets, leading up to the church on the top of the hill and back to the square.

Cynthia, Sandra, Jacqueline and Miranda had lunch in a small trattoria in the town. A selection of freshly made pasta, tricolour salad and fresh bread, dipped in olive oil and balsamic vinegar. They could have eaten the same thing on the ship, but somehow it tasted better in a rustic Italian restaurant on dry land.

"John was desperate to come with us, but I told him it was a girly day out and I would see him later." Cynthia simpered and giggled, and Miranda stared at her in wonderment. The 'astounded' look was beginning to take root on her face. She liked Cynthia a great deal and enjoyed having her as a bridge partner, but when it came to the social side, Miranda found her a little tiresome. Talking to someone with a completely one-track mind was weird.

"Is it official?" Jacqueline asked. "Is he now your

boyfriend, man friend, partner or whatever you would like to call him?"

"For the purposes of this holiday, yes, I suppose he is." She roared with laughter, but none of the others joined in.

"What? I'm just being honest." Cynthia was picking at the salad.

"There comes a time in a woman's life when It becomes undignified to lead men on." Sandra was getting really fed up with that stupid woman thinking she could have any man she wanted.

"I wouldn't say I was leading him on, and the arrangement seems to suit us both. I like John very much, but we're not stuck together like glue and he's married – for now."

"Oh dear, I wonder if his wife knows that their marriage will soon be in trouble. Women who play with men's emotions and flitter from one to the other usually end up with nobody." Sandra said, caustically.

"*You* don't have anyone even with your dignity," Cynthia flicked her blonde hair. "If I didn't know better, I would say you're jealous. There are loads of men on the ship you could flirt with – plenty to go around. It's ever such fun." Cynthia looked at Sandra.

"I wouldn't let myself down. I may not have much, but I still have my self-respect."

"Come on, Sandra, she's only teasing you. We're in Italy, the land of the gigolo and bottom pincher. Embrace it, I say." Jacqueline wanted to burst out laughing but dared not with the pinched faces around her.

"No, it's not funny. Cynthia is a predator. She has an insatiable appetite for men."

"I'll say." Cynthia said with great amusement.

"Why are you getting so uptight, Sandra? What

difference does it make to you if Cynthia gobbles up every single man on the ship?" Jacqueline was beginning to enjoy herself.

"She throws her net out to see what she can catch, sorts through it and throws the rest back into the water. Some of the catch are left floundering on the deck and are left gasping for air, but that wouldn't bother Cynthia."

"You've conjured up quite an image, Sandra; I shan't dignify it with a reply other than to say that if they swim into the net, they get what they deserve." Cynthia's sense of humour was evaporating.

"Come on, girls; let's do some shopping while we're here." Miranda was watching her limited shopping time disappear and was panicking.

Back on the ship, it was time for an afternoon bridge game, after which John came rushing over to their table.

"Time for tea, I think", he said, gazing at Cynthia.

"Oh, for pity's sake, you two go in. Shall we have tea ourselves?" Sandra turned to Miranda and Jacqueline.

"Yes, you had better have tea without me. Poor John has waited long enough." Cynthia laughed, took John's arm and she could be heard filling him in on the day's events as they walked towards the lift.

———

"I'm sorry, but she's impossible", Sandra was pouring tea for the three of them.

"I think she's fun. She's not hurting anyone, is she?" Jacqueline asked. It was a fair question.

It was very clear that Cynthia was a woman of limited intelligence. If she didn't talk about men, she probably wouldn't have anything to say. Jacqueline's friends were interesting – cultivated women who enjoyed music, reading, going to the theatre, and eating in restaurants serving good food and even better wine. She could never be close friends with a woman like that.

"Well, we're not sure if she's hurting anyone or not." Sandra looked suspicious. "She may well be, but that wouldn't be an issue for Cynthia. Treading on other people's toes wouldn't bother her."

———

Cynthia had known Sandra for years, ever since their single days and she hadn't changed at all – still as miserable and heavy going as ever. It was no wonder her husband's left her. Very few men would hang around with a woman like that forever.

Sandra's first husband was a lovely man – good company and kind-hearted. He must have been to put up with her for as long as he did. When things got too much for him, he would telephone Cynthia and unburden himself.

"I don't intend to stay with her for much longer; it's only our children that are keeping me here. I will leave her, you know." He sounded more desperate each time he said it.

"What do you want me to say, Alan, my loyalty is to Sandra. I can't talk about her behind her back." Cynthia genuinely felt sad for her friend but couldn't help feeling that the woman brought misery on herself.

"I want you to say that you'll be waiting for me and that *we* can be together. My life will be so different with a fun, positive person in it."

"No, we can't! In case you haven't noticed, I have a husband."

"He's a sick man, Cynthia. We should both grab a bit of happiness while we can."

"I can't believe you're saying such a horrible thing, Alan. Just because you're stuck with someone you don't love. I love my husband. Yes, he's desperately ill, but I'm going nowhere."

"Who are you talking to?" Sandra walked into the room and saw her husband whispering down the phone. Unfortunately for him, Sandra could make out the shrieking voice of Cynthia on the other end.

He hung up abruptly. "I was talking to Cynthia as a matter of fact, trying to put a date in the diary for another get together."

"But I usually do that, Alan, as you well know. I am in charge of organising our social arrangements." Alarm bells were ringing in Sandra's ears. She wasn't interested in listening to any more of his lame excuses. She knew who was responsible. That bloody woman was trying to break up her happy home. Cynthia was in for a shock if she thought she was going to just sit back and let her move in on her husband.

Cynthia heard Sandra come into the room and the mobile phone went dead. What a wimp! He didn't have the guts to stand his ground. Leave her husband for him? Her lovely, strong, brave husband was more of a man than Alan would ever be, even close to death. She supposed that now Sandra would blame her even more for the crumbling of her marriage.

Not long after that conversation, Cynthia's husband passed away, leaving her and their two daughters bereft. He was still young, fit and as sexy as anything, even after the ravages of chemotherapy treatment. They had been childhood sweethearts and he had captured her heart from the beginning.

After so many years of marriage, the very sight of him still gave her butterflies in her stomach. She ran a beautiful home and she entertained lavishly, knowing when to turn on the charm and who to bestow it upon. Whilst she was in mourning, Alan filed for divorce and of course, according to Sandra, it was all Cynthia's fault.

There had been a few flirtations over the years. She knew she was a good-looking woman – she had been told that often enough from a very early age, but that's all it was – silly flirtatious banter with no substance. She wasn't about to count that one episode with the Managing Director of her husband's firm as a betrayal of her marriage. It wasn't her fault that he was smitten with her after that evening she entertained him and his wife for dinner, at home. He took her for lunch to The Ritz and they had their dessert upstairs in a suite that he had booked for the occasion, but as far as Cynthia was concerned, that was just a fun afternoon never to be repeated – It couldn't be even if she had wanted more. He left the company very soon afterwards.

Cynthia was a pretty, silly, flighty little thing. She left school with no qualifications and went to work in one shop after another as a sales assistant. It wasn't that she couldn't do the job as she was very good at it, but it just didn't float her boat. Some of her friends had rewarding careers, working their way up from the post room to become buyers of big multi-national organisations until they married and had children. To Cynthia, none of it was important. It just didn't matter- her husband was quiet, confident and successful and he knew she adored him. He was the Captain of their ship and generally made the decisions in their household. He was a marvellous partner and father. Cynthia was smart enough to know that she had the best of the bunch.

"I won't have it, Sandra. I allow you get away with murder. You speak rudely to me all the time and accuse me of all sorts with *your* husband and everyone else's. I'm in mourning for my own darling husband and most normal people would understand that and let it go, but not you. You've come to see me to start an argument when others have come to offer their condolences. It's got to stop, otherwise I really will turn my back on you. You can't afford to lose any more friends."

"Admit it! Just own up; you were instrumental in the breakup of my marriage and I'll stop badgering you."

"No, I was not! In fact, I persuaded Alan to stay with you and not to break up your marriage if you must know. I also told him to stop complaining about you to me. There! You would push and push until you made me say it and now you know."

"What do you mean 'persuaded him to stay with me'?"

"Exactly that! Alan would call me all the time, saying how miserable he was and how he wanted to leave you. I told him to stop calling – that I was your friend and wouldn't talk about you behind your back. Those calls were in confidence and I didn't want to make trouble. It seemed to me there was enough of that in your house without my input. If you don't believe me, you can ask him."

Amazingly, their friendship survived all that and even more astonishing was that Sandra found someone else to torment. Cynthia gave the new bloke the once-over and found him wanting. He thought he was onto a good thing; a rich divorcee with a fat settlement was an easy target. Little did he know he was going to earn every penny before he, also, would ultimately divorce her.

———

After the initial shock of widowhood, it would be true to say that Cynthia embraced her single status. At first, she dated frantically – mostly for fear of being lonely. She had seen other women lose their sparkle and zest for life through lack of male company and that wasn't going to happen to her.

She was shocked to discover the number of men who were in unhappy marriages and relationships. How could they be so weak and downtrodden? It would take a very special man to win her over and it hadn't taken her that long to find him.

CHAPTER SIX

Roger Sylvester could still feel the humiliation and embarrassment of being dragged off the coach in front of everyone. As he took the walk of shame down the aisle, the pitying and, in many cases, amused expression on the faces of those stupid people would forever be etched on his memory.

He knew very well why the police were after him, but being a seasoned and plausible liar, he was able to pull the wool over Jacqueline's eyes. She didn't suspect a thing.

His china and glass hire business had gone from strength to strength and he had expanded into the hiring of chairs, tables, and themed furniture. The fashion for the ultimate party was to turn a blank space into a fifties American diner or a nightclub setting with low sofas, colour changing LED cube stools and a funky cocktail bar. He was the man who knew how to do it. Thanks to his wonderful wife and daughter, the company was at the cutting edge of cool party hire. Party planners and caterers were phoning constantly on behalf of their clients.

He was not in the habit of helping himself to large wads of cash from his business account, but a little studio flat had come on the market and the vendor was prepared to do a very good deal for a quick cash sale. It was already nicely furnished and ready to go, should he wish to rent it or even use it from time to time as a little love nest. Either way, it was a good investment.

Other people had invested money in his business as it grew beyond all recognition, but at the end of the day, that's exactly what it was, *his* business and if he needed some cash, he was entitled to help himself liberally to it. As long as their dividends kept coming, that's all that mattered or so he thought. Anyway, if all else fails, a second mortgage on his house should put right some wrongs, help him escape prosecution and shut them all up.

Jacqueline had been right to marry him; she was a good judge of character. He had been loyal and faithful ever since he put a ring on her finger. His past mistakes were long forgotten. He was a happily married man and father to their beautiful daughter, Abby. Walking her up the aisle and into the waiting arms of her soon–to-be husband was the cherry on his cake.

He had made an awful fuss when Abby suggested getting married to Alfie, but the boy seemed very committed and, as Jacqueline said many times, marriage is a leap of faith for everyone.

Everything changed when he took up bridge. At first, it was only once a week. An evening game at a local club which he thoroughly enjoyed. Despite the difficult rules and conventions, he found the game relaxing and addictive.

Once it developed into three times a week, the social aspect developed as well – an endless supply of attractive women. The widowed, lonely, and divorced, ranging from thirty to sixty were only too happy to be his partner for the evening. It was like being a child in a sweet shop, only sweeter. Sometimes Roger would play bridge and sometimes he would be doing other things, but he was never late home. He was always very careful not to arouse suspicion. Jacqueline was like a bloodhound; she could smell if anything were out of the ordinary.

He couldn't believe how easy it was to find women willing to spend time with him – in and out of bed, no questions asked and the sex was fantastic. It was lucky for him Jacqueline had a low sex drive and didn't expect him to perform on his bridge nights. He would have given the game away immediately as he had only ever once turned her down and that was the night before he was about to have major surgery.

Of course, Roger had his favourites, the girls he particularly liked to play with and gradually he narrowed down his selection. That little blonde cutie caught his eye and her cleavage held it. They played bridge together most of the time, but sometimes they would take time off, go to her lovely bungalow and spend a few hours in bed. Cynthia never asked him any questions about his personal life; he could see she wasn't interested. Her only interest was sex, dinner, and the beautiful gifts he bought her.

———

"Nick Lombardo has arranged a bridge cruise and I think we should both go on it."

Roger was sitting having dinner. It was a Friday night and all the family were sitting around the table eating the wonderful food and enjoying a relaxing end of the week evening.

"But you hate playing bridge with me so how will that work?" Jacqueline was surprised he was inviting her to go with him.

"We don't have to play together *all* the time. We can switch partners from time to time, but we'll be together on a lovely holiday and that's all that matters. We'll jump off the ship and explore. What do you say?"

Abby watched her parents and smiled. "We think it's a marvellous idea. If it weren't such a busy time for us, we'd come with you." She placed her hand on her husband's knee and squeezed it.

Abby had asked her father if she could meet his bridge partner, seeing as he was spending so much time on the game and Roger sensibly arranged for the three of them to go out for supper. Jacqueline had no interest in joining them, preferring to stay at home, curled up in the armchair watching her soaps.

Jacqueline was taken aback. Recently, she had started to feel a little unsettled. She wasn't sure exactly when it started, but something wasn't right between them. Up until that moment, life had been one long honeymoon.

Roger was getting twitchy, nervy and a bit short-tempered with her, something that had never happened before. They loved spending time together, whether it was going out for the evening or just sitting at home with a takeaway and a good film. He was happy just to be by her side, but lately she had the impression that he was restless and, knowing him so well, alarm bells started to ring.

"I think it's a marvellous idea, count me in. Give me a few days to buy some fabulous clothes and I'll be ready."

———

"Why on earth would you invite your wife on a cruise with your little bit of fluff?" Cynthia was laughing, but she really didn't think it was funny at all.

"Tactics, my lovely little cactus blossom." Roger was happy to explain it all while he was kissing and licking her neck. "My better half is about to rein in my freedom – I can feel it in my water and I can't have that."

"What exactly do you mean?" Cynthia asked.

"I know when Jacqueline is feeling unsettled and, at the moment, she's watching and waiting for me to do something stupid. I think she's wondering why I enjoy spending so much time at the club and jumping to the right conclusions. I want to show her she has nothing to worry about."

"I've met your wife and she has a lot to worry about and so have you." Cynthia replied, rather nastily Roger thought. "I also met your daughter, on several occasions. You introduced her to me. She's a very pretty girl. Quiet, but pretty."

Roger could feel his temper rising and his voice was steely. "She's a beautiful girl and bloody clever, too and you are quite wrong. I don't have *anything* to be concerned about and neither have my family. Jacqueline will see me playing bridge with all my friends. I will partner her from time to time and she will feel relaxed. She will laugh at the notion that anything suspicious is going on between me and any other woman in the world and be reassured. We will have a lovely week away." Roger had it all worked out. "What's to worry about?"

Cynthia was grinding her teeth with irritation. He thought he was so clever, juggling his mistress and his wife so well, even to the extent that they could both be on board ship with him on a week's holiday. How arrogant was he to be so smug about it?

"Wouldn't the possibility of Jacqueline finding out about us worry you?" Cynthia was smiling.

"Now I *know* you're joking. Who in their right mind would throw away beautiful dinners in the finest restaurants, lovely jewellery and a wonderful sex life by being indiscreet? Nobody I know, that's for sure. I only know clever people."

"You're quite right, but I'm falling in love with you. I know you're hooked on me, too, Roger. Why don't we make it permanent?"

"I know women like you, Cynthia. If it were permanent, you would get bored of me and cast me aside like an old glove. The way things are, I can't wait to see you. We rip each other's clothes off before we make it to the bedroom. That would all stop."

"You must think I'm very shallow if you think that's all I'm interested in." Cynthia was indignant.

"No, I don't think you're shallow at all. I think you're marvellous. That's the point. It's fabulous the way things are. Why make it humdrum? I've got that already."

Cynthia had taken all her clothes off and was standing naked. She walked up to him and stroked him; happy he was instantly turned on. He stripped off quickly and they fell onto the rug.

———

Abby was fully aware that her parents adore her because they were forever telling her so. The apple of her father's eye – actually, of both her parent's eyes, she secretly enjoyed hearing her mother call her their honeymoon baby. It made her feel wanted and loved.

Her parents were unusual in that they always treated her as an adult. She accompanied them wherever they went. When her friends were being looked after by nannies and au-pairs, she was in the back of the car on her way to the theatre, concerts and dinners with *their* friends. As a result, she was privy to almost every conversation.

Growing up, she always had the finest money could buy. Her father sent her to the best private school in the area and she grew to be a fashion leader rather than follower, thanks to her trust fund.

Sadly, her privileged background was not a barrier from getting involved with the wrong crowd and when she and her cool gang of giggling teenagers escaped the confines of the school campus to descend on the local shops, the temptation to steal a souvenir from their adventure was too great to resist.

The store detective, suspicious of a crowd of girls whispering together, watched on camera as backpacks and holdalls were stuffed with valuable clothing. Abby and her friends were prevented from leaving the store, their bags were searched and evidence of the crime found. To her horror, both the police and her father were called and a trip to the police station followed.

Roger took it well, considering. However, Jacqueline did not. There began the blame game of whose genes Abby had inherited to drive her to commit such a needless and avoidable crime, bearing in mind her background.

Unlike some of her friends, Abby was very fortunate that, being her first offence and hopefully the last, she got away with a caution, but her fingerprints were now on the police data base and the knowledge of that kept her on the right side of the law.

As an only child, her parents went to great trouble to ensure that she was never lonely. They encouraged her to invite her friends over for sleepovers, weekends and generously took her closest ones with them on their lovely holidays – always somewhere exotic and exciting.

Roger held court at the dinner table and her girlfriends giggled flirtatiously at the racy stories of his youth, stopping just short of being lewd.

"I hope you don't mind that daddy chats away, darling", her mother would ask. "I know it's a bit embarrassing, but he does love chatting with your lovely friends."

"I know he does, mummy. I don't mind at all. They seem to enjoy it and he's very funny. If it were anyone else's father, I think it would be a bit creepy, but he's such a good storyteller."

Jacqueline laughed. "I should say so – the best you'll

find anywhere."

Abby continued to laugh but looked at her mother quizzically. "What do you mean?"

"Let's just say he's had a lot of practice – I mean in his single days, of course, like most young men. Now, he's a loving husband and father – so I suppose it's lucky he got it out of his system."

The exorbitant fees her parents paid for her education paid off. She was a good student and they had a school file full of, mostly, glowing reports. When it was time to decide on university places, Abby wasn't interested. Against her parent's advice, she decided to go into her father's catering hire and events business.

Her youthful exuberance and natural flair took the company to a different level. She reminded Roger of Jacqueline, with her calm approach to problems and charming way with the clients. The company got a much-needed turbo boost and soon overtook their competitors by miles.

"If you're going to visit clients and talk about helping them make wonderful parties, you'll need a cool little sports car to seal any deal."

"I need them to take me seriously, daddy. I would much prefer to drive a small van with our company name emblazoned all over it. We want people to realise that 'cool' is hiring us to organise their events."

Roger laughed. "My goodness, you really are your mother's daughter."

Abby wasn't worried when she brought her boyfriend home to meet her parents – why would she be? They had never criticised any of her friends and her relationship with them was very open. There was absolutely no need for secrets, but the atmosphere changed when she suggested that she and Alfie wanted to make it permanent.

"Would you agree that I have always gone along with anything you wanted to do?" Roger asked her.

Abby's heart missed a beat. "I would agree, but where is this line of questioning going? You're making me nervous."

"I'm simply saying that for me to advise you not to go ahead and marry Alfie must mean that alarm bells are ringing very loudly in my ears." Roger was trying to stay calm and remain his usual flippant self.

"You haven't said anything about it before. You always seemed to like Alfie – you've made him very welcome." Abby sat down on a footstool in the sitting room and followed her father's gaze to the six o'clock news on the television.

"As a friend, like some of the other boyfriends you've had, he's fine. I wouldn't say he's anything special. He has an average job, earning an average salary. I wouldn't call him exciting or interesting. He's pleasant." For once, her father had no more to say on the subject.

"So, what's the problem with that? He's got a job; he earns a salary and he's asked to marry me. He hasn't pissed me off; he hasn't pissed my parents off – it's all good."

"He actually has pissed me off, Abby. He dumped you a while ago because he thought he found someone better, possibly a girl from a more comfortable family. It didn't just upset you, it upset me and your mother, too. There was no point mentioning it at the time. We just hoped he would be tempted away again."

"That's a bit harsh, daddy. Lots of people think they want something or someone else and then realise that it was a mirage and they go back to their original love."

Jacqueline had been listening to the conversation but

was biding her time to give her opinion.

"I would also like to know why you don't like Alfie." Jacqueline knew the day would come when her husband admitted that nobody would be good enough to marry their beloved daughter.

"He's not good enough for her, Jacqueline."

"Why? It's not just the job or the salary, is it? I know you. What is it, Roger?" Jacqueline wanted him to say it outright.

"I think he's got a roving eye. I think he'll be a womaniser and I don't want Abby to have to worry about that." Roger spat it out. He wouldn't hurt his daughter for the world, but he knew he had by telling her this, and there it is.

As soon as Alfie came into the house, Roger recognised something in him. The familiar swagger and over-confidence, the presumption that he would be welcomed with open arms by Abby's parents and treated royally. What did he have to offer a beautiful girl like his daughter? He was a chancer, that's what *he* was.

"What you're saying is you think she can do better?"

"There she goes again," Roger had always thought Jacqueline was a bloody mind-reader.

"No, I'm not saying that." He lied. "I'm saying that marriage is for life and she needs to be sure she's got the right man."

"Like you were, daddy, when you got married – the first time?"

He felt a sharp stabbing feeling in his heart. Abby had never criticised him in her whole short life. She absolutely idolised him. He didn't miss a beat as he said "Who better to advise you than me? Doesn't that make me the perfect person to understand what's happening here?"

"We love each other, daddy. I'm going to marry Alfie

because I think we're meant to be together."

"Why don't we just think about this for a day or two. Let's have the weekend to chew it over and then Alfie can come over and we'll talk to him." Jacqueline remembered her parents warning and how she totally ignored them. Talking it through for as long as possible, before any action is taken, can only be a good thing.

———

Abby was lying on the bed in her room, crying quietly. Did it really matter if her parents didn't approve of Alfie? Yes, it did. She wanted to maintain the close family unit. She longed for her parents to be happy for her; embrace all the excitement of making the wedding. She was desperate to hear her mother on the phone, loudly talking and laughing to friends and family, pretending to be coy about revealing too many details of the wedding plans.

She heard her father preparing to leave the house to go and play bridge and decided to follow him and waylay him in the carpark for a quiet chat, on their own. He might even forgo the game, finding some excuse, and they could find a quiet café where she could talk him round to seeing things her way.

She waited in her little car for him to pass, knowing he wouldn't notice her parked at the top of the road, in the dark. After a few minutes, she realised he wasn't going to the bridge club after all but driving in a completely different direction. She followed close behind. Eventually, he pulled up outside a sweet little bungalow with a sports car in the driveway. She parked directly opposite and watched. The front door sprang open and an attractive blonde woman threw herself into his arms. Who the hell was she?

Abby's heart sank. She must be mistaken in thinking

what she was thinking. Her devoted father and adoring husband, the man who valued his beloved little family more than anything in the world would surely never jeopardise it. She knew exactly what she was going to do. She picked up her phone and called Alfie. She was ready to set a date for their wedding.

The next day, without revealing what she had seen, she asked her father if she could meet his bridge partner, seeing as he was spending so much time on the game. For a brief moment, Roger thought about procuring some little, plain mouse of a woman to act the part, but his daughter was far too clever to fall for that.

Roger insisted on picking Cynthia up and driving to the restaurant separately. "We'll meet you at Luigi's, darling", he said to Abby, "Just in case you want to go on somewhere afterwards. You won't want to hang around with us the whole evening, will you."

Abby arrived a little early and was shown to the best table in the restaurant. The head waiter recognised the name on the reservation.

Good evening, Madam. Please sit here, away from the draft of the door." He pulled back her chair. "Mrs. Manning particularly likes this table."

She saw her father and Cynthia were laughing as they walked in. He pulled out the chair for her to sit down and walked over to kiss his daughter.

The evening went surprisingly well. So well, in fact, that Abby thought she had imagined an intimate relationship between them. Cynthia avoided any suspicious body language, treating Roger as a dear, but slightly irritating friend. She chatted to Abby as if they were girlfriends, regaling amusing stories and revealing personal details about herself that even Roger hadn't heard before and he thought Abby seemed to be falling for her charms.

Roger, sensing his daughter might need regular reassurance, made a note in his diary for them to meet again in the same restaurant in the near future. It had obviously been one of his better ideas.

_____

"Hello darling, I'm here and on the way to the ship."

Roger was exhausted. He had flown into Pisa and taken a taxi to Livorno ready to pick up the cruise. It had all been a terrible rush as the ship was docking for one day only and he had been worried that, bearing in mind the reputation of the budget airline on which he had booked, he wouldn't make it in time. He was excited to join the ship and start his belated holiday as soon as possible.

On reflection, he was a very lucky man. He had been questioned extensively at the police station after they dropped him home. He was expected to hurriedly produce copies of bank statements and accounts, as well as the contact details of his solicitor and accountant.

It had been difficult to prove that he had innocently removed several hundred thousand pounds from his account, in cash, to buy a flat without the knowledge or say-so of any other signatory on the account, but after several assurances that the matter would be resolved expeditiously on his return, he was a free man.

"Oh darling, that's marvellous, I had given up all hope." Jacqueline sounded very excited. "I haven't been able to get in touch with Abby. I texted her to let her know about the horrible incident on the coach, but she said she was away for a few days. Have you heard from her?" Roger was hoping Jacqueline hadn't told their daughter about it. She was a smart cookie and would ask too many questions and he knew he wouldn't be able to hold it all together.

"No, I've been busy sorting a few things out. It's all to do with money coming in and out of the business account and late payments. The standing orders and direct debits have been affected a bit, but it's all been sorted out now. Why It had to kick off just before our holiday, I will never know."

"Well hurry up and get on board and let's try and enjoy ourselves. I must say everyone has been very friendly." Jacqueline sounded relieved.

"Oh, I see! You don't need me now that you've made lots of new friends."

"I do need you," Jacqueline was laughing. "The bed's too big, so get on board and let's make some waves."

The taxi pulled up and Roger raced up the gangway where security stepped in and whisked him away to be processed.

Finally, he fell through the door and threw himself into his wife's arms. Two glasses of champagne were waiting, fizzing nicely on a tray. "This is an amazing stateroom." Roger opened the balcony door, sipped the champagne and stared out. "Are we port side or starboard side?"

"What can you see?" Jacqueline asked him with a perfectly straight face.

He looked around, curiously, still excited. "Cranes and cargo, some Italian cars, badly parked in a carpark and the gangway."

"Try again."

"Don't tell me, let me guess. I think we're port side." Roger said, noticing his clothes hanging up in the wardrobe and his cosmetics placed neatly in the bathroom.

"I've missed you. I'm so sorry if all this gave you a terrible fright." Roger put his arms around his wife and hugged her.

"Will it affect your bridge?" Jacqueline asked her husband.

"It shouldn't do."

"What a shame, I was hoping to have a head start. I need all the help I can get." They both laughed and fell onto the bed.

———

Miranda saw him immediately as she walked into the dining room. Jacqueline had put on a very brave face throughout but was now laughing happily at her husband's jokes. Lunch would be just that bit more enjoyable.

Before taking her seat at the table, she leant over Roger and, smiling, whispered quietly in his ear, "Oh, wonderful, you're here. Hope all is well now and you can start to enjoy your holiday." She was delighted for Jacqueline.

"Thank you, yes. It was a huge misunderstanding and I will deal with those responsible very harshly when I get home."

"They didn't beat you up or torture you in any way?" Sandra said, sounding disappointed. Everyone at the bridge table winced at her remark.

"Nope, I'm waiting to go back to my stateroom tonight with my beautiful wife for that, with any luck." Everyone at the table roared with laughter, except Sandra.

Roger waited until after lunch and the end of the first round of bridge before he asked, "Where's Cynthia? I'm relying on her to partner me when Jacqueline gets bored."

"We haven't seen her since last night", Miranda said. "I called her room this morning, but there was no answer. I assumed she got off early to explore which in itself is unusual as she likes to have company, doesn't she, John?"

"She does indeed." John said, smugly.

"Perhaps she knocked herself out shopping and had to have a lie-down." Jacqueline wouldn't have been surprised at all if that had been the case.

"I'll go and knock loudly on her stateroom door later and remind her of her duty." Roger felt irritated that John was muscling in on his territory.

Miranda messaged Henry at the earliest opportunity.

"The fugitive is back on board and in very good spirits."

"Oh yes? That's interesting. Did he say anything about it?" Henry was feeling very low. He was missing his girlfriend who would soon be sailing again and out of touch until the next port of call. He was finding it a bit of a strain.

"No, but he was cracking jokes and laughing, eager for his marathon game of bridge this evening."

Henry chuckled. "That's typical behaviour of someone with much to hide. Is he dodgy?"

"No, he's not really. He seems an ordinary bloke trying to have a week's holiday with his wife. Jacqueline seems very relieved to have him back, anyway." Miranda changed the subject. "I haven't heard from Cynthia. I wonder if she's alright. She must be on board; the ship is due to leave at 6.00pm. She's cutting it a bit fine."

"Perhaps she's found herself a new friend, holed up in his cabin and wants to keep it quiet. She already knows what people think of her insatiable sexual appetite."

"Find a new friend and not want to talk about the sordid details? Cynthia? Don't be ridiculous."

"No, you're quite right, that *is* ridiculous. Keep in touch, won't you." Henry regretted he hadn't gone with her. It was the first of many occasions during the voyage that he would feel that.

"What's that noise?"

"It's the ship's horn. We're on the move again. I'll check in soon. Hugs and kisses, over and out."

CHAPTER SEVEN

"What do you mean she's back on the ship? John was asking the Senior Receptionist, just as Sandra and Miranda approached the desk.

"Mrs. Cynthia Manning definitely came back on board, Mr Wood. We have her checked in on our computer. She came back at around 2.00 p.m."

"I've searched the whole ship and knocked on her stateroom door a million times and there's been no answer." John realised he was losing his temper with an innocent person, but he just couldn't help it.

"We are aware that this is a very urgent matter. The First Officer has been informed."

"I would be grateful if you could send me a message when you have found her and I can pass it on to the rest of our little group."

"I most certainly will. Please don't worry, I'm sure she'll be found very soon."

———

Freddy knocked on the door of Ms. Cynthia's stateroom at around 9.00 a.m., two hours after the ship docked at Livorno, to do his usual stateroom service. The room was empty and in a terrible mess which was unusual. The stateroom was usually quite tidy and ordered, compared to many on his schedule. The bedclothes were in a heap, rather than neatly rumpled and there was a bottle of champagne lying on the floor. It had obviously been kicked over and the contents spilled onto the carpet.

Empty champagne glasses stood on the sideboard, next to the ice bucket. They were clean, but he washed them anyway. He assumed Ms Cynthia had been entertaining and things had got a bit rowdy before she felt unwell and called for his assistance. He was used to seeing a lot of alcohol consumed in the staterooms – it was no big deal.

Things were strewn all over the dressing table and the drawers were open. Two freshly ironed shirts still on their hangers and covered in polythene had been thrown across the room, finally landing by the balcony doors.

He had been summoned as he was about to come off duty the night before, to assist Ms Cynthia. He usually tried to ignore the bleep on his pager at that late hour – the callers mostly gave up and waited for the morning, but nothing was too much trouble for this particular lady. She was sitting up in bed, smiling at him and he didn't notice, in the dark, the mess in the cabin. He thought she must be one of his favourite and most generous guests on this sailing.

His last job, before he turned in for the night, was to thoroughly wash down the wheelchair and collapse it before putting it away. It would be needed the next day and was expected to be spotlessly clean and in full working order.

———

"Please will Mrs. Cynthia Manning come to the Reception Desk on the fourth floor? Mrs. Cynthia Manning. Thank you."

Miranda knew the call on the tannoy system was urgent. It could be heard all over the ship, including all the staterooms. She dialled the number of John's cabin. He wasn't in his room, so she left a message on his stateroom answerphone.

"Hi, John, It's Miranda. I'm a bit concerned about Cynthia. I haven't seen her since last night. Have you? If not, can you give me a ring back and if you have, would you also ring me back. I've left a million messages on her answerphone. Oh and by the way, did you remember to order your Dover sole last night? They need 24 hours for a special dinner order. If not, you won't have it tonight."

The food was marvellous, everything you could want and much more, but that only seemed to bring out the greed in many of the guests – a compulsive desire to ask for the one thing the Head Chef of a cruise liner might have forgotten to include on the menu. Miranda was happy to notice that so far, Head Chef was winning.

Miranda stood on her balcony in her bathrobe. The ship had pulled away from the dock and they were heading out to sea. The little pilot boat accompanying it was returning to the port, having safely guided the enormous vessel out into open water. Miranda waved goodbye to it. She thought it was the polite thing to do.

She had been looking out for Cynthia, expecting to see her arrive in a taxi, laden down with shopping and jump on board, but as the ship started to pull away and the ropes were untied from the mooring, she knew it was unlikely.

Her phone was ringing inside the stateroom and she picked it up, expecting it to be John returning her call.

"Have you seen that half-wit?" Sandra sounded angry rather than concerned, although it was difficult to tell, the two usually went hand in hand.

Miranda let the comment pass. "I've just left a message on John's cabin phone. I didn't know what else to do. I assume security has not registered her back on board and that's why they're calling for her."

"Nick Lombardo's been on the blower as well", Sandra's voice had risen to a shriek. "I suppose he must be frantic, too. You can always rely on Cynthia to cause anxiety and drama."

"I don't suppose anyone tries to disappear and miss their cruise intentionally, Sandra."

"Oh yes, they do, especially if you're Cynthia. She must have been bored for five minutes and cooked up a plan."

"Come on, Sandra, think logically. Where could she be and why has she not texted anybody that she'll be late?"

The sound of the call on the loudspeaker interrupted their conversation. "This is an urgent call for Mrs. Cynthia Manning. Please will Mrs. CYNTHIA MANNING come directly to Reception on the fourth floor."

"Now we should be worried, let's go to Reception again and see what's going on." Sandra had given her permission to be concerned, so it must be alright.

———

Miranda looked at the dinner menu, but her mind was elsewhere. She stared out of the window and watched the ship pick up speed now that it was well away from the shore. She could feel the beginning of a panic attack coming on.

She needed Cynthia to be with her for support. There was something about the woman that made Miranda feel secure. Underneath the frivolity was a canny woman not to be trifled with – unless she was doing the trifling and Miranda found that very comforting. Every now and again, Miranda would require a bit of reassurance that this trip wasn't a complete mistake and Cynthia would confirm that she was fully entitled to plan a trip without her boyfriend and for it not be seen by Henry as treachery.

There were five of them around the table, instead of six. Everyone was glancing at the empty chair and taking it in turns to sigh. Roger and Jacqueline were looking at the wine list. They had booked the table later than usual, to give Cynthia a chance to reappear.

"This is most unlike her. We've had dinner all together every night, so far." John was the first to speak. He had totally forgotten about his special order of Dover sole and the waiter didn't bother to remind him.

"Maybe Cynthia got fed up with your conversation and chucked herself overboard", Roger piped up. Jacqueline sniggered into her glass of iced water and nudged him in the ribs.

"It's not a joke, Roger." John couldn't stand the man.

"People do not get on board ship after a day sightseeing, show their security pass and then vanish, or at least I haven't heard of that happening", Roger insisted.

"How many cruises have you been on, Roger? Oh wait, this is your first half of one, isn't it?" John couldn't help himself.

"That's absolutely right! It doesn't happen. So, what is the explanation?" Sandra couldn't make her mind up which of the starters to choose, so she was going to order two.

"You've spent quite a bit of time with Cynthia, Miranda, what do you think has happened?" Roger had a lot of time for Miranda. Her influence over Cynthia must be a calming and sensible one. She just seemed that kind of person.

Roger hadn't messaged Cynthia at all while he was dealing with the police and his only thought, as he was sitting in the back of the taxi on the way to the ship, was to get a message to Jacqueline that he was en route. When, finally, he sent a text message to Cynthia to say he was on board and looking forward to 'playing' with her, he received no reply. He assumed she was ignoring him in a fit of pique.

"I really couldn't tell you, but I think it must be something quite serious. She has enjoyed our company and said so, many times. Why would she suddenly cut off all contact with everyone and spend her time elsewhere?" Miranda felt quite emotional.

"I'm tempted to call her family and tell them she's vanished in a puff of smoke", Sandra said aggressively.

"I wouldn't do that if I were you. You'll look pretty stupid when she turns up and her family are beside themselves with worry." Roger looked menacingly at Sandra and she shut up.

"I think we should leave it to Nick to deal with the matter. He's the main man to sort things out." Jacqueline said. She didn't need any more stress on this holiday.

"I spoke to Nick about it and he shouted at me to mind my own business and get on with my day. I think that's very rude." John had felt like punching him for saying that.

"I think it might be good advice for us all to take", Miranda said, without looking up from the menu, finally making up her mind and ordering dinner.

———

The First Officer, accompanied by a security officer and head of housekeeping, knocked on Cynthia's stateroom door twice without a reply. The housekeeper unlocked the door and they went in.

The stateroom was immaculate, the balcony door was closed, the air-conditioning unit was on and the room was cool.

"Can you open the safe, please?" The security guard used the master key, only asked for in emergencies. Mrs. Manning, like most of the guests on board, would probably have placed certain items in the safe, including her passport and the First Officer wanted to check they were still there. He picked up a lady's watch, a small jewellery pouch and some cash, placed in a plain white envelope and put all the items in a black pouch, leaving a signed receipt with the items listed and where they could be retrieved. The housekeeper proceeded to open the drawers to the dressing table and look inside each one. No passport was found which had been the point of the exercise. He would be reporting his findings to the Captain immediately.

The ship's head of security felt his pager vibrate. He was dealing with one or two matters and ignored it. It continued to buzz in his pocket and he picked it up, walking to the nearest phone.

After a brief conversation, he raced up several flights of stairs to the recreation deck and ran to the cordoned off area where several deck hands were standing. An ex-policeman with thirty years on the force behind him, he was still ill-prepared for what was revealed under the AstroTurf. He stumbled to the corner of the deck and threw up.

He immediately reported his findings to the bridge, but not before making sure his team re-secured the area, putting a guard in place until the ship's doctor arrived.

Captain Edward Van den Burg grew up near the sea in the South West of the Netherlands He was in command of MS *Holland Silhouette*, which came into service in 2008 after having been baptised by Her Majesty Queen Beatrix.

Despite there not being any particular nautical connections in the family, he spent his spare time sailing small boats and decided at a young age he wanted to pursue a career at sea.

He attended Nautical College at the 'De Ruyter' Maritime Academy in Vlissingen where he graduated with a bachelor's degree in Navigation and Marine Engineering.

He was young and good looking, softly spoken and popular with his crew and passengers. His least favourite part of the job was the captain's cocktail parties. On every voyage there would be several, usually one for the passengers on board ship to meet the captain and senior crew members, one for guests who had cruised many times on *Holland Silhouette* and possibly one more for those guests whose voyages on the ship were into double figures.

He would stand in the receiving line and attempt to make conversation with every guest on board, endeavouring to say something a little different each time. Many of the guests would have to be politely ushered in the direction of the waiting glasses of champagne, with some of the ladies having to be peeled off his right arm.

After an exemplary record, he earned his first command of the *Silhouette*, but he was totally unprepared for the sight before him on deck twelve.

It brought back memories of a time long ago on another ship, while serving as a junior officer. On that occasion, the body of a beautiful young woman working as a nanny aboard a Disney cruise ship, simply vanished without explanation.

Her case remains shrouded in mystery while her parents' quest for answers has been thwarted at each attempt. Did she jump? Was she pushed? After what can only be described as a cursory investigation at best, it was concluded she must have been washed away by a freak wave on the second day of a week-long cruise from LA to the Mexican Riviera – an explanation backed by Disney.

The last thing Captain Van den Burg heard on the matter was that her parents are now closer to finding the answers. It is suspected that their daughter was the victim of a sex attack on board, but it will forever haunt him how a young popular woman can just vanish into thin air whilst working on a busy, family-friendly cruise liner.

He naively assumed that once you had witnessed such a heinous crime, it was unlikely to happen again, and he remembered being very thankful that he was not personally responsible for the investigation that followed.

"When was this area last patrolled? Roughly how long could she have been here? His mind was racing, trying to think of the order of procedure.

"I'm not sure, Captain", the Bosun was trying to stay calm and report the events of the last two days in the correct order.

"Have we been monitoring this area?" The captain had a bad feeling. The Bosun looked up at the camera, but he had already noticed it facing the entrance to the deck rather than the cordoned off area.

"We will have footage of everyone who accessed the deck."

"That's not what I asked."

"No Captain, the camera seems to be facing the door."

"Why is that?"

"I think the general consensus was that it should monitor a busier area."

"I see your point, but now I'm going to have to explain it to head office." The Captain was not looking forward to that conversation.

"I think we have enough CCTV footage to be able to gauge what happened. Every deck is well monitored." The Bosun hoped his explanation was sufficient.

"We're missing a vital piece of the jigsaw, are we not? Let's try and wait for the Investigator to arrive before we disturb the scene to remove the body to the morgue. I'm awaiting further instructions. Under no circumstances must the area be contaminated further."

The captain walked back to his office. He had been scratching the skin on his hand with nerves and had drawn blood.

He knew that by passing through international waters, the ship had effectively travelled to a country where there are no police – a no-man's land. In fact, once a ship sails twelve miles away from the shoreline, it is no longer protected by the police force of the nearest country to it.

Instead, under Maritime Law, any crime committed is the responsibility of whichever nation the vessel has been registered with and consequently, under their jurisdiction.

For tax reasons, most ships are registered under 'flags of convenience' in small states such as Panama Liberia or Bermuda. In the case of this 122,000 tonnes ship, it was the Bahamas.

———

Nick Lombardo called an emergency meeting. Everyone, without exception, must come immediately to the games room and the ship's tannoy system helped him by repeating this message around the ship and inside the staterooms.

When everyone was seated, Nick stood behind his makeshift desk looking very solemn.

"Can you all quieten down, please. I'm afraid I have some rather shocking news for everyone. It seems one of our group, Cynthia Manning, has been brutally murdered."

"What? I can't believe it. Are you sure you're not

mistaken?" Sandra immediately became hysterical, sobbing loudly and covering her face with her hands. "Are you sure it's her?"

The noise in the room was deafening with everyone jumping up, talking and gesticulating.

"Can you all please sit down. I haven't finished speaking." Sometimes, Nick wondered if these people had a brain between them.

"I wish it was a mistake, but unfortunately I had to identify her body." Nick was trying to keep it together but failing miserably.

Miranda glanced around the room at everyone's reaction to the news – just to make sure that this wasn't some awful joke that only she didn't find amusing. She couldn't believe that such an inconceivable thing could happen to her friend on a holiday.

John stood up and approached Nick, turning to address the rest of the room.

"Someone must know something about this. Did anyone hear or witness anything? If so, for God's sake, come forward. How is it possible that Cynthia was murdered on board ship and nobody noticed?"

He turned to Nick. "We have to do something. We have to find out what happened."

Nick sat down, lifting his hand to massage his forehead which started throbbing. "I'm leaving it up to the Captain and his security team to deal with it and I suggest you all do the same. If they need any information, I have already said we will all make ourselves available. Obviously, I am here round the clock for anyone who wants to talk to me, confidentially or otherwise."

Roger stared in front of him, too afraid to look anyone in the eye. He reached for Jacqueline's hand, shook his head and shrugged, but his face had paled from the shock.

Back in their respective staterooms, each member of the little group expressed their true feelings away from prying eyes.

Sandra ran into her cabin, letting the door slam shut behind her, even though she reprimanded everyone for doing the same thing. She closed her balcony door so nobody could hear her scream into her pillow.

It seemed to take an eternity for John to get back to his room. The corridors were never-ending, like they appear to be in a bad dream. Finally, he arrived at his cabin door and fumbled with the key card until eventually it worked and the door opened. He poured himself a whisky – his eyes still filled with tears. He walked out onto his balcony and stared out to sea, waiting for its calming effect to kick in. Unfortunately, a rising sense of panic which started in his stomach could not be quelled and he rushed to the bathroom, just in time.

———

Miranda stood in the middle of her room for quite a long time. She didn't feel like opening the balcony door, although she was staring unseeing at the blueness of the sky from behind the glass, nor did she feel like pouring herself a drink. She sat down in the armchair and phoned Henry.

"Cynthia's been murdered, horribly and brutally. We thought she was just late back from a shopping trip or visiting a new friend in their cabin."

Henry was silent for rather a long time while he was taking in the news. "Oh darling, you must be in shock. I'm so sorry for you. I feel so helpless stuck here."

"There's nothing any of us can do for her. It's too late. We weren't there when she needed us, Henry. How horrible is that? Nick told us to leave it to the captain and security and that's what I'm going to do, but I'm scared – really scared."

"Try not to be, just make sure your door is locked at night and don't go back to your cabin alone. See that someone escorts you at all times."

"I don't want to make a fuss, Henry, the staff have enough to do."

"It's very important that you take these precautions Miranda, and I will feel a lot better if you do."

Miranda agreed. She wished she could get off the ship right now and go home.

———

Roger and Jacqueline locked themselves in their stateroom and poured themselves a gin and tonic.

"I can't believe it. Who would want to kill Cynthia? She was harmless." Roger's face was still ashen.

"I can believe it," Jacqueline said, "She was a very strange woman."

"Why strange?" Roger wasn't expecting his wife to use that particular word to describe Cynthia.

"She alienated everyone with her behaviour, Roger. You must have noticed that. She was far too familiar with men and women. Eventually someone was going to give her a slap."

"Someone did more than 'give her a slap', darling. They finished her off."

Jacqueline walked towards the balcony, deciding it was safe to open the patio door. "Perhaps it was a game that went too far? Perhaps whoever killed her, hit her a bit harder than they intended."

"Bludgeoning someone to death doesn't sound like a sex game to me, but what do I know?" Roger made a decision. "As much as I liked Cynthia, I'm not going to meddle. I'm going to leave the investigation to the experts."

Jacqueline looked sternly at her husband. "I think that's very wise."

———

Many of the police forces from poor countries with questionable human rights records are stretched to the limit when it comes to their own domestic workload, let alone a crime which takes place at sea thousands of miles away.

The pilot boat pulled up alongside, just as dawn was breaking. The captain was grateful that it was early in the morning before most of the guests were up and about. He was keen to keep the investigation into the murder of Mrs Manning as discreet as possible.

Samuel James had a heavy heart as he nimbly jumped from the pilot boat onto the large cruise liner. He was exhausted from his long journey to the ship. As an under-resourced, ill-equipped police officer from a police station in Arawak Cay, he knew this would be a testing time and he was unlikely to have much success. He should have been accompanied by another senior investigator, but only he could be spared at such short notice.

Back at the station in the Bahamas, he would now be working his way through a substantial workload, mainly consisting of theft and petty theft, domestic violence, a significant increase in drug dealing and addiction, not forgetting an assortment of crimes against the tourists flooding onto the island. At this moment, he longed to be assigned those laborious tasks.

Just one man, he thought, to interview the 2,400 passengers and almost 1000 crew on board this $580 million liner? The staterooms would have been thoroughly cleaned, evidence disposed of and certain guests may have disembarked. With no forensic equipment, he was going to need some help.

Captain Van Den Burg felt sorry for the young policeman after the AstroTurf was lifted up and the body of Mrs. Manning was revealed in all her decomposing glory. He ran to the corner of the deck and threw up – in the same corner as the head of security used to discharge the contents of his stomach. It was evident that she had taken a vicious blow to the head hidden under a cheap nylon wig, but he didn't think that would have been enough to kill her. He urgently needed to secure the scene of the murder and immediately gave orders for Mrs. Manning's stateroom to be secured.

Samuel might not be the most experienced murder investigator in the world, but he knew a hate crime when he saw one and this was one of the most calculated, vicious attacks he had ever seen. Stab someone, shoot a person, even spike a victim's drink with poison – all of these methods he could relate to, but this was the devil at work.

He had been very lucky in his life. He was a good-looking lad and as bright as a button. His grandparents paid for his schooling because they thought he was the best bet out of their five grandchildren and would benefit from it the most. They noticed he was a thoughtful child, unperturbed by the chaos around him and happy to sit down in the sunshine next to his grandmother leafing through the pages of books, pointing out the pictures and quick to learn to read the words. That's not to say he didn't like a kick around with his friends. He knew how to get along with everyone and the right things to say to both young and old. His grandmother was confident that her faith in him would be rewarded.

His mother worked very hard as a hotel chamber maid,

quickly being promoted to housekeeper through sheer hard graft – his father spent his time smoking and drinking away her earnings. Despite this, they were a close family, supported by a network of grandparents who had scrimped and saved all their lives, rarely dipping into their nest egg.

When Samuel showed promise, preferring to read and study at home rather than spend every waking moment hanging around with his friends, the elders in the family decided it was time to speculate to accumulate.

He read the application form to join the Royal Bahamas Police Force (RBPF) and studied the list of requirements. His excitement knew no bounds.

Be a Bahamian citizen

Be of good character and without a criminal record.

Be between the ages of 18 and 30.

Have good academic qualifications.

Meet medical standards.

Be successful throughout the assessment process.

For the first time in his life, he would be able to stand up proudly in the knowledge that he has as much chance of success as anyone else applying for the coveted job.

Samuel's senior officers recognised his talents. He was methodical, focused, and relentless in his pursuit of the bad guys combined with empathy for the victims and he rose quickly through the ranks. Massively under-resourced, Samuel never baulked at orders from his superiors, rarely getting paid over-time.

———

"You can insist on some legal representation, you know", Henry advised Miranda during a very costly ship-to-shore phone call.

"Do I need it? I think I'm right at the back of the queue of suspects, Henry. It would sound guilty as sin for no good reason to ask for it." Miranda could feel her blood pressure rising.

"Tell them everything. Every tiny detail about your conversations, however irrelevant it may seem to you and if you have to name the people that Cynthia said she didn't like or of whom she was suspicious, do so."

"Do you mean be a snitch? That's horrible, Henry." Miranda didn't think her simple witness statement was going to be deemed that important to the enquiry.

"Yes, Miranda. I'm not a criminal lawyer, but I do know that withholding information is a criminal offence so snitch away, sing like a canary, spill the beans and whatever else you have to do to get off the ship quickly and come home to me. Oh, and Miranda?"

"Yes, Henry…"

"I've missed you terribly. I'm not sure I can bear being separated from you for such a long time again."

Miranda was squeezing the phone to her ear so she didn't miss any part of what he was saying and smiled happily. She thought that when she returned home, the first thing they should do is talk about making their relationship more permanent. She wouldn't bottle it this time.

CHAPTER EIGHT

Makisig couldn't believe his luck when he got the job on a luxury cruise ship. Things were definitely looking up for him and his family, at last. The only problems he had with the job was being away from home for months at a time and remembering to answer to his new name. Freddy is not a usual name in the Philippines.

He was just finishing cleaning his tenth stateroom when the housekeeper came rushing up to him, a look of fear on her face. She was fearful that the staterooms would not be cleaned in good time. She took great pride in the fact that the guests, upon leaving, rarely came back to their stateroom without finding it clean, neat and tidy.

"The captain would like to see you. I think it's to do with Mrs. Manning in stateroom 8323. Salvatore will take over until you get back."

Freddy started to silently cry. He hoped this terrible thing wouldn't affect his job on the ship, but if he told the truth, he couldn't get into trouble.

He knocked cautiously on the captain's office door and waited. After about five minutes, he knocked again. The door was flung open and the Captain filled the whole entrance. Smiling down at him, he ushered Freddy gently to a chair and nodded towards the man behind his desk.

Captain Van Den Burg had a whole team of staff on hand to assist the Bahamian Assistant Superintendent, should it be required.

"Good morning. I am Assistant Superintendent Samuel James and, of course, you know Captain Van Den Burg." Freddy nodded, his hands clasped tightly behind his back.

"Please sit down. Do you answer to Makisig or Freddy? Which are you more comfortable with?" Samuel asked the steward as he was glancing through Freddy's employment file.

"Freddy, Sir – I always answer to Freddy."

"There's no need to be nervous – this is just an informal chat about Mrs. Manning, the lady who occupied one of the staterooms on your floor."

Freddy looked like he was going to burst into tears. "She was a very nice lady – very kind."

"Was she kind to you, Freddy? More than some of the other guests?"

"She was a very kind lady. She always asked for everything very nicely – not roughly, you know - and she never asked me to work late, except one night."

Samuel looked up from the file. "Except one night? What happened on that night?"

"Ms Cynthia – she asked me to call her that – was feeling unwell and asked me to remove a wheelchair and some dirty towels from her room - she sounded very ill." Freddy was frowning, trying to remember the exact details. He had cleaned a lot of rooms since then.

"Did she look ill?"

"I couldn't see her very well. She was lying on her bed in the dark, but she sounded terrible. Her voice was different – not soft like usual."

"What did you do?" Samuel was listening intently and so was the captain.

"First, I asked how she was, of course. I would always ask that." Freddy wanted to make sure he showed he followed procedure.

"And then…"

"I took the wheelchair away and washed it thoroughly - it looked like there was a little bit of blood on it, but I think that was just from Ms. Cynthia's nosebleed."

"How did you know the blood was from a nosebleed?" Captain Van Den Burg managed to ask the question a millisecond before Samuel.

"She told me about it." Freddy hesitated and then had a thought "And it must have been quite a bad nosebleed because there were some bloodied towels, too."

"I suppose there's no point asking what you did with the towels?"

Samuel smiled, nervously. "I know what you are saying, sir, but yes – I put them straight in the laundry."

"Quite right, Freddy. What else would you do with bloodied towels? Can you remember anything that seemed strange when you were cleaning the stateroom?" Samuel looked kindly at Freddy, hoping that a piece of evidence would magically pop into his memory.

"Yes! – I remember thinking how untidy the stateroom looked in the morning when I came to give it my usual thorough clean."

"How did it usually look and why would you notice the difference in the amount of mess?" Samuel was interested in the details.

"Ms Cynthia's stateroom was very neat and tidy. Everything in its place – but that morning it was very untidy – the drawers to the dressing table were left open and it looked like she was searching for something that she thought she had lost. A champagne bottle had fallen on the floor and left a big stain, but the glasses were clean. I washed them anyway, just in case."

"And you say all of that was strange?"

Freddy looked at the captain, silently pleading for help and an excuse to go back to his duties. "Not strange-strange – just not like Ms Cynthia's stateroom." He didn't want them to think he was criticising the guest's habits. "There was one very out of place thing I want to tell you."

"You can tell us anything that's on your mind, Freddy. That's what we need you to do." The captain was very impressed with Freddy's statement, so far.

"There were ironed shirts on hangers left on the floor." Freddy sighed. That would be something very important, he was sure of that.

Samuel and the captain looked disappointed. "Can you tell us, again, why you think that is 'out of place'?"

"They were men's shirts and Ms Cynthia was the only occupant in the stateroom."

"She may have had a male visitor?"

"I've been doing this job a long time, Captain. If there were shirts to iron, Ms Cynthia would have asked me to see to it. I also know if one or two people sleep in the bed – you can tell these things just by the crumpled sheets."

"Thank you very much for your help, Freddy. I hope you don't mind if we call you again after we've looked at the CCTV footage." Samuel stood up and held out his hand.

"Wait a moment!" Captain Van Den Burg was looking on his computer screen. "Why was there a wheelchair in Mrs. Manning's stateroom? She's not registered as disabled on our records."

"Ms Cynthia told me her friend was feeling unwell and she put her in a wheelchair to get around the ship."

Samuel and the captain looked at each other, both shaking their heads in puzzlement. "I would say out of all of these details, that's the only one that's strange." Samuel was looking at Freddy who had clearly had enough and needed a break.

—

Nick Lombardo walked quickly to the lift and pressed 'basement'. He proceeded to walk along the rabbit warren of corridors until he saw the door marked 'Captain' and knocked loudly.

Captain Van den Burg threw open the door and greeted him like an old friend. The reason for this was that he hoped Nick could supply some important and detailed information on every member of the bridge club sailing with him, thereby reducing the interview time and amount of paperwork.

"Good morning, please sit down. This is Assistant Superintendent Samuel James of the Arawak Cay police department in the Bahamas. He will be conducting the initial investigation before we dock at Southampton and would like to interview some of the guests, particularly the ones connected to the bridge cruise. Can I offer you some coffee?"

Nick nodded. His hands were feeling shaky.

"I would firstly like to thank you very much for identifying Mrs. Manning. I'm sorry that I had to ask you to do so, but I'm sure you understand..."

"Absolutely, Captain. I appreciate that I am responsible for the group while they are on board the ship."

Nick took a large sip of his coffee, put the cup and saucer down and continued. "It must be a nightmare for you – I know it's a logistical nightmare for me."

The captain was right in his assumption that Nick would be super-efficient with the paperwork.

"I have taken the liberty of making a list of the few people I noticed spending considerable time with Cynthia Manning during this cruise. I'm not a lawyer and have no legal experience, so if I've missed any crucial evidence or any particular person off the list, it is completely unintentional. Does this cover me for any negligence on my part?"

"Please don't worry about how much or little information you give me," Samuel could see that Nick Lombardo was trying to help. He could also see the poor man was wishing this unfortunate event had happened on someone else's group holiday.

"It's all very useful. At this stage, I'm just having a chat with people. You would be surprised what people remember when they have to, but also how much detail has to be sifted through to extract something small that might help with our enquiries." Samuel took the list from Nick's outstretched hand and glanced quickly at it.

"How well did you know Mrs. Manning?" Samuel wasn't expecting a great deal of information.

Nick sat back in his chair, picked up his coffee cup and took a few gulps. "Cynthia Manning has been learning bridge with us for a few years. She would be a very competent bridge player if she put her mind to it, sorry – would *have* been. She was one of our more colourful members. If she didn't like you, she would show it. If you showed her the smallest chink in your armour, she would play on it. Some people complained she was a bit of a bully at the bridge table. I would argue that if she were guilty of it, it would have been in a semi-playful way."

"Was she romantically involved with anyone; do you know?" Samuel squirmed. He had better get used to asking this question.

Nick often wondered about his clients' personal lives but would never pry. He was happy to share his musings with Samuel.

"It's always difficult to say for sure if two people are romantically linked and seeing each other outside of the bridge club. Most of my clients have been coming to the club for years and years. Some know each other better than they know their own family."

Nick continued, warming to the subject.

"Cynthia was a friendly person. Some would say over-familiar, but I didn't receive any serious complaints about her. She played with lots of people but had her favourite partners - they're on the list. We're a very nice, quite respectable group, Assistant Superintendent, and I'm not just saying it because they're *my* group. If anyone gets a parking ticket, it holds up the game while it's discussed ad infinitum. Should there be a murderer lurking amongst us, I would be very surprised."

Samuel nodded. Mr. Lombardo would be amazed how many murderers hide behind a façade of respectability.

"Finally, Mr. Lombardo, can you think of anyone who might want to kill her for any reason?"

Nick laughed nervously. "I can't help being flippant in reply to this question. Can someone be murdered for being annoying? As far as I know, that was her only crime. I can't think of any other another reason."

"Thank you. I might need to talk to you again, possibly to discuss anything that flags up on the CCTV." Samuel got up and shook Nick's hand.

"If I can help you in any way, please don't hesitate to ask." Nick hadn't finished his coffee. He couldn't get out of there fast enough.

Samuel and the captain were already weary and the interviews had only just began.

"Please sit down, Mr. Wood. Can I offer you some tea or coffee?"

"Coffee would be lovely, thank you. Could you manage some of your excellent biscuits too, please?"

The Captain picked up the telephone to place the order.

"My name is Samuel James and this, as you know, is Captain Van den Burg. I'll try not to take up too much of your time, but I would like to ask you for a few questions.

First, the Captain and I would like to say how sorry we are that you have lost a dear friend in such terrible circumstances."

"Thank you very much. That's very kind of you." John looked suitably distressed.

"Anything you can you tell me about your relationship with Mrs. Cynthia Manning will be very helpful." Samuel spoke first.

He and the captain were interviewing in the small meeting room, off the captain's office. John noticed the table had notepads, pencils and a jug of ice-cold water with half a dozen glasses. It looked as if they were about to conduct an Annual General Meeting.

The 'invitation' to attend an informal chat with the Investigating Officer dealing with the murder of Mrs. Cynthia Manning was left in the pigeon hole outside John's stateroom the night before. He read it and re-read it. It was only a few lines on ship notecard, but its impact hit home.

He lay in bed tossing and turning through the night, reliving every word and deed over the past five years they had known each other.

At first, he thought Cynthia a silly, empty-headed blonde and gave her little thought. It wasn't until much later that he saw a manipulative woman, accustomed to toying with men's affection and getting her own way.

He couldn't quite remember when she started getting under his skin, but she made him feel more alive and sexier than any other woman he had ever known, including his wife.

He ordered breakfast to be delivered to his stateroom. He ate half a bowl of cereal, nibbled on a croissant and discarded the rest. He looked in the wardrobe and wondered what to wear.

"When you say 'relationship', I assume you mean as a friend and fellow bridge player?" John said, determined to make it very clear from the start.

"If that was the nature of your relationship, then yes, but let me make myself clear, Mr. Wood, I am not here to judge you on your morals. If Mrs. Manning had a close relationship with you or anyone else on this ship, I would like to know only so that I can narrow down the list of person or persons of interest. I really would rather not have to interview thousands of people who have never met or heard of Mrs. Manning and, therefore, are not relevant to my enquiries."

John visibly relaxed. "Cynthia and I were very good friends; bridge partners and I am a happily married man. She was a terrific woman - full of life and I shall, frankly, be lost without her. It doesn't take long, Superintendent, for life in the fast lane to soon veer over to the slow lane and eventually end up on the hard shoulder."

"I understand, Mr. Wood. Do you have any idea why anyone would want to kill her?"

"I have absolutely no idea. I can't imagine why anyone would plan to kill her, but whoever knew Cynthia could not be ambivalent towards her. You either loved or hated her. She was very outspoken about her views on everything and made a big impression."

"Did you love her or hate her, Mr. Wood?"

"If you want to know the absolute truth..."

"That would be very helpful", Samuel held his breath.

"I fancied her like mad, but I certainly didn't kill her."

"Thank you very much for your co-operation, Mr. Wood. We will, if you don't mind, want to talk to you again to discuss any CCTV footage that may come to light." Captain Van den Burg stood up and showed John out.

John raced back to his stateroom and thought he would make an outrageously expensive phone call to his wife. It was comforting to hear her lovely voice.

"Hello, darling. Are you having a wonderful time on the ocean waves?" his wife trilled down the phone. She was having a great time without him.

John could hear she sounded very relaxed. "It was lovely until a terrible thing happened. Cynthia has been murdered."

"Is this a joke?" His wife was stifling a giggle.

"No, dear - it's absolutely not a joke. It's horrific. We're all being treated like suspects – giving statements to a policeman from the Bahamas. That man has very piercing eyes and they bore into you to make you confess."

There was silence at the end of the phone while she processed the information. "Why do you sound so concerned. You have nothing to worry about unless you physically chucked her overboard."

"I know that, but it's very unnerving. Nobody chucked her overboard. She was bludgeoned to death." John felt nauseous every time he thought of it.

"Good God! Who would do such a thing. Couldn't they just have tipped her into the sea? Isn't that what usually happens to people murdered on board ship?" His wife was being far too flippant for his liking, but he wasn't about to pull her up on it.

John tried to stay calm. He didn't want her to hear how truly devastated he was about Cynthia's death.

"It's just been a terrible shock for us all, really." John kept a chatty tone to his voice. "One minute you're playing bridge with the woman and the next she's lying stone cold dead."

"Oh darling, that's horrible. When will you be home?" She really didn't care for the woman. Cynthia would often call the house to speak to John, asking for him as if she was the housekeeper rather than his wife. She often wondered whilst watching John getting ready for his bridge nights, taking pains to look young and trendy, whether there was anything going on between them. Had she cared a bit more, she might have hired a private investigator to follow him, but that would be very costly, and she would rather buy herself a new outfit with the money.

"Very soon, I hope. I do love you, darling, very much. I can't wait to see you."

His wife was secretly rather glad that unpleasant woman wouldn't be troubling them again.

———

The conversation at dinner was very stilted. Even Roger wasn't his usual chirpy self, but the turn of events didn't seem to have dampened anyone's appetite significantly.

"Can I order anything special for my ladies and gentlemen tonight?" The waiter asked. He couldn't believe that he wasn't being sent to the kitchen a hundred times during dinner service to request the chef provide several main courses and side dishes *not* on the evening's menu.

"Thank you so much, but everything is fine for us, tonight." John said. "Unless you people fancy anything?" He glanced at Roger, Jacqueline, Miranda and Sandra.

"My dinner is lovely, Alex, thank you." Miranda looked at the waiter and smiled. "Perhaps we could have another bottle of sparkling water on the table."

"I can see there's crepes on the menu tonight. Will they be warm or cold, Alex?" Roger hadn't finished his main course, but he was already thinking about dessert.

"I couldn't eat another thing. I feel uncomfortably full." Sandra sat back in her chair and patted her stomach. "I think I'll just have two scoops of ice cream, one chocolate and one strawberry please, Alex. I hate vanilla."

Jacqueline sat very quietly, staring into her plate. She would have preferred room service in her stateroom this evening, but Roger persuaded her to join him in the dining room. She was getting really fed up. She wanted to go home and spend time with Abby and get back to normal.

"Very good. I will give the order to chef. If you need anything more, please let me know." Alex cleared away the dirty plates and quietly disappeared.

"Has anyone been downstairs yet?" John wasn't going to ask. He intended to be discreet and keep the details of his meeting a secret, but he couldn't contain himself.

"Oh, my Lord! Trust you to be the first person they called down for interrogation." Sandra stared at John furiously.

"I wasn't interrogated. I was asked a few questions about Cynthia. It took all of ten minutes." John felt very calm. The old bat wasn't going to rile him.

"I hope you mentioned all the visits to her stateroom, half-naked." Sandra had a new weapon to use now. She didn't have to pretend to be civil now her dearest friend was dead,

"Damn! I knew I forgot to mention something. I'll pop down now and tell them, or you can tell them when they drag you down, kicking and screaming." John laughed in Sandra's face.

"I'll have plenty to say when it's my turn", Sandra said conspiratorially.

"Don't forget to mention that Cynthia couldn't stick you." John muttered.

"As a matter of fact, that's not true. We were very close friends. You don't know anything about our friendship." Sandra's lip began to quiver and tears appeared from nowhere.

"Friendship, you call it? If you say so." John had finally upset her and felt empowered. It serves her right.

"Let's not be unkind to each other. I'm happy to say that I've got nothing to contribute except that it's very dull without her." Miranda missed her chats and bridge playing with Cynthia. She looked at John and changed the subject. "Were they nice to you?".

"They were very nice to me. I expect the Assistant Superintendent and the Captain are making a sort of 'short list' of the people with whom Cynthia came into contact and spent time with." John looked over the table. He was annoyed that Roger had been keeping very quiet – saving it all up to blurt out to the captain, he supposed. "It's not like you not to add anything to the conversation, Roger. You know, the usual interruption when I'm speaking."

"What do you want me to say?" Roger was seething. Why did that odious man always have to start with him. "I did it. I murdered my lovely friend, Cynthia. I wasn't on the ship, but I managed to murder her anyway. Do you feel better – now that you've solved the case, Sherlock?"

"You're a man with secrets, Roger and I suspect they're going to be revealed fairly soon."

Roger couldn't understand why John was suddenly so bloody cocky and arrogant. "Have the police decided that you're no longer a person of interest?" Roger wanted to smash John in the face with his wine glass. "Is that why you're crowing like an over-sexed cock?"

"It certainly looks like that to me. They were very courteous, and they wouldn't be if they suspected me of murder now, would they?"

"Are you an expert in helping the police with their enquiries now?" Roger said.

"No. I defer to you for that. This is your second interrogation in a few days, is it not?" John was in his element. "I'm not sure you'll wriggle out of this one quite so easily."

"What do you mean by that? Can you really afford to make slanderous comments to me, you poor excuse for a man. You can expect to hear from my solicitor when I get home. Start emptying your piggy bank." Roger's face was purple.

"Who else but Roger Sylvester would come on board a ship, in the middle of a cruise, strutting like a peacock, after previously being hauled off to a police station with no explanation." John blurted out what had been on his mind from the start.

"Ah that's it, isn't it. You're so bloody nosy, you just want to know what it was all about, don't you? Well it's got nothing to do with you or anyone else. You really are a stupid arse and you're going to get what's coming to you. Whether it's to do with Cynthia's murder or not." Roger stared menacingly at him.

"Let's all calm down. One minute we're eating our dinner very nicely and the next we're at each other's throats. Let's leave the investigation to those who know what they're doing. Hurling insults at each other won't help. Personally, I would like to go home and forget all about this trip." Jacqueline's voice was raised which was most unusual. She wondered why Roger was going head-to-head with John and being so vicious. She was beginning to feel very alarmed by it all. The old distrust was slowly seeping in - again.

"I agree. There's nothing we can do and getting

agitated isn't helping. We have to make the best of it until we get back to Southampton." Miranda was feeling tired and excused herself from the table.

———

"I've found a note outside my door suggesting - inviting - commanding me to go down to the captain's office tomorrow at 10.00am. Someone is coming to escort me downstairs." Miranda was so happy to be chatting to Henry. She held the phone tightly to her ear as if she were cuddling him. "It almost came to blows at the dinner table when John mentioned he had been interviewed. I don't think I'm going to mention mine to the others."

"You don't have to tell anyone, darling – it's nobody's business." Henry felt anxious for her.

"It'll be fine. I don't suppose I'll be in there for very long." Miranda was beginning to feel tearful. Enough was enough – it was time for all of this to end.

———

"Good morning. My name is Samuel James, I am the Assistant Superintendent heading this investigation. Please sit down. Can we offer you a tea or coffee?" Samuel stood up and shook Miranda's hand, wearing a friendly smile.

He felt less tense about this interview, due to the comment written in the margin next to her name on the list that Nick Lombardo had handed to him. He looked down and re-read his notes.

"She has been an unofficial peacekeeper during this bridge cruise with a good understanding of the many and complex personalities in the group." It was like a very good school report.

He looked up and smiled. "I hope you don't mind if I ask you a few questions about Mrs. Manning."

"Please do", Miranda felt surprisingly relaxed.

"Now I believe you were quite close to Mrs. Manning, not just on this cruise, but during the period of time you've been playing bridge. She was your bridge partner, is that right?" Samuel looked at his notes.

"Yes, we usually play together, but Cynthia played a lot of bridge and had other partners. I only play once a week."

"It's difficult to phrase this, but has Mrs. Manning's murder come as a complete surprise to you?" Samuel looked nervously at Miranda.

"Absolutely! I actually feel traumatised by it. What exactly do you mean by 'surprise'?"

"As a close friend, you will be in a position to know whether Mrs. Manning was frightened about anything, scared of anyone, threatened by someone..."

"Oh, I see. Yes, I think she would have told me, but she was quite secretive. There was more to Cynthia than people know...knew." Miranda was frowning as she spoke.

"Like what?"

Miranda leant forward and spoke quietly, fearful of being overheard. "She gave the impression that she was a bit of a dumb blonde – all giggly and simpering, but that couldn't be further from the truth. She was as sharp as a razor and knew exactly what she was doing. From what I understand, Cynthia had a very happy marriage and nursed her husband for some time before his death, after which she started making up for lost time."

"How do you mean?" Samuel looked fleetingly at the captain. This could be interesting.

"Cynthia was a very nice woman and took to me immediately which was lovely, because I was new to the club and needed a friend. I found her very amusing and great fun, but my feelings were not shared by everyone, particularly other women." Miranda felt she was treading on eggshells.

"Why was that?" Samuel was trying to coax out more but didn't want to interrupt Miranda's train of thought.

"She was free to come and go as she pleased and had no qualms in accepting invitations from men that she liked or fancied." Miranda was feeling a bit of a traitor revealing Cynthia's secrets.

"Do you mean married men?"

Miranda looked at Samuel and the captain and squirmed, but she had to be honest for Cynthia's sake.

"Married men, younger men and any man that amused her, really. She said that if they were attracted to her, wanted to give her a good time and be generous, why should she deny herself? She wasn't betraying her husband or children, so why not?"

"Is there anyone you know, in particular, whose toes she was treading on or who she was betraying and would likely fight back?"

"Everyone in this group is very outspoken. If Cynthia were getting on anyone's nerves which she did, regularly, they would tell her in no uncertain terms. She took it all in good faith – she didn't hold a grudge. Nobody fell out over it." Miranda was confident about what she was saying.

"Someone wanted to fall out over it, Ms. Soames - evidently!"

"Evidently", Miranda repeated. "It's quite horrible, really. I mean - there isn't one person in this group that I could accuse of doing this – that I would suspect of being capable of murder. Is it possible that she was murdered by someone else on the ship that she came into contact with? It could be anybody."

"It is possible, but due to the nature of the crime,

unlikely. I would say that Mrs Manning knew her murderer." Samuel hoped Miranda wouldn't ask for any further details."

"May I ask how she was murdered?"

"She was bludgeoned to death and strangled and that leads me to believe it was very personal." Samuel watched her reaction. "We will be looking at some CCTV footage and I may need to call for you again."

"Absolutely. Whatever I can do to help." Miranda face had turned pale. She thought she was going to be violently sick and hoped she would get back to her cabin in time.

"May I offer you a drink, Ms. Soames", Captain Van den Burg had been very quiet throughout the interview, but he thought Miranda needed something to put the colour back."

"No, thank you, captain. I'll go back to my stateroom and help myself liberally to the contents of my fridge and when its empty, Freddy will fill it up."

———

It would be an exaggeration to say that Captain Van Den Burg was invigorated by having the policeman on the ship, but it certainly was making life a bit more stimulating. A distraction from the daily grind of dealing with the problems of guest relations, personnel and the engine room, but he knew that it would have limited attraction and he would soon be wishing for more mundane duties.

At first, he thought as Assistant Superintendent, Samuel James was rather junior in rank to be dealing with a murder investigation, but he couldn't have been more wrong. The two hit it off immediately – both having a professional and formal attitude towards their work.

"I think I should start interviewing as quickly as

possible, before memories start to fade and details forgotten, however minor." Samuel was keen to get started.

"I've been looking through the CCTV and I can't see anything suspicious, but I was waiting for you to come on board before we really went through it." The Captain trawled through the thousands of images frame by frame, but it was almost impossible to spot anything out of the ordinary - 'ordinary' on board a luxury cruise liner had its own special meaning.

Guests who choose to holiday on an exclusive cruise liner such as *Holland Silhouette* assume they can behave any way they wish with a certain amount of anonymity. Miles away from the shore, in the middle of the ocean, they can be excused in thinking that nobody can see their sometimes outrageous behaviour, as they wantonly let their hair down in the pursuit of the 'perfect holiday'.

As the captain watched the CCTV, he smiled – as a parent might smile watching their children frolicking in and out of the swimming pool and jacuzzi or sunbathing topless on a secluded area of sundeck holding glasses of champagne and cocktails – totally unaware of the hidden cameras installed for the sole purpose of monitoring their safety – nothing more. The film in the cameras were filed away, never to be scrutinised, unless a murder investigation is underway.

His phone rang on his desk and broke his concentration. It was the Port Authority Agent from Livorno with some interesting information and, hopefully, crucial evidence.

———

"Good morning, Mrs. Sylvester – please sit down. Can I offer you any refreshment?"

Captain Van den Burg smiled to himself and thought

that Samuel sounded very confident and self-assured. A far cry from the nervous Assistant Superintendent who first boarded the ship.

Jacqueline and lifted her invitation to be interviewed from the rack outside her stateroom door and showed it to her husband.

"I am to be escorted to my appointment with the Assistant Superintendent at 10.00 a.m. tomorrow. It's my turn, it seems, to be interrogated." She showed the note to Roger, who stared at the two lines for an age.

"I didn't know the woman, other than the fact that she seemed a bit stupid and Sandra thought she was lacking moral backbone, both seem to be the in thing at the moment. Men seem to go for that kind of woman." Jacqueline took the note back and put it in her handbag.

"It's all part of the process, isn't it? I mean, look how I've just been treated by the police. Appallingly!" Roger struggled to look indignant.

"What shall I say?"

"Wait to hear the line of questioning I suppose and then make your decision." Roger was reading his book on the balcony. He had nothing more to say about it.

A young, junior officer knocked on the stateroom door at exactly 10.00 a.m. to escort Jacqueline into the off-limits area of the ship.

In answer to the first question, Jacqueline said, "I'll have a coffee, please. De-caffeinated if possible." Jacqueline settled down in the tub chair and put her handbag down beside her.

"I'm sorry to interrupt your holiday, Mrs. Sylvester, but I am interviewing everyone who had contact with Mrs. Manning."

"Limited contact, Assistant Superintendent." Jacqueline looked thoughtful. "Four of us got off the ship at one of the stops and explored the town. We had a light lunch and returned to the ship. I haven't had much more contact with her since then."

"What did you make of her? Was she pleasant, friendly, chatty...?" Samuel tried to sound light.

"She seemed an okay sort of person. She wasn't someone I particularly wanted to keep in touch with after this holiday." Jacqueline didn't want to run the woman down.

"Why was that?

"Why didn't I want to be close friends with Cynthia?"

"Yes", Samuel asked. "Why did you feel you couldn't be close friends with her?"

"She was just not my type, Superintendent. She was a bit of a bore – only wanting to talk about men and her conquests. I'm sure she was a very nice woman - probably a very good mother and wife, but she would have made a terrible friend."

"That's quite a lot to have gleaned from spending so little time together." Samuel sat upright in his chair. Jacqueline Sylvester had more to say. She just didn't know it yet.

"Not really. It doesn't take very long to know whether one is intellectually suited to someone. I would say one can assess that quite quickly." Jacqueline hadn't wanted to get too involved in describing Cynthia's personality. It seemed a bit cruel now.

"Who would you say was particularly close to Mrs. Manning?" Samuel sat back and tried to sound casual. He could feel Mrs. Sylvester was feeling a little intimidated.

"I suppose she was quite close to her bridge partners. I believe she played with two people – John Wood and Miranda Soames. They both seemed to get on very well with her - no problems there." Jacqueline was mindful not to tell tales about anyone, after all, there was nothing to report out of the ordinary.

"Did she have any romantic connection with anyone specific, as far as you know?"

"I really couldn't say for sure." Jacqueline was going to tread very carefully over this point. "I believe she had a bit of a reputation in the bridge club for being a man-eater, whatever that might mean. I take gossip like that with a pinch of salt and I have found, in my experience, that women get very jealous and territorial."

Samuel nodded in agreement and hesitated before asking his next question.

"But if you had to stick your neck out on the point of her having a romantic connection, what would you say?" Samuel was hoping his amiable demeanour would give the impression that her comment would be 'off the record'.

Jacqueline was ready to go back to her stateroom and decided to just blurt out her thoughts on the matter and get it over with. "I would say that there were 'a number of irons in the fire', so to speak – both at home and on the ship."

"Thank you so much for your help, Mrs. Sylvester. I will be looking at some CCTV film and may need to talk to you again, if you don't mind."

Jacqueline got up and shook Samuel's hand. "I'll be here."

CHAPTER NINE

Captain Van den Burg was having a very bad day. Not only had he suddenly found himself in the middle of a murder investigation, but now the ship's doctor was sitting in his office, reporting the need to immediately disembark a passenger in need of hospital treatment. The patient had a very high temperature and could well be carrying a potentially contagious and life-threatening illness.

"Other vessels are, at present, reporting a surge in cases of fever and difficulty breathing. The symptoms include the loss and change to one's sense of smell and taste. They are desperately trying to contain whatever it is and hoping to disembark any guests showing early signs of a fever off the ship and straight to hospital. I am concerned that if it gets too much of a hold and the numbers on board increase, the hospitals will refuse to take the passengers, so I would like to act quickly."

Captain Van Den Burg had his orders to move expeditiously on this matter. "Have any other guests reported feeling unwell?"

"Not at the moment, Captain." The Doctor continued with his report. "I'm not sure masks and gloves will be sufficient to contain the virus, Captain, should it take hold. At this stage, it is unknown whether it is airborne or caught only from direct contact. The good news is that the passenger is travelling alone, and we have quarantined her in her stateroom for the time being. Her meals will be brought to her and left outside the stateroom door. The cleaning of the room and changing towels and bed linen have been put on hold."

The Doctor was feeling the strain. This cruise was turning out to be a complete logistical and medical nightmare.

"I will request, as a matter of urgency, for the Port Authority to send an ambulance to remove the passenger to hospital as soon as is possible. I simply cannot take no for an answer." The Captain was on the phone before the doctor had left his office.

Three hours later, following conversations with The Crisis Management Team at head office, Captain Van Den Burg watched several of his medical staff, dressed in hazmat suits, always included as part of the ship's emergency kit, escort the passenger onto a tender to be taken to the port in Nice. There, a waiting ambulance with its emergency lights flashing would take her to a hospital twenty minutes outside the town. Both the tender and crew would not be returning to the ship until the results of any tests have been established.

———

"I see it's your turn next." Jacqueline was looking over Roger's shoulder at his invitation to an informal meeting with Assistant Superintendent James.

"I'm quite looking forward to it. I'm happy to talk endlessly about our bridge partnership and answer any other questions he may ask." Roger walked over to his wardrobe and stroked his chin, wondering what outfit to wear for his interview. Jacqueline watched him and shook her head in disbelief.

"Why are you looking at me in that tone of voice?" Roger said, jokingly.

"I do believe that if they were escorting you to the executioner's block, you would be worried about your appearance," Jacqueline sighed. "You're not the star of the show here, you know."

"I'm fully aware of that, darling, but I can't help feeling very lucky that my family are okay. They're well, happy, and unharmed. We're on a cruise – yes, it has been spoiled by Cynthia's untimely death, which is horrible, I know, but it could have been a lot closer to home. How awful would that be? I certainly wouldn't be sorting through my wardrobe for a suitable outfit if that had been the case."

Jacqueline settled herself on the balcony with her book to wait for Roger's return. "I wouldn't bet good money on that", she said as the door closed behind him.

———

Roger Sylvester sauntered along the corridor towards the Captain's office, softly whistling the first two bars of 'Jerusalem'. He knocked on the door a bit too loudly, announcing his arrival.

"Good morning, Mr. Sylvester. I am Assistant Superintendent Samuel James."

"...And I am Captain Van Den Burg." The Captain held his hand out before Samuel forgot he was in the room, again. "Before we start the meeting, may I offer you some refreshment?"

"I could murder one of your very nice cocktails of the day, please." Roger threw back his head and roared with laughter. "See what I did there? – sorry, that was in rather bad taste."

Samuel chose not to respond to the comment but looked at the captain before launching straight into his line of questioning.

"I've been looking forward to speaking to you, Mr. Sylvester. First, both the Captain and I would like to say how sorry we are for the loss of your close friend and bridge partner. You may well be the one person on this ship who knew her best."

"I certainly knew her very well, but I would dispute knowing her better than anyone else. I wouldn't presume such a thing." Roger looked very comfortable and confident sitting in the tub chair.

"Can you tell us a little bit about your relationship with Mrs. Manning, please?" Samuel was looking forward to this.

Roger sat back in the chair and crossed his legs. Samuel wondered how anyone could look so relaxed, while being asked by the police to give a statement in a murder enquiry.

"Cynthia and I have been playing bridge for a few years. She's a great family friend and we're all heartbroken by her very untimely death. You don't understand, Superintendent, what a wonderful woman she is – was - and how much we're all going to miss her. I mean, her personality alone was fabulous – she is – was - a real firecracker." Roger felt that was a pretty honest character assessment.

"How often did you see her? Once a week? More than that?" Samuel asked,

"Once or twice a week. Occasionally more if there was a bridge competition on. We might go out for dinner, either before or after a bridge game, to make an evening out of it. In fact, my daughter started to come out for dinner with us recently, too."

"Your daughter? Does she play bridge as well?" Samuel needed to focus hard on this interview. There was something different about it that he couldn't quite put his finger on.

Roger uncrossed his legs and stopped looking quite so relaxed. "No, absolutely not. It wouldn't be her scene at all. Not that she lacks intelligence to learn the game or anything like that. I think she just wanted to know what the fuss was all about – you know, what was so fascinating that I had to go out of the house in the evening a few times a week. Once she saw how social the game is and how much I enjoyed it, she completely understood." Roger was very happy with the overall image of respectability he was creating.

"Is your daughter married, Mr. Sylvester?"

"Yes, she is. Very happily married."

"Why did her husband not join the three of you for dinner?" Samuel asked innocently.

Roger was now leaning forward with his hands clasped in his lap, twiddling his thumbs nervously. "I hadn't really thought about it, but you're quite right, I should have asked him to join us. Abby, my daughter, sort of invited herself and I just went along with it."

"So your daughter suggested she join you and Cynthia for dinner, without her husband or your wife?" Samuel glanced over at Captain Van Den Burg. The Captain took this as a sign that something interesting might be forthcoming.

"It does sound a bit strange, but my daughter and I have always been very close. She used to follow me around when she was little and we would often do fun things together, just the two of us. I suppose she didn't think about whether to include anyone else. She was just curious to get to know Cynthia." Roger was wondering why the interview was focusing on his daughter joining him and Cynthia for dinner.

"But you said Mrs. Manning was a family friend?" Samuel persisted.

"Well, I obviously knew her, my daughter met her at dinner and got on well with her and my wife was friendly with her on this cruise, so that's what I meant by 'a family friend'. "

"I would like to remind you that anything you tell us in this office, during this interview, is confidential so I will ask you, Mr. Sylvester, if your relationship with Mrs. Manning went beyond just being bridge partners?" Samuel had a hunch there was more to it.

"Absolutely not, Superintendent."

"I realise that you are on the ship with your wife, but I do know that you boarded quite a while after the rest of the group. I believe there was some misunderstanding with the UK police...?" Samuel waited for the gaps to be filled in.

"Oh that was just something and nothing. All to do with money coming in and out of my business bank account. It was all very boring and certainly nothing to do with this enquiry. I hope you are not making a connection with this crime?" Roger started to feel very hot.

"What I am asking is if you have anything more to tell me about your relationship with Mrs. Manning, now would be a good time. If you had a close relationship with Mrs. Manning, it does not automatically make you a suspect. We are not here to judge you, Mr. Sylvester. It just makes life easier to know the exact nature so we don't waste time."

"I'm not perfect, Superintendent. I like the ladies and enjoy their company. That's part of the attraction of belonging to a bridge club – there are lot of lovely ladies to meet there. I am, however, first and foremost a happily married man - a family man and that is the most important thing to me."

"Thank you for your candour, Mr. Sylvester. Should I need to call upon you again, I hope you won't mind."

"I think you've taken a shine to me, Superintendent, so I expect we will be meeting again soon."

―――

"I hope they'll be wrapping up the murder enquiry soon, darling and I can come home to you." Miranda was crying softly down the phone to Henry. She felt very isolated and homesick and on top of everything there was a rumour that one of the guests has been taken off the ship in a hurry.

She held the phone away from her whilst Henry's voice boomed down the phone. "There's no point in me asking the ship's doctor why, Henry. Please don't shout!"

"I'm not shouting, Miranda, I'm agitated. Why have they tendered one of the guests off the ship and is their condition a danger to the other passengers? We need to establish this." Henry insisted.

"So should I go into the captain's office and demand to see the guest's medical records?" Miranda wasn't being serious about this, but Henry thought she was. "The guest has gone, Henry. He or she is no longer a danger."

"Yes, good idea. Do that first thing in the morning. We don't know if this guest was carrying some horrible contagious disease picked up from goodness knows where, do we? And if so, we also don't know if it's spread in the air-conditioning unit or something. Have they finished interviewing everyone?"

Henry knew he should be strong for her, but he felt very emotional. He couldn't wait to have her home and get back to normal.

"Please don't alarm me more than I am already, darling. It's not helping. I think they have one or two people left to interview and that'll be it. Nick said that he thinks the group won't be needed to assist with anymore enquiries and we can start planning our escape."

"I love you, Miranda. Every day I blame myself for not coming with you. At least we would be together. I'm so sorry. I would hate to be the boyfriend that wasn't there in a crisis."

"You have no reason to blame yourself. How were we

to know this would prove to be such a disaster? I just thought the trip would be something a bit different – I was right on that score. By the way, the captain has waived the cost of phone calls for the time being."

"That's the least he can do. I know all this is not his fault, but he's not the only one feeling the strain." Henry was running out of things to say to help.

"I'm sure he realises that." Miranda changed the topic.

"The food is still good and we're being looked after, but nobody is really eating very much and in between, we're playing bridge – lots of it and sitting by the pool. Poor Cynthia is dead and lying in the morgue on the ship and nobody wants to talk about it. I still expect her to breeze in, looking immaculate, saying something inappropriate. I found her wind-up remarks really quite funny, but far more amusing was certain people's reaction to them. It was definitely one of her skills." Miranda was smiling thinking about Cynthia's expressions on her face as the barbed remarks spewed forth.

"Probably a skill that got her murdered." Henry shook his head. Some people asked for trouble and he thought poor Cynthia was that type of person.

"Keep your chin up, my darling and we'll see each other soon. I'll be the one waving the Union Jack on the horizon as you sail into Southampton." Henry hung up. If anything had made his mind up about his commitment to Miranda, it was this nightmare.

—

"I am very worried that my lovely people are not having their favourite food." Alex complained to the dinner guests at the table. He had become very fond of the people he had been serving, twice a day, and felt a close bond with each of them, getting to know their likes and dislikes even before they voiced them – which they didn't hesitate to do several times during each meal.

He felt very sorry for the loss of the blonde lady. It was the first time he had heard about anyone being murdered on a cruise ship, let alone one of his customers in the dining room. The atmosphere at the table had changed and he was trying very hard to keep everyone in a good mood.

Once his shift was over, he was expected to repeat any titbit he managed to pick up from the conversation at the table. He had achieved a sort of celebrity status in the staff quarters.

"If I have to choose from this menu for much longer, I'm going to go completely mad." Sandra threw herself back in her chair, pointing at the list of dishes and staring at the beautiful penmanship on the page.

"It's terrible to watch how cruelly you are being treated." John said caustically. "You have been made to sit in a beautifully appointed dining room, with the biggest crystal chandelier both you and I have ever seen and forced to order culinary delights from a full and extensive menu, catering for every possible dietary requirement. Poor you!"

John was watching the waiting staff running around, taking care of the many tables allocated to them. They made it look effortless, but he imagined that if every waiter served the sort of demanding guests that were sitting on his table, they would all be heading for nervous breakdowns. He will be giving Alex a very nice tip at the end of the cruise. He was doing a sterling job.

"You're always the first to put me down." Sandra would have liked to say more, but she had been worn down by the whole experience.

"We've all done so well. Let's not spoil it now. I spoke

to Henry today and he thinks we'll be home soon. At least we've done our best to help the police."

"It's been a waste of time. What could any of us say that might help to find who murdered Cynthia?" John said, irritated.

"You would think that. Bloody know-all. How do you know what technique the police are trained to employ to question people? What questions might give away the perpetrator of a murder?" Roger didn't bother to look up from his plate. He didn't even look sneeringly at Jacqueline, which he often did when he thought he had said something witty.

"You're very prickly tonight. I wonder why. Could it be anything to do with your interview with the Assistant Superintendent? Did he rattle your cage?" Roger had walked straight into John's trap.

"I haven't been interviewed yet", Roger lied.

"Yes, you have. I have a reliable source who saw you go down to the captain's office. Why lie about it? How ridiculous to lie when we've all been so open about it. That says volumes about your character. Not that I needed any more proof that you're a weirdo."

Jacqueline banged her fist down hard on the table and caused the surrounding diners to look up from their meal. "That's enough from you tonight, thank you. How dare you speak like that. I've spent this whole trip listening to you, and others, speak rudely at the table without any filter at all and I've had enough, do you hear me?"

"I'm very sorry, Jacqueline. I didn't mean to offend you. Please forgive me." John felt very badly about upsetting her. She had enough to contend with.

"You all think because I sit quietly, eating my dinner and minding my own business, that none of this warring and back-biting bothers me. Well, it does!" Jacqueline was thoroughly fed up with all of them. Sitting there smugly with hardly any real thought for the poor woman lying on a slab in the bowels of the ship.

"If you must know, I did have a meeting with the Assistant Superintendent today." Roger spoke quietly, trying to keep his voice measured for Jacqueline's sake. For the first time, he could see she was at the end of her tether. "It was a very short meeting. I suspect I was asked the same questions as you."

Roger looked at everyone sitting at the table. "How well did we know each other, whether our relationship was intimate and such like."

"The difference is *you* would have had more to say, being on such close terms with Cynthia. I know she confided in you about personal things. Why wouldn't she confide in her 'bridge partner'?" John couldn't shut up.

Jacqueline got up from the table and left the room.

"You're a buffoon. You know nothing about the relationship between Cynthia and me, but it was a damn sight more meaningful than yours, that's for sure." Roger pushed his plate away, got up and left the dining room.

———

Captain Van Den Burg was now feeling upbeat on two counts. The first, was that he thought the interviews carried out by Assistant Superintendent Samuel James were really very professional and efficient. A pretty good job, all things considered.

He had been concerned about supervising a murder investigation whilst at sea, but the statements given by the key people who knew the victim had been more than satisfactory. Further information would be gleaned from the CCTV and ready to hand over to the police in Southampton when the ship eventually docked.

The second reason was the arrival of the police pilot

boat from Nice, bringing certain items sealed in an evidence bag.

By sheer luck, the items had been handed to the Port Authority Agent at Livorno by beachcombers scouring for lost valuables amongst the sand and pebbles. The agent had the items sent immediately to Nice where they were carefully labelled, bagged and transported to the ship, anchored offshore.

Samuel James and Captain Van Den Burg peered at the items through the plastic bag. It contained an iron from the ship's laundry room with the cord tied up in a tight knot; a small metal tag with the name of the ship fixed to the bottom and a champagne glass, one of thousands ordered regularly as a stock item on board. How it remained in one piece and not smashed to smithereens was surely a miracle, but even if it had been broken, it would still be useful evidence. Finally, the prize piece and star of the collection, a mobile telephone.

———

Sandra was lying on her bed with an almighty headache when she heard a scratching noise outside her stateroom. She got up and raced to the door, hoping to catch whoever was disturbing her rest to give them a good telling off. She saw a card in her cubby hole addressed to Mrs. Dearlove, inviting her to an interview with Captain Van Den Burg and Assistant Superintendent Samuel James of the Arawak Cay police station in the Bahamas.

"About time!" she shouted out loud to herself. "The first thing I want to know..." she muttered to herself "is why am I the last bloody person to be called for interview. I wouldn't mind, but I knew Cynthia longer than any of these other shmucks."

She went out onto her balcony, sat down to eat her breakfast and read the card again. It was just two lines, nevertheless the words hit her hard. She just couldn't get her head around Cynthia's horrible, brutal murder, mainly because her punchbag was gone. She gave that woman plenty of grief, but by God did she deserve it.

Cynthia spent her time mincing around after her husband and anyone else's that took her fancy. The innocent expression on her heavily made-up face fooled nobody. She may as well have said, "Who me? I haven't done anything wrong. It's not *my* problem that you can't hang on to your man."

"Well, Cynthia? You sure as hell won't be treading on too many toes, now - unless that sort of behaviour is rife where you're going." Sandra wanted to shout it out to sea. Instead, she turned to go back into her cabin to choose her interview outfit – something appropriately sombre.

———

"Good afternoon Mrs. Dearlove. My name is Assistant Superintendent Samuel James. Please sit down." He said.

"Captain? Could you order Mrs. Dearlove some refreshment?"

Captain Van Den Burg looked at Samuel who was starting to get on his nerves. What a shock the 'little policeman' was going to get when he was back in his hut on the Island. He wouldn't be helping himself liberally from a five-star buffet there.

Sandra fiddled around in her handbag, just to delay things as a stand against the injustice of being overlooked.

"Before we start, I would like to know why I'm the last person to be called to give a statement? Do you know who I am?" Her voice could probably be heard several floors above in the vodka lounge.

It was at this point that Samuel was very pleased with Nick Lombardo and his list of bridge guests. "I know exactly who you are, Mrs. Dearlove and that is precisely why I waited until last to call you in. I don't want our interview to be rushed or hurried in any way. Please sit down and relax. Shall we wait until you have had your coffee and biscuits?"

Sandra was mollified. She knew a clever man like the Superintendent would see, immediately, that she had plenty to say that would be crucial to his investigation. "No, it's alright. We can start straight away."

"Firstly, I would like to say, from myself and the Captain, how very sorry we are that you have lost a dear and close friend in such a manner."

"Thank you. I appreciate that."

"I'm very interested to know about your relationship with Mrs. Manning. I won't fire questions at you, just let it flow." Samuel sat forward in his chair with a nice new notebook and a collection of pens. This was going to take a while.

"Moral backbone? That woman didn't know the meaning of the word. We've been friends for years, we mixed together socially with our partners – the four of us went everywhere. We dined out frequently, went to the theatre and concerts, it was marvellous until the trouble started." Sandra was already breathless.

"Oh dear. What trouble was that?" Samuel hadn't written anything down yet.

"Cynthia's husband became very ill. Pancreatic cancer, I think. It was very sad, but she changed overnight. I suppose she was preparing for widowhood – casting her eyes for a suitable replacement, maybe."

"Did Mrs. Manning care for her sick husband during that period?" Samuel asked, gently.

"Yes, she was wonderful in that regard. She wouldn't leave his side and their two daughters would take over to give her a bit of a break now and again."

"Did you see much of her and her husband?"

"Not a great deal. Her social life dried up a bit. I popped into see her from time to time, bring her some shopping if she asked – that sort of thing."

"What makes you think that Cynthia didn't have moral backbone?"

"She had a very unhealthy relationship with my husband, Alan."

"In what way?"

"Secret phone calls, intimate looks when they thought my back was turned. It was very upsetting." Sandra was working herself up nicely.

"Did you have it out with her about this?" Samuel knew the answer.

"Of course I did, but she denied it. She told me, quite recently actually, that my husband kept telling her that he wanted to divorce me and that she repeatedly told him that she didn't want to get involved in 'our marital troubles'. We didn't have any 'marital troubles' until she stuck her nose in."

"But you're still with your husband?" Samuel was very happy the captain was sitting in the room with them.

"Alan and I did get divorced and I remarried." Sandra sipped her coffee and finished the last of the three biscuits.

"Was Mrs. Manning friendly with you and your second husband, too?"

"She didn't have time to get her claws into him – flutter her eyelashes at him. It was not a successful marriage and we are now divorced."

"So the breakdown of your second marriage wasn't Mrs. Manning's fault?" Samuel was feeling giddy with all the details but making copious notes which he hoped will make sense when he read them back.

"No. I suppose she wasn't responsible for that." Sandra looked disappointed.

"Can you think of anyone who would want to kill Mrs. Manning?" Samuel scribbled 'brace yourself' on the notepad and showed it to the captain who struggled not to laugh.

"Is everything I say to you strictly confidential because I can tell you, you won't have to look very far for the murderer. I don't have any proof, before you ask." Sandra was ready to whistle blow.

"Anything you say in this room is strictly confidential, Mrs. Dearlove."

"You have obviously interviewed John Wood. He's a married man, sucked into Cynthia's web. I'm surprised his wife allowed him to go on this trip." Sandra was warming up.

"Yes, we interviewed Mr. Wood."

"Did he tell you that he's becoming increasingly infatuated with Cynthia? That he lurks around every corner, waiting for her? He's very jealous of anyone who goes near her, you know. Especially Roger." Sandra's eyes were blazing.

"Why would Mr. Wood be jealous of Roger? I assume you mean Mr. Sylvester?"

"Roger is another married man sucked into that ever-growing web. How did she manage it? Having sex with all these men - it's disgusting. I'm sure their wives knew about it. You'd have to be pretty stupid not to know your husband was sleeping with that woman."

"How do you know Mrs. Manning's relationship with these men was physical and not just platonic?"

"I'm a woman, Superintendent. I might not be having sex with several men all at once, but I can still spot one who can hardly keep it in his trousers when he's around Cynthia. Take my advice, I would be looking at both of those men for answers, if I were you."

"Thank you so much, Mrs. Dearlove. We may have to call upon you again after we have scrutinised the CCTV on the ship."

"Oh my goodness me. In that case, you most certainly will be calling on me again."

———

"Show Tunes from the Musicals" was about to start in the Ship's theatre. It was such an amazing space, considering it was on a ship.

The 1,150 tip-up seats, with drink holders on the arms of each one was designed in exactly the same way as those in a regular theatre, as well as room for the orchestra and Miranda thought it was just fabulous. There were two shows every night, one for those who dined early and a later one.

The choreography and costumes were magnificent, and the evening's entertainment was as always, glorious. The little group were sitting six rows back from the front, enjoying the show and yet, even something as simple as the seating plan couldn't be agreed upon.

Miranda was sitting next to John. She noticed tears slowly trickling down his cheeks as the familiar tunes were playing and the showgirls dancing and she felt her eyes welling up, too. John was thinking how he had betrayed his beloved wife chasing a silly dream and Miranda was longing for Henry to be by her side. She reached out and squeezed his hand.

"Cynthia would have loved this. She loved a good sing-song." John said.

"The bawdier the better", Sandra said, nastily. "I hope you pull yourself together before you get off the ship and go home to your wife. She'll be expecting to see a smiling face. We're a bit close to the stage here, aren't we?"

"My wife is a wonderful human being. She will expect me to be sad about the murder of a dear friend and we're sitting in exactly the right place. You're damned lucky I reserved you a seat."

"You reserved this seat?" Sandra laughed at her own joke.

"The production is as good as the West End. They must rehearse for months before the season." Miranda was staring at the costumes, enjoying every minute of the show.

"They have the most amazing talent apply to be part of the entertainment crew and audition the best before they choose the cast", Jacqueline said. "I read about it in the brochure."

"I've had my interview with the Superintendent and the Captain", Sandra whispered to Roger. "Good fun, wasn't it?"

"The most fun I've ever had," Roger said, sarcastically.

"Don't start, Sandra – we're having a nice, light-hearted evening watching this lovely production. Please don't spoil it." Jacqueline decided not to wait any longer before stepping in.

"I'm not saying anything controversial. I just didn't want you all to think I was being secretive. I was in there for ever such a long time. I think he got the picture."

"Who got the picture?" Miranda asked.

"The Superintendent. I told him exactly the sort of woman they were dealing with." Sandra sat back and smiled.

"And the Assistant Superintendent must have seen exactly the sort of woman *he* was dealing with when you did." John said, through gritted teeth.

"Will you please be quiet." A voice hissed from the row behind.

"We'll see." Sandra always had to have the last word.

———

Nick Lombardo ordered a gin and tonic, even though the captain had only offered him tea or coffee. He felt he had earned it after this awful fiasco.

"Good morning, Mr. Lombardo. Would you just have a quick look at my computer. I have some footage downloaded from the CCTV." Samuel turned his screen around. "As you can see, the date is a couple of days before Mrs. Manning's body was found on the recreation deck. Can you confirm that this is you leaving her cabin? Do you remember what that conversation was about?"

Nick could see himself walking down the corridor and knocking on the stateroom door. He disappears within for a few moments and then the door is thrown open and he is coming out of the cabin, looking a bit irritated.

"Yes, absolutely. That's me. I had been receiving a few silly complaints about Cynthia from other members of the group - nothing major. They asked me if I would have a word with her about her - how can I put it – tendency to be outspoken."

"How rude was she to these people?" Samuel asked.

Nick wasn't going to beat around the bush. "Rude and rather personal towards several people in the group. Cynthia had a very high opinion of herself, which is fine – why not? But if you're on a holiday with a group of people, you have to behave yourself, try and get along with them. Insulting people left, right and centre because you imagine they're attacking you personally, is not acceptable. I won't have it, Superintendent - not in my group, anyway."

"So you decided to step in and deal with it?" Samuel coaxed. He could see Nick was getting annoyed just thinking about the conversation he had with Mrs. Manning.

"I called her and made an appointment to see her – I didn't just barge in."

"No, of course not."

"I explained to her that I heard a few complaints about her rather distasteful comments and asked her if she could be a little more patient and refrain from attacking them verbally for every remark they made." Nick continued. "She wouldn't have it. She denied that she was behaving unreasonably - she took umbrage to the fact that I felt the need to come and see her about it and she was pretty cross with me for 'taking sides' as she saw it. It was a complete waste of time and, as you can see by my gesticulation, I got absolutely nowhere with her."

"Thank you so much, Mr. Lombardo."

"Please call me Nick. How are you getting on with your enquiries? You must be nearly finished with us by now?"

"We're working quite nicely through the statements. Everyone has been very helpful. I have just one more question to ask you before we wrap this up."

"By all means, ask away." Nick tipped his glass up and drained it.

"Do you know who this is?" Samuel pointed to a person in a baseball cap, turning up at Cynthia's door, holding a bottle of champagne and two glasses. He watched Nick's reaction closely.

Nick couldn't believe what he was looking at. He could see two people, Cynthia, and an odd-looking person whom he had never seen in his life before leaving the cabin, arms entwined, going into the laundry room across the corridor.

"What on earth are they doing in the laundry room and who the hell is that?"

"If we knew the answer to both of those questions, I suspect we would be closer to solving the murder."

"How long are they are in there?" Nick was entranced."

"Wait! See what happens next", Samuel fast-forwards the clip.

The door opens and Cynthia emerges, pushing her friend, now holding two freshly ironed shirts, in a wheelchair.

"Where on earth are they going now? What time is all this activity?" Nick was still staring, mesmerised, at the screen.

"It's close to midnight. As you can see, the ship was very quiet that evening."

"What happens next?" Nick asked the captain.

The captain leant forward. "That's the funny thing. They seem to be having a lovely time – walking around the recreation deck, looking out to sea and chatting very nicely and then we lose track of them for a bit. They reappear in the lift, getting out and going along the corridor back to Mrs. Manning's stateroom."

"Fine, well that's it, then. Can I go now?" Nick's interest in all of this had waned days ago. All he wanted to do was to get back home to run his successful bridge club which had not been quite so lucrative since he had been away.

Captain Van Den Burg looked at Samuel. "Do you have any more questions for Mr. Lombardo?"

"I don't think we'll be needing to talk to you again."

Samuel got up and showed Nick out of the office.

"Are we drawing a line under his name?" Captain Van Den Burg certainly hoped so.

"Oh yes, I think we can be fairly certain that we have a full statement from him. I wouldn't like to have his job trying to keep that lot in line."

———

"I wasn't expecting to be called back so soon." John sat down heavily in the chair and smiled, confidently. This was just a formality. His 'cocktail of the day' arrived on a tray, the ice cubes bobbing around nicely in the long glass.

"It's very nice of you to help us again, Mr. Wood. We have downloaded some images from the CCTV, and we wondered if you could take a look at them."

"No problem at all. Let's have a peek." John leant forward at the same time as Samuel James turned the screen of his computer towards him. At first, he was looking at an empty corridor and then he saw himself getting out of the lift and approaching Cynthia's stateroom. It must have been late as there was nobody about.

"Oh look! that's me visiting Cynthia" John said, merrily and then his heart stopped. The footage showed him opening up the flies of his shorts and exposing himself to the woman who had opened the door of the stateroom.

"Oh my Lord – I was just having a little joke. I did tell you, Superintendent, that I fancied her like mad, didn't I. I was just proving it, that's all." John felt ready to pass out.

"Now, if you look closely, you can see she reaches out and drags you into her cabin." Samuel's attention was focused on the screen. "An hour later, you seem to have had a falling out." It was very clear that John was being unceremoniously kicked out of the cabin and sent on his way. "Can you remember what happened?"

"Okay, Superintendent, I may not have been one hundred percent honest with you. Cynthia and I enjoyed a bit of slap and tickle now and again. I can see that from where you're sitting, I look like a stupid, idiotic schoolboy, but that's how she made me feel. She liked me acting like a love-struck adolescent. She was a very horny lady."

"I'm not interested in your sexual prowess, Mr. Wood, what I want to know is why Mrs. Manning kicked you out of the cabin afterwards. You do see that, from our point of view, it needs explaining."

"That's what she was like, Superintendent. When Cynthia was up for it, she was all smoochy and flirty – you had to peel her off you. As soon as the deed was done, you were history, until the next time you were summoned. I was okay with that - it was just a bit of fun for me just as much as it was for her, but I would think that if someone wanted more from her – it could be very annoying."

Samuel scrolled down and showed John another clip. "And what was this all about, do you remember?"

John saw himself walking along the corridor, holding a bottle of champagne and a couple of glasses. "I think that was the day we boarded the ship. We were all so excited about being on a bridge cruise – oh, I remember now – I knocked on Miranda's door, by accident of course, thinking it was Cynthia's stateroom."

"I've got one more picture to show you, Mr. Wood. Do you know who this person is wearing a baseball cap?"

"Is it a woman? She seems to be standing right behind me in the queue to get off the ship. I didn't notice her. Should I know her?"

"And here she is again. Still no bells ringing?"

John watched in horror as a tall person, wearing a most unfetching baseball cap and holding a champagne bottle in one hand with two glasses in another, knocked on Cynthia's door. A little while later, the two of them went into the laundry room.

"Cynthia seems to be drinking rather a lot of champagne. It's no wonder her bridge playing was suffering. I wouldn't have told her that, of course." John's eyes were still on the screen.

"This clip appears to be shortly after you left Cynthia's stateroom, Mr. Wood. I can't help feeling that there was a lot of traffic in and out of Mrs. Manning's cabin that night. She must have been a very sociable lady." Samuel stared at John, making him squirm in his chair.

"You are correct. I left Cynthia's room quite late, actually – we do like our nightcaps and they tend to go on a bit. I said "goodnight" and assumed she was off to bed, but what on earth are those two doing?"

"I was hoping somebody could tell me."

"Who is in the wheelchair? As far as I know, there isn't anyone in our group disabled enough to require a wheelchair and why are they frolicking around the recreation deck?

"A very good question, Mr. Wood."

"I don't mean to be unkind, Superintendent, but Cynthia is not a person full of the milk of human kindness. Helping someone into a wheelchair and pushing them around is not a service she would normally offer."

"I hoped you would know. Thank you for your help, Mr. Wood."

"Just one more thing, Superintendent. I hope you're putting Roger Sylvester through his paces. He is a much closer friend to Cynthia – some would say too close."

"From what I've witnessed on here, Mr. Wood, I'm not sure it's possible to get any closer to Mrs. Manning."

John turned and marched out of the office, bumping

into a steward on his way to the lift.

"What do you think?" Captain Van Den Burg asked Samuel.

"I'm not sure. Something new, however trivial, always seems to pop up when we speak to Mr. Wood. I'll keep him as a person of interest for a bit longer, I think."

John couldn't relax until after the lift doors closed and he was on his way back to his stateroom. He hurriedly opened the cabin door, poured himself a drink and went to sit on the balcony. What a horrible shock to see yourself performing like a complete plonker. He should have known that there were cameras all over the ship. He hoped the Superintendent wouldn't put him in the frame for Cynthia's murder. No! That was a ridiculous thought and as for that other scene he saw in the clip – Cynthia running around pushing a wheelchair? What a crazy arrangement was that?

———

"If this is a real art auction, I'm Marilyn Monroe." Sandra was spoiling the evening for everyone, yet again.

"They've got some lovely pictures. Some of them are terribly expensive." Jacqueline was looking through the catalogue.

The group were sitting in the atrium of the ship. A gorgeous space, usually reserved for a trio of musicians serenading the guests as they walk around, dipping in and out of the lounges and bars drinking lychee martinis, flavoured vodkas and an array of frothy coffees.

The floor was black and gold marble and there were usually little coffee tables and comfortable chairs arranged in circles between the columns, but on this occasion, chairs were crammed into every available space to provide comfort for the prospective purchaser in a holiday spending mood.

On sea days, the shops were open and busy with people mingling around looking at cosmetics, spraying themselves with perfume from the sample bottles available, before ambling over to the jewellery shop to admire an array of gems.

The boutique offered a large selection of men and women's fashion in an assortment of sizes. Some guests purchased the same item in two sizes, a little insurance of one becoming too small during the sailing.

The auction was a highlight of the ship's list of 'things to do and enjoy on board' and the space allocated was intentional – designed to attract, like a magnet, to the beautifully framed prints, posters and occasionally original paintings by some famous but mostly obscure, artists. Easels were brought in to display the largest and most expensive pieces of art in the collection.

Suddenly, the piped music stopped, and a pair of green alligator-skin cowboy boots could be seen walking towards the podium. They were the best thing about the man wearing them.

"Good morning, fellow art connoisseurs. It's wonderful to see you here in such great numbers. I must have got my collection just right for this cruise." The auctioneer was dressed in a well-tailored suit, with a black shirt and tie, but all eyes were drawn to his feet.

"Is your name down for the Rembrandt or will you go for the Picasso?" John asked Roger, leaning over, hardly able to control his sniggering.

"You couldn't afford a copy, let alone an original. I'm sure they've got some postcards of the paintings somewhere you could drool over." Roger replied, without hesitation.

Miranda reached out and grabbed a glass of champagne from a passing tray. "I think it's lovely to buy one of these limited-edition prints or a lithograph as a memento of the holiday. I may consider buying one for Henry if it's not too expensive."

"I can't believe you would consider buying any of these, Miranda. The paint is still wet on half of them." Sandra laughed and so did Miranda.

The auctioneer was busy. The auction was in full swing and he was doing a roaring trade. There was a run on the Chagall, Erte, Dali and Picasso and he was perspiring from the excitement and dollar calculations.

"Oh look! Some fool has brought that brightly coloured picture of something completely unfathomable. I would get the most awful migraine looking at that every day. Surely you shouldn't have to co-ordinate your wardrobe to match your painting." Sandra's voice was very loud.

"I think that's a Britto, Sandra. He's very collectable. You must keep your voice down." Jacqueline whispered.

At that point, an auction assistant marched purposefully up to Sandra "Madam, if this auction is not your sort of thing, I suggest you find another activity on the ship that suits you. Please let the other guests enjoy the auction, without interruption."

"Jacqueline, look at that sweet Disney print of Dumbo. Shall we buy one for our grandchild?" Roger was smiling softly. He had noticed one of the guests buying several of the Disney lithographs. She must be a collector.

"We don't have a grandchild yet, darling." Jacqueline would have loved to have purchased it.

"I'm sure it won't be long. We can put it away in a cupboard and bring it out when it's required." Roger looked very keen.

"It would be cheaper to go to the cinema and buy a large tub of popcorn. The kid would love it just as much." Sandra interrupted.

———

Miranda Soames sat down in the tub chair and smiled at the Assistant Superintendent.

"Can I offer you a drink, Ms Soames? The cocktail of the day, perhaps? I'm told it's very delicious." Samuel sounded pleasant and light-hearted.

Listening to Samuel casually offering cocktails, Captain Van Den Burg gave Samuel a sideways glance and shook his head. He had stopped caring that he was showing some annoyance.

"I would love a cocktail. Thank you very much." Miranda felt better already.

They all waited for the cocktail to arrive before Samuel turned his computer screen around. "I wonder if you could just tell me a bit more about this clip, please?"

Miranda watched the screen for a while. She could see an empty corridor and then she spotted herself walking towards Cynthia's stateroom. Her friend welcomed her enthusiastically. The screen showed Cynthia reach out and hug Miranda, before gently drawing her into the room. Shortly afterwards, two officers, in ship's uniform, could be seen walking down the aisle towards Cynthia's stateroom. They checked the number on a piece of paper and knocked on the door.

"I just want you to know that the captain and I have no objection to anyone having guests in their rooms. Would you mind just telling me the reason for their visit to Mrs. Manning's stateroom that evening, please?" Samuel looked down at his notepad and waited for Miranda's explanation.

"Oh dear, it does look rather suspicious, doesn't it, but it really wasn't at all. Cynthia talked to everyone on the ship and flirted with the officers every time she saw one standing around, or on their way somewhere on the ship." Miranda was still staring at the screen.

"Did she invite them all to her cabin or just a select few?" Captain Van Den Burg asked the question. He had spoken to the officers in question. They had reported that, as they were both invited for drinks, they didn't see a problem and assured the captain that their behaviour had been professional and correct at all times.

"On that particular occasion, she must have asked them to her cabin. I can hear her now – pretending to be surprised to bump into them, whilst suggesting that she was inviting a lovely young lady into her stateroom and would they like to meet her. It was exactly her style – She was incorrigible, Captain. It was very wrong of her to do that."

"I won't deny that it was a surprise." The Captain's face was unreadable.

"I have a boyfriend – I hope soon to be fiancé, waiting for me at home. Cynthia met him as we were getting ready to drive down to Southampton and was flirting with him, too. He didn't like her very much – he thought she was very silly and giggly for a woman of her age. I was unaware that she had planned to invite other people to join us for drinks on her balcony that evening, but it was very enjoyable and, as you can see if you fast forward, quite brief.

"And how about this? Can you remember what this was all about?" Samuel again turned the screen around to face Miranda.

She could see John racing down the corridor to Cynthia's room. He knocked, looking around to see if anyone was watching. The door opened and Cynthia stepped out. It looked like she was shooing him away. He grabbed her face and kissed her on the mouth before racing back down the corridor.

"I was with her that evening – on the balcony, Assistant Superintendent.

"How did that look to you?" Samuel asked Miranda.

"It looks like Cynthia saying "Hi, I can't talk now, I'll catch you later" or "Miranda's on the balcony, come back later and we can chat." - "There could be a million scenarios, Superintendent. I wouldn't like to say - I try not to get involved in the personal lives of people in my bridge group more than I have to. That's how you fall out. They're too busy doing that amongst themselves and, as you can tell, they *are* falling out."

"Just one more question before you go, Ms. Soames. Do you know who this person is wearing a baseball cap?"

For this sequence, Miranda decided to reach into her handbag and grab her glasses. She peered at the screen and saw - either a woman or a man, wearing a baseball cap – she wasn't too sure - standing behind her in the queue to disembark the ship. It was difficult to decipher the gender of the person in the queue. The person was of an average height and weight. Apart from going to great lengths to avoid being seen by a camera, there was nothing particularly unusual about them.

"I didn't notice that person standing behind me and she doesn't look familiar." Miranda kept staring at the screen.

"Here she is again. Mrs. Manning obviously knew her."

"Oh my Lord! She's holding a bottle of champagne." Miranda couldn't believe what she was seeing. "Cynthia would have told me if there was something to celebrate – she just wouldn't have left me out. The more the merrier was Cynthia's approach. What's going on there? No, that's all wrong." Miranda was shaking her head. None of this made any sense. "Why was Cynthia going into the laundry room? Cynthia's idea of doing laundry was to call our steward and have him collect dirty and deliver clean and pressed."

"This is just the beginning. Watch what happens next." Samuel was quite enjoying this.

"Who is the person in the baseball cap? Cynthia didn't mention someone wearing a cap calling on her. She always took great pleasure in telling me, in great detail, everything about everyone she met - what they were wearing, where it was purchased and how much the whole outfit cost. I'm sure I would have known about this visitor to her stateroom." Miranda was agog.

"What happens next?"

"The two ladies go on a jolly around the ship." Samuel had the resigned smile of a man completely confused.

Miranda could see Cynthia pushing the wheelchair around the deck. The two women gaze out to sea and the wheelchair is hastily wheeled away. However many times the shot was replayed, the faces of the two women were obscured.

"Are you sure you have the right person, Assistant Superintendent? Is that Cynthia's stateroom. It certainly looks like her leaving with that stranger, but..."

"A stranger to you, Ms Soames, but obviously not to her."

"It must be a man, Superintendent. Cynthia Manning would only go for a jolly, late at night, with a man."

"Thank you for your help, Ms Soames. I shouldn't need to speak to you again." Samuel got up and showed Miranda out of the office and sat back down.

"I think we can cross her name of our list."

"So you're satisfied that her alibi for the night of the murder checks out?" Captain Van Den Burg believed in checking and double checking everything.

"I'm sure she wasn't with Mrs. Manning and nowhere near her stateroom at the time of the murder. I don't think Ms. Soames had any reason to hurt her friend. They were living completely separate lives, neither one in competition with the other and that's what I'll be putting in my report."

Samuel and the captain both agreed.

———

Captain Van Den Burgh and Samuel looked, for the umpteenth time, at the evidence bag. Wearing gloves and very carefully, they extracted the mobile phone. The Captain managed to find the correct charger and now it had a full battery. The call list was most revealing, as were the text messages. Had the phone been a more up to date model, it certainly would not have been retrieved.

Cynthia had been very busy reporting her activities, daily. Samuel assumed that some of the text messages were to and from her children. He didn't recognise their names, saw no connection to the events that had taken place on the ship and the tone of them was chatty and light. Many of the messages had been sent several weeks before the cruise, but he wanted to start focusing on the most recent ones, shortly before Mrs. Manning's murder. Samuel scrolled down, passed the trivia, until he saw a familiar name.

"...I'm ready for you, gorgeous. Don't keep me waiting too long. I need to keep up my hard man image." Samuel could picture John Wood's hand shaking as he wrote that message, so keen would he have been to get together with Mrs. Manning.

"...I'm having a rest in my cabin before dinner and I think I'm rested enough – Get in here – I can't wait."

Samuel hated looking at other people's phone messages, but it had to be done. He never stopped marvelling at the content of some of the texts, emails and letters he had read over the years.

"...I couldn't believe how they hauled you off the coach. I hope you didn't expect me to jump to your defence, not with your wife sitting with you. I'm missing you terribly, obviously, but you know me - I'm making the best of the situation. I just want you to know that I can't wait for you to come back so that we can resume our wonderful sessions in bed. Nobody touches me the way you do – makes me feel as horny as you do. Making love to you is divine. Hurry back on board, you stallion."

Samuel showed the captain the message. If they didn't already know, it reaffirmed their belief about not putting things in writing that couldn't be shouted from the rooftop.

"...I've got good news – well, I hope you think it's good news. I will be meeting the ship in Livorno. It's a pretty civilised place and easy to get to. I'll book a flight to Pisa and get a taxi from there to the ship. Get your knickers off, Cynthia – I'm on my way. – make sure you delete this message."

"And this text message is from a successful business man?" Captain Van Den Burg asked Samuel.

"In my line of work, Captain, you would be amazed to read the things people write down."

"...Are you okay, Cynth? Do you need me to escort you down for drinks? I know how you hate to be alone; you shy thing."

"...You are funny, but seriously - I don't know what I would do without you, Miranda. Sandra still has the power to upset me, even after all these years."

"...I won't come to your cabin again if you stash any more handsome officers under the bed – but really, Cynthia, you know I love Henry. He would go mad with me *if he knew."*

"Keep your hair on, darling – it was only a bit of fun. I won't do it again, I promise."

Samuel continued to scroll, careful not to miss the most innocent of messages that might have a hint of malevolence.

"Here's a particularly nasty message", Samuel pointed out - handing the phone over to Captain Van Den Burgh.

" ...I really would like to slap you; do you know that? You're supposed to be my friend, but you shame me at every opportunity. I think you get off on it."

"You imagine it, Sandra. We came on this holiday to play bridge and socialise with our friends. It's a hobby we both enjoy. Why can't you embrace it? Why can't you just be nice to me? I'm not going to continue texting if you're going to send me a whole stream of vitriol. Byeeeee – see you later."

"No, I won't be pushed off. You listen. If you keep running me down, Cynthia - I won't be responsible for my actions."

"Cynthia? Where are you? We're all trying desperately to get hold of you. The ship's about to leave and they say that you're on board, but nobody has heard from you. Just send me a quick message where you are, even if it's just a smiley face emoji. I don't care what you're up to." Samuel could hear Miranda's voice sounded pretty desperate.

Samuel continued scrolling down, showing the captain the messages that made even him blush. "Apart from the usual tripe, I haven't yet seen anything sinister, but I'll continue searching."

"I think we should hand it over to the police in Southampton. Do you agree?" Captain Van Den Burgh made a record of their findings in the ship's diary.

"Absolutely. That's exactly what we'll do."

Samuel reached into the bag and carefully took out the iron. Both men looked at it, noticing that it had been wrenched from the fitting on the wall of the laundry room. There was no doubt that the iron had caused some of Mrs. Manning's injuries, but the cord finished the job.

The murderer had made no effort at all to clean off any evidence of the crime from the iron. Just looking at it, it was obvious to Samuel that it was the murder weapon.

They must have assumed that it would all be washed off by the sea into which it was thrown. Very careless - Samuel was thrilled to notice that. There would be a wealth of evidence taken from it when the forensic team get their hands on it. For now, both men noticed blood and hair all over it – caught in the grooves of the sole plate at the base. Having seen the damage to Mrs. Manning's skull, it wasn't surprising.

As far as Captain Van Den Burg was concerned, he felt that he and Samuel had left no stone unturned. They had made an exhaustive effort to collect statements and gather as much evidence as possible.

His relationship with the Assistant Superintendent had taken a turn for the better. They had made a pact that conversation at lunch in the self-service restaurant should be devoted to the day's events, dedicated to the serious matter of the ongoing investigation and pooling their brainstorming skills, whilst dinner would be spent appreciating the fine food and wine, focusing on the exceptionally good entertainment in the theatre or news of their respective families.

Samuel had noticed the Captain had thawed towards him. At first, he was very distant and reserved and nothing Samuel said or did seemed to make any difference. Gradually, purely down to professional courtesy, Captain Van Den Burgh began to see that they were both on the same side and wanted the identical outcome – for Samuel to get back, as soon as possible, to his island police station on Arawak Cay, having assisted in solving this difficult and horrific murder.

He felt enormous respect for Captain Van Den Burgh. A man in command of a luxury cruise ship of this size, responsible for the thousands of people on board who relied on him for a variety of reasons, most certainly deserved it.

He had no idea when he boarded the ship, that the man would be such a hero. Some days, Samuel thought he had the worries of the world on his shoulders, but it seemed like nothing, compared to the responsibilities of this quiet and capable man.

———

"Good morning, Mrs. Dearlove. What can we offer you by way of refreshment, this morning?" Captain Van Den Burgh asked, pleasantly.

"Just a cup of tea – with lemon, please." Sandra was not in the mood for alcohol - in fact, she was very depressed.

After the furore and shock over Cynthia's murder had died down, she suddenly realised that, more than anyone else on the ship, she had been most affected by it.

Admittedly, her friendship with Cynthia wasn't perfect – most people would argue it wasn't a friendship at all. To outsiders, it seemed very clear that Sandra was the aggressor, the tormentor, and Cynthia was the poor downtrodden victim of her vicious tongue, but that couldn't have been further from the truth.

Sandra had always adored Cynthia - particularly her energy and lively spirit. She envied – in an admiring way – her glamour and her sex drive, both of which Sandra could only dream of having. She longed for Cynthia's petite little figure, rather than her own large, big-boned and ungainly one and most of all, she wished she could sparkle – Cynthia could have sold it by the bottle and made a fortune.

She could run rings around Cynthia intellectually. Cynthia's conversation was vapid and idiotic, but it didn't seem to get on anyone's nerves, for the simple reason that she was so decorative and enormous fun. It could take a person hours to process all the components, mostly artificial, that made Cynthia look so good. Only now did it dawn on Sandra that all the intellect and experience in the world was valueless, compared to Cynthia's 'joie de vivre.'

By the time Sandra realised that Alan was being a disloyal husband, rather than Cynthia behaving like a predatory friend, it was too late for the two women - the trust had gone. The damage had been done and Sandra was more upset about that than about her divorce.

There was no question that Cynthia got a thrill from teasing her. It was her fault for getting so worked up over it. It fuelled Cynthia's inner bully and made her worse. Cynthia could never have been friends with a woman as attractive and appealing as herself, other than Miranda – a much younger woman with her whole life in front of her was no threat – even Cynthia could not compete. Sandra valued other attributes over and above just good looks, so it worked well between them.

The problem now was how the hell was she going to function without her poor, dead friend. There had been many a time Sandra could have happily murdered Cynthia. The thought of pushing her in front of a bus or suffocating her by ramming one of her favourite cream cakes down her throat was, sometimes, all consuming, but the details of Cynthia's horrible death would haunt her for the rest of her life. Even in death, Cynthia was poisoning what was left of Sandra's pitiful little life.

"Would you mind explaining this altercation for us, please." Samuel asked, sighing heavily.

Sandra saw herself marching down the corridor towards Cynthia's stateroom and it looked like she was hammering on the door. "You may well sigh, Superintendent, but you haven't just lost a beloved friend."

"Can you remember why you were calling on Mrs. Manning?" Samuel asked, reasonably.

"It wasn't an altercation at all. I think it must have been something to do with our bridge game. We often chatted about conventions and how to learn to use more of them in our game." Sandra lifted her chin up and blatantly lied.

Captain Van Den Burg had the threatening text that Sandra send Cynthia ready and showed it to her.

"This looks pretty sinister. While you were visiting, were you planning to harm your friend, Mrs. Dearlove?"

Sandra looked at the phone message, horror struck. "Absolutely not, Captain. You have to believe me. I've got a big mouth, but I wouldn't murder anyone."

"I wouldn't make a habit of sending threatening messages, if I were you - and isn't this interesting? - After you go into the room, Mr. Wood comes along and listens outside the door. As you can see, something he hears makes him knock. It's quite clear he's very keen to be let in." Samuel knew Sandra wasn't telling the truth and was determined to find out the reason.

"Yes, I think he wanted to discuss the game, too. Cynthia was a terrible cheat."

"You're the first person I've spoken to that said that about her."

"No really, Superintendent, she was. She didn't cheat in the normal way – slipping an ace up her sleeve, or anything. She just wouldn't stop bloody talking – even when you were trying to concentrate. I'm sure it was a ploy to distract you."

"If you don't tell me the real reason why you were in Mrs. Manning's cabin, I won't show you the next clip which happens to be very interesting."

"Okay, Superintendent, but you must be getting so fed up with hearing about Cynthia and me falling out all the time. I'm sure it's filling up your notepad and not leaving much space for the really important stuff."

"I may be young, but please don't underestimate me - I'm not as wet behind the ears as you think. It's necessary for me to take a full statement, leaving no stone unturned. With respect, Mrs. Dearlove - I need to be the person to decide what is trivial or not." Samuel was trying very hard not to get annoyed. "If it was so innocent, why is Mrs. Manning physically throwing you out of her room after such a short visit?"

Sandra was really fed up with being seen as the outcast in the group – the one included, only to make up the numbers. Looking back, she wished she had been able to spend more time with Cynthia, just talking about the weather - or her ever-expanding wardrobe of clothes and yes, even joining in with Cynthia's giggly, smutty view of the world – teenage girl talk that Sandra found mind-numbingly boring, even when she was a teenager.

Her relationship with her friend could have been much better, lasted longer and might even have saved her life. She could have protected Cynthia if they were sharing a stateroom on the ship, like many friends do. Sandra would have gone along with that; had she been asked and it would have reduced the cost of the holiday significantly.

"This is all my fault, Assistant Superintendent. The whole nasty business could have been avoided if I had insisted we shared a stateroom. I noticed several women were sharing rooms on this cruise and, after all, Cynthia and I were best friends - so I went to see her to tell her so. I knocked on her door and barged in. I know that was rude, but I had things on my mind that needed to be said. I told Cynthia that we should have been sharing a room to keep the cost down."

Samuel felt he had finally made a break-through. "What did Mrs. Manning have to say about that?"

Sandra looked down to hide the tears that sprang up. "She laughed in my face. She said I was the last person she would want to share with as I was such a bore – no fun at all and worse – an embarrassment to be seen with."

"That was very hurtful. You were only trying to be helpful."

"...And then that idiot, John, knocked on the door," Sandra blubbed, "and Cynthia told him why I was there. He started laughing, too. They both made me feel very small."

"How did you deal with that, Mrs. Dearlove. Not well, I assume."

"I told Cynthia that she would come to a sticky end with her ridiculous behaviour. I said that she should be biting my hand off to accept that I was in a position to protect her from herself. Who wouldn't want to take an offer like that?"

"Mrs. Manning, it seems." Samuel looked at Sandra - unknowingly shaking his head.

Sandra took the gesture as approval of her plan. "I'm sure that I could have talked Cynthia into seeing the error of her promiscuous ways and agree with me that it would have been the right decision if John hadn't pushed his way in at that moment. He encouraged her to be spiteful, Superintendent. Anyway, he took it upon himself to eject me from the stateroom, muttering something about protecting the feelings of his dear friend. How ridiculous! He would say and do anything to get her into bed."

"Please don't upset yourself, Mrs. Dearlove – it's in the past. Would you mind having a look at the screen and telling me if you recognise this person, please." Samuel swivelled the screen around to face Sandra.

She saw herself standing in a queue to disembark the ship. She recognised Miranda, looking very young and excited, Jacqueline wearing a brightly coloured headscarf, a wisp of Cynthia's blonde hair and a part of those infernal sunglasses could be seen in the corner of the clip. The person behind the group was wearing a baseball cap and was half a head taller than the rest of the crowd. It was difficult to see the face, which was kept low, out of full view.

"I'm sorry, Assistant Superintendent, but that person doesn't look familiar at all. Do you think they could have had something to do with Cynthia's murder?"

"He or she has popped up a few times near or around your group of friends. It's probably a complete coincidence, but on a ship of this size, it seems odd that every time you were all together, there they are, wearing the same cap.

"Oh my goodness. I doubt any of us noticed her. I think she's a woman, Superintendent. I can see why you're having trouble – she's not a particularly attractive one, wearing all that loose-fitting rubbish, but it's definitely a woman."

"Have a look at this and see what you make of it."

Sandra looked up with a start. Samuel had interrupted

her jabbing the lemon in her tea with her teaspoon to get the most she could out of it.

"Would you like another cup of lemon tea? Samuel asked, hoping the answer would be "No."

"Yes, please and some more biscuits would be lovely."

Sandra could not believe her eyes. The same woman she had just seen standing behind her in the queue was knocking on Cynthia's stateroom door. It had to be someone Cynthia knew and, worse still, the two must be celebrating something special – the woman was holding a bottle of champagne and a couple of glasses.

Samuel fast forwarded the film and waited for a reaction.

Sandra could feel the anger well up inside her as she saw Cynthia and this odd person, arms entwined, walking along the corridor into the laundry room.

"Who is this stranger, Superintendent - we must find her." Sandra was livid. "Cynthia never once mentioned this person to me or anyone else." If she had a dark little secret, it wouldn't be one for very long.

Cynthia was now reversing the wheelchair out of the laundry room with her new friend sitting in it. "What a wonderful, kind hearted person Cynthia is – not! What's going on here? Is that a laundry room or shop mobility, Superintendent?"

"The Captain and I are finding it quite hard to fathom it all out, ourselves." Samuel never tired of watching the clip.

Sandra started to roar with laughter. Captain Van Den Burgh found the sound sinister. Women like Sandra only laugh spontaneously when it's at someone else's expense.

"It must be a man in the wheelchair - it could be Cynthia's idea of spicing up her sex life." Sandra couldn't take her eyes of the screen. "Maybe she thought wheeling someone around the ship could shake them up into feeling randy, who knows?" She leant over the desk, her face almost touching Samuels, and squinted at the screen. "...But I'm sure it's a woman."

She watched in silence as the final scene played out.

"She's obviously blowing kisses to her visitor if they're responding like that, but, quite rudely I think, Cynthia doesn't see her out – so maybe not such a special friend, Superintendent. What happens next?"

"The person disappears through a doorway."

"...And that's it? They just vanish into thin air?"

"They seem to have done exactly that." Samuel sighed, again.

"Thank you very much for coming in and assisting us, Mrs. Dearlove." Captain Van Den Burgh stood up and held out his hand. "I appreciate it's been an emotional rollercoaster watching the tape."

Captain Van Den Burgh felt drained. In fairness, he felt like that after every interview, but Mrs. Dearlove was particularly hard work. The note taking wasn't the problem. It was the treading on eggshells in order to extract the necessary information that was so tiring.

He was continually impressed with the way Samuel handled every interview. He, better than anyone the Captain had ever known, instinctively understood the fragile psyche of most of the guests and staff, questioning them accordingly. It was a masterpiece in progress.

"Are we ready to cross Mrs. Dearlove off our list?"

"Yes, we should. She's an extremely volatile woman, but is she capable of murder? I really don't think so. I don't believe Mrs. Dearlove has the cool headedness to carry off murdering Mrs. Manning."

Captain Van Den Burg disagreed. "I would say Mrs. Dearlove is exactly the type of loose cannon capable of committing a heinous crime."

Sandra ran back to her stateroom. She stood with her back to the door, debating whether to throw herself on the bed and weep, or sit on her balcony and slowly burn at Cynthia's betrayal as a friend. Ignoring the feeling of unnecessary extravagance, she helped herself to a large gin and tonic from the fridge – not included in the pre-paid drink's package and decided to do the latter.

———

"One–two–Chachacha, three-four-chachacha..."

Vladimir Sokolov was busy supplementing his income by giving private ballroom and Latin dance lessons. It was quite early in the morning and the ship was quiet. Most of the guests were otherwise engaged, deciding whether to have a simple breakfast in their stateroom or help themselves to the huge buffet on the eleventh floor.

Vladimir and Irina, the husband-and-wife team employed to head the entertainment's programme, had a wealth of experience between them. Irina had danced with the Bolshoi Ballet Academy - the world-famous school of ballet in Moscow, since she was very young. She would have been promoted to prima ballerina had it not been for an accident - putting an end to her dancing career and, very nearly, her life.

Vladimir had been choreographing the shows on board ship for about ten years. They were responsible for everything visible - the design of the wonderful outfits and the complex dance routines which took a year from start to finish to complete.

Miranda was sitting in the front row, changing into her silver ballroom dancing shoes, still nestling in their suede bag, hardly used. She had wisely kept them for an opportunity such as this. She hoped that the dance lessons, so long ago, would put her in the intermediate category rather than a beginner.

She had been most impressed by the romantic scene of Vladimir instructing some of the guests on the intricacies of the Viennese waltz and the rumba. In some cases, it looked like he was dancing with sacks of potatoes, but Miranda was hopeful that nobody would think that of her.

Miranda saw Jacqueline and Roger across the dance floor, watching the last lesson ending. She waved for them to join her in the front row of plush velvet seats.

"Are you going to have a go?" Jacqueline smiled. "I can see you being gracefully led around the floor by handsome Vladimir."

"I'll give you a spin around, Miranda, and I'll only charge you half the price. How much *is* he charging for a private lesson?" Roger asked.

"She wants to learn the chachacha, not the Highland fling – heavy on the fling." Both Jacqueline and Roger fell about laughing at the joke.

Miranda hoped Vladimir didn't think they were laughing at him. "An absolute fortune, but I have to give it a go. It's an opportunity too good to miss. He makes it look so easy."

"If Henry isn't learning with you, isn't all this a waste of time and money?" Roger asked.

"Henry isn't interested in ballroom dancing. He may agree to learn a wedding dance if and when the time comes, but I very much doubt he'll be willing to rumba the night away." Miranda looked sheepish.

"Oh that would be marvellous. You've missed him, haven't you?" Jacqueline often noticed Miranda, sitting quietly, preoccupied with her own thoughts, and assumed they were of Henry. "Please let us know when you get engaged, so we that we can mark the occasion – invite you and Henry for dinner with our daughter and son-in-law. They're quite recently married, too. You've been so lovely to me and Roger – thank you, Miranda."

"Of course I will. I hope I have the opportunity. He's been hinting about taking our relationship to the next level for some time and I've just sidestepped the subject – frightened of commitment, I suppose, but I'm ready now. If Henry thinks I'm not interested, he may well have given up on the idea."

"There's only one thing for it", Roger said with a perfectly straight face – "you will have to propose to the divine Henry. There's no shame in it. Jacqueline begged me to marry her."

"Somehow, Henry, I find that hard to believe." Miranda laughed.

"Thank goodness you know me better than that. Of course I didn't. My recollection of the event is that Roger proposed to me and he was oh *so* lucky that I accepted."

Sandra had been searching all over the ship for the three of them and, before sitting down next to Miranda, made a big show of pointing at the dance floor.

"If he can teach lumbering Lola how to dance, he can teach anyone."

Roger leant forward, smiling at Sandra. "Make an old man happy - let's see you quickstep out of here." Very occasionally, even he felt guilty telling her off, but someone had to keep her in check. She had no filter.

Sandra watched for a while. She was very tempted to ask whether any of them had been asked down for a further chat with the captain and the Assistant Superintendent. There was no way she was going to tell the group about her meeting. Roger and John's teasing would be unbearable – it took her days to recover from the last bout of it. No! She would keep it to herself.

How could she ask them whether they were suspicious of Cynthia's visitor to her stateroom late at night? The woman was entitled to receive guests – it would sound ridiculous. Now was definitely not the time.

Her attention focused again on the dancers. "I have to admit it can look very elegant with the right person. I might give it a try."

"Goodness me, Sandra. Did I hear correctly? Are you going to have a few dance lessons. This I must see." Jacqueline said.

"You go, girl." Roger nearly fell off his chair. "Will you need a muzzle or will he?"

"Rude!" Sandra couldn't care less what he thought.

"I would love you to learn with me, Sandra. We could practice the steps together." Miranda was very happy. It was her efforts alone that had finally found a way to thaw the most miserable woman in the group. "If I had known you fancied it, I would have booked us both a lesson. Let's do it."

Sandra held her hand up. "Hold your horses. Let's see how good this fella is, first."

Vladimir was in the process of trying to teach his second pupil a heel turn, when he saw them watching him. He didn't miss a step but gave an imperceptible nod at Miranda. She was next.

The dance floor had a lovely sheen and Miranda felt the soft suede soles of her shoes glide in time with the Latin rhythm. She already knew to lift her chin and keep her arms at shoulder level.

"I'm sure your bottom shouldn't be sticking out like that." Sandra shouted at Miranda and turned to Jacqueline – "Her posture should be much better."

"Shut up, Sandra. You'll make her feel self-conscious." Jacqueline couldn't wait for the moment when she could turn her back on Sandra, forever. Enough was enough.

Vladimir whispered something into Miranda's ear. He strolled unhurriedly over to Sandra and held out his hand, a gesture that demanded she take it and allow him to escort her onto the dance floor.

"Madame, Let's try this routine together and see what you think", he said, smiling.

Sandra took his hand and followed him onto the floor. Drawing herself up to her full height and pulling in her stomach, she positively 'glided' around the dance floor. It was impossible not to follow Vladimir's lead.

It was obvious to the onlookers that the only thing keeping Sandra upright was Vladimir's firm grip.

"Very good for a beginner – It takes time and practice to perfect any dance." Vladimir had made his point.

———

"Good morning, Mrs. Sylvester. Please sit down. May I offer you anything?" Captain Van Den Burg motioned for Jacqueline to sit in the tub chair.

"I think I'll try a hot chocolate, heavy on the marshmallows please. Before we start, Captain, I would like to say a big thank you, both from myself and my husband, for how well you and the Assistant Superintendent have handled everything to do with the investigation into poor Cynthia's death." Jacqueline hoped she was showing some appreciation. "We have all felt the strain of it."

Samuel was delighted to hear some praise – he could have easily burst into tears, had the captain not been standing right behind him. It had not been easy for him on board *Holland Silhouette*, as not everyone was friendly. Some of the staff were positively hostile - refusing to spend any downtime in his company or include him in their social group. He was neither fish nor fowl. If the captain hadn't spent so much time ensuring he was comfortable, Samuel would have found himself completely alone.

He had experienced coolness and standoffishness before – it was part of the course in police work, but he didn't expect hostility. Even though *Holland Silhouette* was the biggest ship he had ever seen, it was still a confined space, with few places to hide should anyone be planning an unlawful act. He really should not have been surprised that the presence of a policeman, especially a murder investigator, would be unnerving.

The captain looked at Samuel and smiled warmly. "Thank you very much, Mrs. Sylvester. That's very nice of you. The Assistant Superintendent and I have tried hard to put everyone at ease, while at the same time attempting to get to the bottom of this unfortunate affair."

Samuel nodded in agreement. "Would you mind looking at the screen, Mrs. Sylvester, and tell me if you recognise this person, please."

Jacqueline scooped up the marshmallows that were floating on top of her delicious hot chocolate with her teaspoon and sipped it. She leant forward and looked at the screen. There was her little group, bundled together in a queue, walking slowly towards the exit and on to terra firma.

She noticed Miranda, busy trying to keep everyone upbeat and positive. Sandra was looking around - ready to pounce on anyone that might jostle her, even by accident. She spotted a bit of Cynthia, wearing her usual dark sunglasses - even though they were all in a tunnel and, finally, she recognised herself as the frump - wearing a brightly coloured headscarf.

She almost gave up looking, until she spotted the

person Samuel wanted her to see. A tall woman wearing a sports cap - keeping her features out of the way of the camera. The person did look very strange..

Samuel watched her processing each person, individually. "What are you seeing, Mrs. Sylvester? Is anything out of place?"

"That woman standing behind us all. There's something about her. I don't think I know her, but she's going to an awful lot of trouble to intentionally look odd. Why would someone do that?"

"This person — we think it's a woman. At first we thought it could have been a man in disguise, but we are now working on the basis that 'he' is a 'she'." Samuel watched Jacqueline's reaction. "We think that this could be a someone of interest in our investigation."

"Yes, I think she must be. With all that ill-fitting gear she's wearing, she could be anything." Jacqueline smiled, but it didn't reach her eyes. Samuel felt a little niggle in his stomach and knew he was going to need to find out why.

Jacqueline's eyes kept darting back to the woman. "Do you mean it could be the murderer, Superintendent? She looks like a youngish woman to me, despite all the frippery. I just assumed — I think we all did, that it would be one of Cynthia's discarded lovers — or one of their wives responsible for her demise." Jacqueline would have put money on it.

"Let's move on to another frame. What do you make of this?"

The camera switched to the corridor outside Cynthia's stateroom. Jacqueline could see a figure walking along, looming larger as she approached the screen. The woman was casually holding a bottle of champagne by the neck in one hand, and two glasses in the other. The stateroom door opened and she walked straight in.

Jacqueline couldn't take her eyes of the screen. Her flippant remarks had dried up and, unknowingly, her breathing had quickened.

Samuel fast-forwarded the clip and waited.

Jacqueline watched as the two woman made their way to the laundry room and Cynthia begin wheeling the visitor around the ship. It was the walk that was sending alarm bells ringing in her head. She recognised that walk, but it couldn't be. It looked like Cynthia was pushing the wheelchair around, but she wasn't walking like Cynthia.

When the clip came to an end and the visitor was busy blowing kisses to Cynthia, before letting the stateroom door slam shut behind her, Jacqueline leant back in the tub chair. "That was very strange, Superintendent – it's almost as if I were looking at two strangers, not just one."

"What makes you say that?"

"I'm supposed to recognise one of those two ladies, am I not? – but I have to say that they both look weird." Jacqueline felt very confused and rather upset. "Cynthia isn't looking or behaving like herself on camera. I think I've just been too exposed to all of this and am now starting to imagine things."

"What does it look like to you? It doesn't matter how ridiculous it sounds; I still would be interested to hear it." Samuel said.

Jacqueline shook her head, as if shaking off her thoughts. "It just looks like two silly women messing about late at night on deck, Superintendent, and all my musing and pondering on the matter won't change that. This chocolate is delicious. I'm not leaving until I've drained every drop of it."

After a few minutes, Samuel got up from his chair and walked around the desk - that little niggle in his stomach was still there. "Thank you for coming in, Mrs. Sylvester", he said, shaking her hand. "It's a very odd case, but ultimately it will be for the UK police in Southampton to finally wrap it up."

Samuel just slipped that little piece of information into the conversation just in case she thought once everyone was off the ship, that would be the end of the investigation.

Captain Van Den Burg had been holding his breath for ages. The atmosphere in the office changed as soon as Mrs. Sylvester watched the CCTV footage on the screen and Samuel had picked up on it immediately.

"Are we crossing Mrs. Sylvester off our list – I get the feeling there is some unfinished business there."

"You're absolutely right, Captain – that's exactly how I'm feeling. I can't explain what it is, but something upset her during the interview. I think I will leave her on my list, for the time being.

___

"Has he arrived?" Sandra asked. "What sort of celebrity chef can he be if he's on board and nobody knows about it?"

"There were only eight places in his 'masterclass'. I applied before the sailing, so I suppose they don't want to broadcast his arrival in case people are disappointed." Miranda replied.

"Who would be upset? It's a cookery class." Sandra just didn't understand.

"I assume there must be a lot of disappointed people – men and women, who would have liked a private cooking demonstration with the great Franco Fratelli." Jacqueline explained.

"Can you remind me, how are we so privileged to get a ticket?" Sandra asked Miranda.

"I managed to get two, one for me and one for Cynthia. We had to pay in advance before we boarded the ship. It's quite expensive – I hope it's worth it." Miranda wouldn't have put it passed Cynthia to try to seduce the handsome chef. What a feather in her cap that would have been.

"Roger found out about it and thought I would like it", Jacqueline said. "If it cheers us all up, it will be worth every penny."

"So I've inherited my ticket from Cynthia?" Sandra asked.

"I thought you would enjoy it. I couldn't let the ticket go to waste. I'm sure Cynthia would have wanted you to have some fun with it." Miranda wasn't sure at all.

Oh, great! *Now* Cynthia wants me to have some fun. What happened to having fun together? "You're not expecting me to pay for it, are you?"

Jacqueline sighed and gave Sandra a steely stare over her spectacles.

Sandra shrugged. "Just checking."

Sandra, Jacqueline and Miranda were the last to be seated at the bar. They were interested in the display of several books written by the famous chef. The inflated price included a personal message on the fly leaf. After a quick glance, they all decided it would be easier to continue using the tried and tested family recipes.

"I think a book should be included in the price. It would have been a nice gesture." Sandra didn't need another book to gather dust on the shelf. "It's not as if buying the book will bring happy memories of the cruise."

"I'm sure it will for others in the class. Life must go on. We can't allow ourselves to get bitter about things, can we?" Jacqueline looked around, not catching Sandra's eye.

"...Fry the onions until they're transparent – make sure they don't stick to the pan", Chef Fratelli was dancing around a beautiful, copper-bottom frying pan – "...and then add the kidneys."

"As if, after thirty years, I didn't know how to fry kidney and onions? And you paid good money for this?" Sandra watched everyone making notes in their newly acquired *Holland Silhouette* notepads.

"In every chef's kitchen there must be preparation. It's the finishing touch that makes the difference." Jacqueline assumed this was the message the Chef was promoting, but she was also hoping that things in the kitchen would get a bit more exciting.

The gathering of six women and two men were huddled together, watching Chef Fratelli. He was more used to working in a fully functional, fabulously well-equipped modern kitchen than fumbling around trying to get to grips with the space allocated to him for the day.

There were several tiny kitchens on the ship, just big enough to knock up a small snack for the guests who felt a bit peckish after walking up a flight of stairs to the next level.

Franco struggled to turn down the heat on the portable cooker – throwing around a few more bowls and spoons as he did so.

"As you can see, I am rolling the shortcrust pastry out very thinly. I cannot abide thick pastry. I will line this loose bottom tart tin and blind bake."

"As soon as this 'demonstration' is over, I'm going to get our money back. What a bloody liberty!" Sandra was making a scene and people were staring at her.

"Is there a problem, madam?" Franco had tried to ignore the woman, but realised it was probably quicker to just confront her.

"Tell me something, Mr. Fratelli. When you were invited onto the ship to give a cookery demonstration to these lovely people, did it not occur to you to look in a grown-up recipe book? - To choose something maybe with the wow factor. A dish we could be proud to serve as the centre piece of our dinner table?"

Miranda was very pleased that she had been placed at the other end of the bar next to a very nice man, most excited at the prospect of making Chef Fratelli's kidney pie. On this occasion, however, she had to agree with Sandra that the dish wasn't really doing it for her, either.

Franco stared coldly at the upstart and probably would have enjoyed humiliating her, but he wisely decided against it.

"I agree with you, madam. Kidney is not to everyone's taste and, of course, one has to take into consideration allergies and vegetarian options. As the head chef of this beautiful vessel will tell you, he has at his disposal a plethora of ingredients in readiness to please his guests, should kidney be unsuitable."

He played to the room, gratified to hear many murmurs of approval. "I am, however, rather more limited with my ingredients and time, but I would say that this dish is very popular in my restaurant. Why would I not wish to recreate it?"

Sandra was about to argue, but Chef Fratelli interrupted her. "While we are waiting for the pastry to cook, would anyone else like to ask any questions? Anything at all?" Franco asked, anxiously.

"Chef Fratelli – I would like to ask you a question, please." Miranda was desperate to get the vibe back on track.

"Please do. Ask my anything. Now's your chance."

"When you visit your friends for dinner, what dishes to

they prepare for you? How do they deal with entertaining a celebrity chef?"

Everyone in the room applauded – all were agog to hear the answer to the question.

"They always try and make my favourite food – a beautifully prepared omelette with freshly picked chives or cheese on toast. I know it must sound strange to you all, but the simpler the better for me." Chef Fratelli was satisfied that the calm atmosphere in the room had been restored.

———

Once again, a note was sticking out of the pigeon hole outside Roger's stateroom when he returned from breakfast and he quickly put it in his pocket. He thought it best not to mention his second visit to the captain's office to Jacqueline – there would be too many questions that he really wasn't in the mood to answer.

At the start of his last interview with the Assistant Superintendent, he was confident that he came across as just another guy enjoying a holiday with his wife, on board a luxury cruise liner - it couldn't be simpler. By the time the meeting ended, he started to feel that he was under suspicion for Cynthia's murder.

Obviously, that would be ridiculous. He may be a lot of things – a chancer, a womaniser, very slightly light fingered in his business account, but not a murderer. He supposed this was a tactic, used as part of the interview technique.

He had messaged Abby and kept her up to date with what was going on in the investigation. She was as surprised as him with the news.

"I can't understand why anyone would want to kill Cynthia. She was such a very friendly person, Dad. What will you do now?"

"I'm not sure I feel like finding another bridge partner, just yet. I'm playing the game with your mother on the ship and that's working out very well."

"I'm very pleased to hear that. She comes in handy now and again." Abby laughed, warmly. "I'd stick with her, if I were you."

Now that he had been summoned for another meeting, the nerves kicked in again. He hoped he wasn't going to be sick and arouse Jacqueline's suspicion.

He settled Jacqueline by the swimming pool on the recreation deck, popping a couple of her paperbacks on the little drinks table at her side and casually walked towards the lift.

As he descended in the glass elevator, he watched other guests mingling around the ship, darting in out of coffee and cocktail lounges without a care in the world, and he longed for the same feeling. He comforted himself with the thought that they, too, may be harbouring dark secrets they would go to any lengths to hide.

Once again, he navigated his way along the winding corridors until he reached the Captain's door. On this occasion, he knocked cautiously.

"Hello, Mr. Sylvester. Do come in and take a seat. May I offer you a drink?" Captain Van Den Burg greeted him warmly.

"I could murder one of your cocktails of the day." Roger laughed, again at the tired joke.

"Thank you for coming in to see us. Could you have a look at some footage on the screen for us, please."

Roger put on his spectacles to see the screen. "What should I be looking at?"

"Do you recognise this woman?" Samuel pointed to the woman with the baseball cap.

The cocktail arrived and Roger was satisfied to see it

was heavy on the fruit and maraschino cherries. "I can see lovely Miranda. My god, she's got her work cut out cheering up Sandra. Her boyfriend should have come with her on the cruise. She would have had a much better time. Oh, look! - there's my wife, wearing a fetching headscarf."

"...But do you recognise the woman standing very close behind the group?"

"She's an odd-looking woman. She should be arrested by ship security for bad dress sense. It's difficult to see her face as she's hiding it under that awful cap."

"Let me fast forward to another clip and see if it helps." Samuel turned the screen around further.

Roger saw the same woman confidently walking down the corridor towards Cynthia's stateroom. He watched as she almost pushed her way into the cabin.

"Who is she, Superintendent?"

"I was hoping someone in your group would recognise her", Samuel appeared to be looking at the screen. "Just a moment, there's a bit more footage."

Roger watched as the two women went into the laundry room, followed by the wheelchair adventure around the ship and back.

"Can you play that last clip for me again, please", Roger asked Samuel.

Samuel rewound the tape to the point where the woman approaches Cynthia's stateroom, holding the champagne bottle and glasses. It was not a coincidence that he chose that part of the tape to stop.

"There are two things wrong with this," Roger couldn't take his eyes off the screen. "The first is, why is Cynthia being so helpful to a complete stranger or for that matter, a friend? This person is not with our bridge group – all women in the group have been closely scrutinised by me.

I would know if she was."

"And the second thing…"

"There's something about that woman. It's nothing physical – I'm trying to work out what it can be?" Roger was thinking aloud. "It's her walk - she has a particular stride that seems familiar, but the most out of character part of this is the whole late-night shenanigans. It's not like Cynthia at all. Unless there were bedroom antics on offer, she would be fast asleep at that time of night."

"Would you say that it is possible Mrs Manning was forced out of the stateroom against her will?"

Roger drained his cocktail, inspecting it to see if he could suck another drop through the straw before putting it down. "It doesn't look like it from the tape, Assistant Superintendent, but I do know that one would need to prize Cynthia out of her cabin with a shoe horn to get her into a laundry room anywhere, even at home and to march around the ship playing carer would certainly not be her scene either."

"Thank you very much, Mr. Sylvester. Once again, you've been a great help."

Captain Van Den Burg was relieved that they were coming to the end of the interviews and would soon be docking at Southampton.

"I take it both Mr and Mrs Sylvester will remain on the list".

Samuel was furiously writing up his notes. "There is no doubt in my mind." he said, emphatically.

CHAPTER TEN

He was just getting to the part of the dream where they announced the amount of his multi-million-pounds lottery win when the shrill sound of the alarm awoke him with a start.

Detective Inspector Edward Springer of Hampshire and Isle of Wight Police Constabulary had a busy day ahead, gathering his team to meet *Holland Silhouette* at Southampton Dock. He quickly reached out and pressed the 'off' button so as not to wake the whole house.

Just having returned from a couple of weeks on annual leave, he was struggling to get his mind focused on another murder case. The family had taken a much-needed break away in the sun, but more importantly, his marriage had needed some loving care and attention, too.

In the twenty-five years on the job, he still gave it hundred and ten percent and at some point, something had to give. During that time, he watched, in horror, as the marriages of so many of his colleagues fell apart. It didn't surprise him to know that the reason was not attributed to the absence of love or commitment. It was more likely the fact that there were only so many pieces of a person to hand around before they cracked.

As a boy, his parents made the mistake of buying him a policeman dressing up outfit and he arrested and cuffed most of his relatives and friends far beyond the time when he should have grown out of it.

He was a copper through and through and the people upstairs recognised that about him. Most of the big, juicy murder cases landed on his desk and they trusted him and his team to sniff out the murderers, fraudsters and law breakers, bringing them to trial with all the loopholes plugged.

Edward Springer was a lucky man and didn't he know it. His wife was a wonderful mother, a home-maker and great in bed, even after fifteen years and three children. She never complained about having to put her life on hold so he could work his way up the promotion ladder.

He could see that even a patient woman such as she was getting to the end of her tether and it was time to start thinking more about his personal life and less about the department.

There had been an episode where he nearly got sucked into an extra-marital affair - too close for comfort as far as he was concerned, but he pulled himself back from the brink just in time. It would have undoubtedly meant the end of his marriage and everything that meant the world to him. As he made passionate love to his wife, he could tell in her eyes that she knew how close they both had come to ruin and he held her even tighter.

This was the second murder on a cruise ship that he had investigated. The first time, he and his team had been asked to travel to Norway to board a large vessel with registered offices in the UK.

The DI heading that case had phoned around to gather his preferred team of detectives, knowing full well their passports were current and ready to go. It was an exciting time for him. A police force in a foreign country has no jurisdiction and just getting a simple witness statement involves obtaining a Letter of Request, granted by that country, which has to go through Interpol who are then required to grant permission. It was certainly a change from the usual run of the mill stuff chucked onto his desk.

On that occasion, a staff member had brutally assaulted a colleague, working in a similar capacity, but earning a fraction more money and showing off about it. The injured party had been flown off the ship by helicopter to hospital, but on arrival was pronounced dead. An assault had turned into a murder. Edward hoped that this investigation, on his home ground, would be a bit more straight forward.

Currently, he was taking one Detective Sergeant, two Detective Constables, a photographer and a Crime Scene Investigator. He would also need a pathologist from the Coroner's Office to determine the cause of death.

From extensive telephone conversations with Assistant Superintendent Samuel James, he was required to take over the ongoing investigation of the murder of a woman on board a ship that would be arriving in port early that morning. Why it had been necessary to call a policeman from an outpost in the Bahamas he would never know, despite the ship's registration documents. The whole episode was bound to be a complete cockup.

Edward realised that the 'golden hour enquires' would have been lost. This related to the first twenty-four to forty-eight hours being the most critical in identifying the victim, suspect and witnesses, thereby maximising the chance of securing evidence that will be admissible in court. Furthermore, the crime scene would have likely been contaminated by the removal of the body to the ship's morgue.

Fortunately, the rest of the murder scene had been protected and preserved. There were no witnesses to the murder, but a list had been compiled of close associates and possible suspects detained. He was left with the small job of dealing with forensics, arranging for the photographing of the murder scene and the victim's stateroom, deploying a Family Liaison Officer as a conduit between the enquiry team and the family of the victim and checking and re-checking the statements taken by Samuel James of the Arawak Cay police force. God help him.

———

"Am I to understand that you suspect the murderer is no longer on board?" Edward had a cup of cold coffee sitting in front of him that he hadn't had a chance to drink.

"My instincts tell me that the perpetrator has already left the ship."

Samuel James poured over his vast file of notes, relieved to be handing everything over to this competent and experienced Detective Inspector. He could see, immediately, that the man was itching to get his hands on everything and take over the investigation and Samuel was only too happy to oblige.

"I have interviewed all the relevant people, Detective Inspector. None have disembarked the ship, as yet. I'm sure you can appreciate it would be impossible to take witness statements from every passenger and staff member on board.

"We did a risk assessment and decided that the rest of the passengers were in no danger. The captain and I will be submitting our reports to you, together with the evidence that was handed in from Livorno, our last stop. We have also examined the CCTV a number of times."

"And yet you sailed with nobody missing on board?" Edward asked.

"That is correct, Sir."

"How can that be?"

"Both the captain and I are baffled."

Edward nodded. His team would certainly have their work cut out trying to make sense of this lot.

"Thank you for your help, Samuel. I can see you've

done a sterling job. It's not easy being dumped on board a floating city to crack a murder investigation. I hope you don't think it sounds patronising if I say that I'm sure you're relieved to hand the whole thing over to us. We'll take it from here."

Samuel wasn't offended in the least. He had done the job to the best of his ability and was more than satisfied that this new team of investigators were completely up to speed. It was time to pass it over. He would certainly miss Captain Van den Burg. A more upright and caring person committed to his job as a Sea Captain would be hard to find. He would even miss the characters he interviewed - such an eccentric and colourful group of people. A case such as this one would probably never come his way again.

"If you need anything at all from me, Detective Inspector, I'm always at the end of the phone day or night."

Captain Van den Burg felt a sense of relief, too. He would be setting sail later with a ship full of new passengers and some new crew, adhering to his schedule, but with a few extra people on board. He had a backlog of paperwork urgently requiring his attention and needed to get back to the job of running a cruise ship.

Early that morning, on the bridge as dawn was breaking, Captain Van den Burg stood straight, hands behind his back and watched as the ship approached Southampton. A modest man, he was not interested in standing out in a crowd or courting a lot of attention. He would rather just know that his superiors thought he was proficient at his job – a good and safe captain.

This particular morning, he couldn't help feeling a huge sense of achievement that he had 'navigated his ship through 'choppy waters' in more ways than one. He felt satisfied that the unfortunate murder of poor Mrs. Manning had been thoroughly investigated from his end and that he, Assistant Superintendent Samuel James and all his staff had behaved impeccably. All courtesy was shown to the guests who had a personal connection to the victim and to the vast number of over-anxious passengers needing reassurance that a mad axe murderer wasn't running amok.

As the ship drew nearer, he noticed a crowd had gathered on the dock. Not the usual ship's fan base, the interested cruise-loving public who enjoyed viewing the ship as it unloaded its happy and relaxed passengers, but a hoard of plain clothed and uniformed police, standing by their vehicles waiting to board.

———

"So, what have we got, so far?" Edward was pacing around the makeshift incident room, given to them by Captain Van den Burg for the purposes of the investigation.

The team had been working full on for twelve hours and it was starting to show. The room was relatively comfortable, with a long table at one end covered in a crisp white tablecloth, laden with constantly replenished refreshments. It was so nice to occasionally be appreciated.

"We have followed on from the interview statements in the file, Sir. They have all filled in an MG11 and they match the statements previously given. We have the elimination fingerprint forms ready and have had no resistance to us taking finger prints and DNA mouth swabs. They have been all given voluntarily. We have also taken Polaroid pictures of all the interviewees, again given voluntarily. Finally, we have put exhibit labels on the items ready for forensic testing."

"Thank you DS Long. Have we had the pathology report yet?"

"It took a while to come through, as usual, Sir, but it's just come in." The pathologist would like to see you.

Edward looked to see who was on duty and nodded to himself, satisfied.

"The victim had Diazepam in her system. She was bludgeoned over the head, at least twice and strangled. The first blow was more forceful than the second. She wouldn't have seen it coming so no defence wounds. Interestingly, she also had a tumour on the brain which, in a very short time, would probably have killed her anyway."

Edward liked Johnny Martin. He was a forensic pathologist with a sense of humour and they were thin on the ground.

"I hope you're not saying that the murderer did her a favour?" Edward said with wry expression on his face.

"Well they did really. She would have been not that far off from having a hellish time and a painful death. Seriously though, it might have been responsible for a change in her behaviour that could have triggered her murder. Any pressure on the frontal lobe could be responsible for anti-social or excessive behaviour which could present as normal."

"How very unpleasant. Does it sound like a cold, uncalculated murder?" Edward was hoping it wasn't. It made it easier for him to crack a murder that was personal, rather than random. His mind took a different turn. "Mind you, the Diazepam may have nothing to do with the murder. Could she have been prescribed it for anxiety?" Edward was thinking aloud.

"It's more likely the drug was used to subdue her. I think the murderer got cold feet when they saw the amount of blood and changed tack. There's a lot of nylon fibres in the hair and wound, so the head must have been covered up before she was moved. If I find anything else for you, I'll let you know."

Edward stared at Cynthia lying on the table and felt sad, as he always did, when he was looking at premature death. She was a woman in the prime of life and took good care of herself - obviously comfortable enough to be able to afford to go on a luxury cruise. It seemed she had everything to live for.

"Yes, I know what you're thinking", Doctor Martin saw the expression on Edward's face. "I feel like that every time. Most people would think she had the perfect life."

―――

"Have we checked the CCTV yet?" Edward was in a hurry.

"You have to come and look at it, Sir. It's very weird." DI Long was staring at the computer screen.

Edward stared in disbelief at the footage. "Good God! We need to show this to the Crime Scene Investigator. Mrs. Manning had some interesting callers and she, together with her probable murderer, seem to have had a lovely time going all over the ship. Let's hope they touched everything."

―――

"...I've got good news – well, I hope you think it's good news. I will be meeting the ship in Livorno. It's a pretty civilised place and easy to get to. I'll book a flight to Pisa and get a taxi from there to the ship. Get your knickers off, Cynthia – I'm on my way – make sure you delete this message."

"Fortunately for us, she didn't delete the message." DI Edward Springer and Roger Sylvester were both staring at the message on the mobile phone, neither one was smiling.

"I can explain, Detective Inspector..."

"I think you had better, Mr. Sylvester."

"Please don't tell my wife. My relationship with Cynthia was just a bit of fun. It was never meant to be anything serious and she knew that. Two consenting adults having a good time – trying to stave off the advancing years by pretending to be giddy young things." Roger laughed nervously and wiped some perspiration off his forehead.

"Mrs. Manning was entitled to behave anyway she wished. She could afford to be silly and frivolous because she had nothing to lose. You, however, have a lot to lose."

"I do indeed, Detective Inspector and I am fully aware of it. That's why I made it clear that I was never going to leave my wife, in fact, Cynthia didn't want me to."

"Did you arrange to go on the cruise together?"

"As part of a group of bridge players, yes and with my wife."

"I think Cynthia had you over a barrel and you were desperate. Did she blackmail you? Threaten to tell your wife?" Edward threw it into the mix to gauge Roger's reaction.

"Absolutely not. She was a simple woman – a lovely lady. Not a scheming harlot – well, not with me, anyway. She was happy with a bit of attention and a few presents."

"But you were not on board at the start of the cruise."

"No. Unfortunately, there was some mishandling of funds going from one account to another and I had to deal with it personally."

"I could be barking up the wrong tree, Mr. Sylvester, but I always follow the money – exactly where did it came from and where was it going." Edward found that tracing the cash inevitably exposed something interesting.

"Did you arrange for Cynthia's murder? Is that where the money was going, Mr. Sylvester? Was it on its way to someone's account in payment for getting rid of a problem? After all, you had an alibi by not being on the ship."

"You couldn't be more wrong, Detective Inspector. I was using the company's money to buy a little flat."

"A little love nest, do you mean?" Edward raised his eyebrows. He hadn't expected that.

"Possibly, or just a sound investment. Either way, it's not illegal, is it?"

"One final point, Mr. Sylvester. We believe your wife may have recognised the woman on the CCTV, knocking on Mrs. Manning's stateroom door, late at night on the evening of her murder."

"Jacqueline certainly didn't mention anything to me. We're both completely flummoxed as to who it could have been and their connection with Cynthia."

———

Miranda stood on her balcony for the last time and watched the ship approach Southampton. Dawn was just breaking and she was about to call Henry. This was the call she had been itching to make.

A note had been left in her cubby hole to inform her that she would be required to see the Hampshire Police before disembarking, just to go over a few points on her statement. She wasn't sure what more she could do to help, but she would make her way down to the theatre after breakfast. Her luggage had been collected and would be waiting for her in the luggage hall near the port exit.

"I've come home to you, Henry," she said, excitedly.

"Have you docked? Oh, that's marvellous. I know you

said you will have to be processed one more time by the police so I'll leave now. I should be there in a couple of hours. That should be enough time for them to do whatever they need." Henry sounded like he was jumping out of bed and she could hear him switch on the shower.

"Henry? Don't let's bother to book a cruise for our honeymoon."

"Oh damn it, I wonder if I can get my money back." Henry was laughing.

———

Miranda had arranged to meet Sandra and John in the breakfast room. Jacqueline and Roger said they were leaving early and wouldn't be joining them.

"As if we haven't had enough to contend with." Sandra shrilled as soon as Miranda sat down at the table.

"This is it now, guys. We're home at last." Miranda tried to hide her excitement, although she still felt miserable about Cynthia, but life must go on.

"I managed to put a call through to Cynthia's family. It's all terribly sad. They're boarding the ship this morning. Apparently the police have an officer who will help them get through this nightmare." Sandra looked terrible. The events of the past week were catching up with her.

"You know you can call me any time to chat, Sandra, don't you? You both can. I'm so sorry for all of this."

"Oh for goodness's sake, it's not *your* fault, Miranda. No, I won't need mollycoddling, but thanks for caring anyway."

"I think I will." John stared sorrowfully at his poached eggs, "as the offer extends to me, too. I still can't believe it. One minute, she's there looking gorgeous and bringing colour into my life and the next – gone forever."

Sandra looked at him disagreeably. "Poor you. You'll have to rely on your wife for your entertainment from now on, won't you. I've no doubt she'll be as disappointed as you. Cynthia's family have to live with what's happened, *that's* the travesty. I don't think they'll ever recover from the shock of how she died and nor will I."

"After breakfast, shall we all go down together for the final interview to give each other moral support?" Miranda asked, pleasantly. She wasn't going to let the conversation descend to its usual depressing level.

Miranda very much regretted suggesting such a thing. As they walked into the theatre, Sandra rushed up to DS Long, forcing him to take a step back and verbally assaulted him.

"Detective, are you any closer to solving my friend's vicious murder?"

"I'm sorry, Madam, who are you?" DS Long was an experienced officer, accustomed to dealing with every kind of person that walked on earth.

"I'm Sandra Dearlove, best friend of Mrs. Manning, you know who I mean - the poor victim?" She said, sarcastically. "You will, no doubt, have read my fulsome statement." She looked around the room sheepishly, hoping nobody heard and therefore arrive at the right conclusion that she had pointed the finger at almost everyone.

He ushered her along. "Would you mind following my colleague who will be taking a photograph, a swab and some prints, if you don't mind." He immediately turned away to deal with others before she could respond.

Miranda had requested that she wished to be processed as quickly as possible. She had kept Henry waiting long enough. Now, all that was left to do was to get on with their lovely lives, together.

She wondered if she would find the time to devote to

any of her cruise buddies in the future, or indeed the game of bridge itself. It was the one thing they had in common and without it, there wouldn't be much else to talk about.

———

Edward Springer was sitting in his chair, swivelling back and forth whilst staring at more CCTV footage on his screen. *Who is that woman?*

He had to look long and hard at the grainy footage of the person knocking, late at night, on Mrs. Manning's stateroom door holding a bottle of champagne, in order to decipher whether it was a male or female, so strangely were they dressed – similar to a comedic drag act. Why bring two glasses and not one? All the staterooms had a well-stocked drinks cabinet with glasses and a constantly replenished ice bucket. Unless, one glass had already been spiked with the Diazepam, but not enough to kill someone. So why not just dispatch Cynthia with the drug?

The person didn't match any of the guest or crew identification photos he and his team had trawled through.

Reviewing the statements given to Samuel James, Edward and his team found some to be quite entertaining and others sinister. Mrs. Manning had left a big impression on a lot of people.

Mrs. Sandra Dearlove's interview, for example, a sometime friend of the victim, could easily be read as a confession had the Assistant Superintendent not established otherwise. It seemed the woman had every reason to bear a grudge.

Mr. John Wood's statement seemed relatively straightforward, except for his jealousy of his rival for Cynthia's affection, Roger Sylvester. Watching him darting in and out of Mrs. Manning's stateroom in a permanent state of arousal was rather comical, but that would not necessarily rule him out.

Who would suspect a sweet girl like Miranda Soames? The only woman on the trip that Mrs. Manning trusted and confided in. Perhaps Cynthia threatened to reveal an indiscretion on board that Miranda didn't want her fiancé to find out about?

Then there was the enigmatic Roger Sylvester, whose statement was a piece of art. Reading between the lines, Edward had his work cut out with this interview. Here was a man who felt he could get away with anything, just by being urbane and charming.

Samuel James had a lot to say about this gentleman, however, having already had a run-in with the law, Mr. Sylvester couldn't have been responsible for Cynthia's murder as he hadn't yet boarded the ship. On further interview, Edward should have been satisfied with the explanation as to why Roger Sylvester was hauled off the coach on the way to Southampton. He wasn't! Did it have any bearing on the events that unfolded?

Another statement that stood out from the others was from Jacqueline Sylvester. She certainly had Cynthia's measure, but did she think her husband and Cynthia were having an affair? A very cool lady indeed. So cool, in fact, that Samuel almost missed the slight change in her expression upon seeing the person walking around, pushing Cynthia. She was certainly not a person to dismiss.

He followed the apparition around the ship on his screen. Mrs. Manning must have already been murdered, but he had to admit, at a quick glance, they looked like two people enjoying the evening air on deck.

Forensics had examined the laundry room and had found some evidence of blood stain which had travelled to the furthest corner of the room, just under the ceiling. The room had been thoroughly cleaned and the team had almost given up finding anything at all. They had pored over all three wheelchairs known to be on board ship during that sailing and luckily managed to find one with some transference of nylon hair from a wig or hairpiece that had stuck to the base of the handle under a microscopic spot of blood.

Edward originally thought the crazy golf, pitch and putt, or whatever that place on the recreation deck was called could have easily been the murder scene. There was no camera working in the area and the murderer would have seen that. It certainly would have kept the blood and gore in one area, but there was evidence that the victim had been placed there after she had been murdered, such as the positioning of the body and the blood seepage under the hairpiece.

Assuming this murder was a one-off, a crime of passion committed by a person consumed with hate and rage, it all seemed very contained.

CHAPTER ELEVEN

Abby couldn't get the vision of her father trotting up Cynthia's driveway out of her head. How humiliating that she had been forced – yes, forced, to sit in the car and watch him sneak around behind her mother's back. It was her responsibility, as their daughter, to know the full extent of what was going on – to protect Jacqueline and save Roger from making an irreparable mistake. Since then, her feelings had hardened towards him and the situation.

Dinner with them both had been a nightmare. Abby played the events of the evening over and over in her head, recalling that every mouthful of food eaten had stuck in her throat. Never again would she put herself through such torture.

Her father sat at the table, trying to pretend he and his bridge partner were just good pals. His jokes were coming thick and fast, making Cynthia roar with laughter at every punch line. His attentiveness towards Cynthia's comfort in the restaurant reminded her of the way he treated her mother and she wanted to scream.

She looked around at the other diners – some eating, others chatting over the top of their wine glasses and wondered whether she was the only person in the restaurant trying to rescue her family from falling apart.

Abby could tell that her father was congratulating himself for managing, successfully, to pull the wool over his daughter's eyes. He had a certain self-satisfied look on his face when he thought he got away with something. It was obvious there was chemistry between him and

Cynthia and that their friendship had become more intimate.

After dinner, Abby drove straight to Alfie's flat. She rang the bell several times, but he didn't answer the door. She called and messaged on her mobile phone and still received no answer. She needed to talk to him – why was he not answering her calls?

She sat down on the floor outside the front door and waited, thinking she could hear movement inside the flat, but the sound must have been coming from somewhere else. She couldn't be trusted to think rationally. Tears trickled down her cheeks as she got in her car and drove home.

Jacqueline was waiting up, sitting in the living room watching television. The log fire was burning itself out and Abby sat next to her mother on the sofa.

"How was your evening, darling?" Jacqueline put her arm around her daughter. She couldn't think of anything more boring than spending an evening talking about bridge.

Abby wanted to blurt it all out. She wanted to confide in her mother that she suspected her father was betraying them both, but how could she? She couldn't prove anything. Why would she make trouble between her parents that could never be put right unless she was absolutely sure? Once that seed of doubt was planted in Jacqueline's mind, it would torment her. She had to tread very carefully; her mother wasn't stupid.

"Just about bearable. The food wasn't particularly good, Dad's bridge partner was over made up, banal and ordinary – not exciting or clever like you and I can't think why I wanted to meet her. The whole evening was a waste of time. I should have spent the evening with Alfie or stayed in and had a girlie night with you."

"I know why you wanted to join them, Abby. You're my daughter and we think alike, but you have no reason to be concerned, darling. I gave up being suspicious of other women years ago. Our family means everything to your father. He wouldn't do anything to jeopardise it, purely because he knows if he does, he will live to regret it."

Abby wasn't convinced. Mother and daughter held hands, both staring at the television, occupied by their own thoughts. She didn't bother to tell Jacqueline about her visit to Alfie's flat. She wasn't ready to hear her mother's misgivings about him.

Later, when Alfie finally returned her call, Abby was rather cold towards him.

"I called, messaged, turned up at the flat – all for nothing. Where were you, Alfie? We arranged that I would come over and report back to you after my awful dinner with my father and his...well, I don't know what to call her."

"I'm so sorry, Abby. I was there all along. I must have fallen asleep."

"And I thought I heard movement in the flat. What's going on? It's not like you. I hoped you would be there when I needed you and I really could have done with my fiancée's support at that moment, Alfie."

"Like I said, Abby, I must have fallen into a really deep sleep. I didn't hear a thing. Please forgive me – it won't happen again. I will make sure I'm always there for you in future. You can rely on me."

As it turned out, Abby couldn't rely on him. Their wedding went ahead, despite the persistent warning voice in her head and it was a lavish affair. She had wanted more modest nuptials, in view of the fact that Alfie had lost his job, again.

"Why can't we just get married in a registry office and use your parent's money to help set up our home?" Alfie hated to see it wasted on people he didn't know or care about.

"My parents have one child and they have been dreaming of making a wedding and seeing their daughter happily married and settled since I was born. We can't deprive them of that pleasure." Abby felt very strongly about it.

"It's just wasteful, Abby, when we could really use the money." Alfie thought she could be really stupid sometimes.

"My parents think that you intend to find a job and pull your weight, Alfie, and so do I."

"This is just a blip. I'll find something soon and it will be the best job I've ever had. There's no point rushing into something if it's not right. You want me to be happy, don't you."

"Of course I do, but my salary won't be enough to support us both indefinitely, especially when we start a family."

"Don't you fret. Your parents won't let us starve." Alfie smiled confidently.

Before she knew it, her mother had booked everything and large deposits had been given to the wedding planner, venue, band and caterer. Abby found that being in the catering industry was helpful, but she didn't want to abuse her contacts – they were the lifeblood of her business.

By the time her mother sat quietly weeping with joy, while her daughter was being fitted for her wedding dress, Abby knew that it was too late to change her mind.

The couple spent their honeymoon in Venice, famous for being the most romantic city in the world, but for

Abby, it was the loneliest place.

The weather was glorious, as was the food they ate in every café and restaurant in piazzas and alleyways around the city. Alfie managed to devote the first few days to be the caring, loving husband, but then, bored, decided he wanted some space to explore the city on his own.

"We're not joined at the hip, darling, and you like to look at different things. We can meet at the little restaurant behind the hotel for lunch." He looked at Abby's disappointed face and stroked her cheek.

"We've got a wonderful life planned together. It will be more enjoyable if we respect each other's space, don't you agree?" Not bothering to wait for an answer, he gathered up his backpack and guide book and disappeared into the crowd.

Abby was ready to pack it in, come home and get back to normal.

———

The coach house, hidden at the bottom of a quiet lane, was the most beautiful house Abby and Alfie had ever seen and the view from the sitting room was of endless green open space, only changing with the seasons.

A little gate at the bottom of the garden opened onto a bridle path and one could be forgiven for thinking that the house was situated deep in the heart of the countryside, rather than a London suburb.

It gave Roger and Jacqueline enormous pleasure to buy the house for their daughter and son-in-law and it should have been a little haven of peace and tranquillity – somewhere for them to lay down roots and produce much wanted grandchildren.

They had invited Alfie's parents over for tea and tactfully brought up the subject of purchasing the little cottage.

"Isn't it a pretty place for a young couple to start their married life?" Jacqueline said brightly, offering a plate of cupcakes around, hoping that she and Roger might be offered a modest contribution towards the purchase. "But if you've seen something more to your liking, we're open to suggestions?"

They picked up their teacups simultaneously and chorused "All in good time."

Abby didn't have the heart to mention, during the many daily conversations with her parents, that as they had predicted, she had made a terrible error by choosing Alfie as her life partner. Since she had matured and developed into adulthood and was responsible for a team of people who worked under her direction, she had made very few mistakes – she couldn't think of even one, until now.

It was still dark when Abby woke from a troubled sleep. She got out of bed, carefully, so as not to wake Alfie and went downstairs.

The sitting room was a mess with dirty plates and wine glasses lying on the coffee table in front of the television. It looked like friends had dropped around and helped themselves liberally from her fridge.

Much earlier, she had cleared up from dinner leaving the kitchen clean and tidy. She fell into bed exhausted from a hectic day at the office, hoping Alfie would join her a little later. Evidently, coming up to bed for a romantic night with his wife was the last thing on Alfie's mind, as was a day of job interviews.

She showered, dressed and headed out to the office. She could see the lights were switched on and could smell the coffee machine. Her father was already at his desk.

"Why is a newly married woman coming to the office at this ungodly hour of the morning?" Roger was teasing, but Abby found it hard to be amused.

She tried to be as flippant, "Oh, you know – things to do, people to see…"

She busied herself pouring two cups of coffee and was satisfied to notice that the milk in the fridge was still fresh.

"Is Alfie going to be busy today?"

Her father meant no harm by his remark. He assumed that Alfie would have a diary full of interviews and be systematically working through them. How could she tell him that all the signs were pointing to the fact that Alfie had little intention of finding a new job any time soon?

Abby sighed. "He's waiting for the Prime Minister's job to become available. Judging by the newspapers, he shouldn't have long to wait."

Roger got the message. "Did I mention Mummy and I are off on a bridge cruise. I'm not sure how I managed to persuade her to come along. Give me a kiss and tell me how clever I am."

Abby shot up from her desk and threw her arms around her father. She was delighted to hear they would be going away for a few days.

"Now don't get into mischief while we're away and I simply forbid you to discuss starting a family."

"Just because you said that I think we will intentionally get right to it."

Father and daughter roared with laughter. There was nothing like a morning dose of Roger Sylvester in a good mood to cheer her up.

"Tell me more about this wonderful bridge trip. Is the lovely Cynthia going?"

Roger intentionally continued to look in his diary and took his time answering. It wouldn't do to appear too excited.

"I think so – all my bridge girls are going. Apparently, it's the first time the club have organised this sort of thing. Cynthia and I got roped in, which is hardly surprising – I mean, it wouldn't be much of a bridge group without me, now would it?" He looked at Abby and waited for an amused reaction that didn't happen.

"Anyway, I immediately reported back to headquarters with all the details. I mentioned that it would be a shame for Mummy and me not to take advantage of the opportunity to go on a lovely cruise and, guess what? – she jumped at the chance."

Abby wished her father wouldn't underestimate her. He really knew how to spin a web of rubbish. She never remembered her parents going anywhere as part of a crowd as underneath all the laughter and joking around, they were private people – just the three of them was the perfect number. Her mother would certainly not have 'jumped at the chance.'

Roger looked at his daughter's expression and continued.

"So the plan is that we drive to Southampton, leave the car, jump on board and sail away to sunny climes. We don't have to play bridge all day – we can just explore the beautiful Italian and French riviera. We will probably eat with friends in the evening and dance the night away, followed by a nightcap on our balcony – Heavenly!"

"It does sound like a great trip." Abby digested the information, "But I'm going to miss you both terribly."

"No you won't." He reached over and took her hand in his. "You'll be too busy nesting."

———

Abby calculated that Alfie had been sitting around like a slob in every room in their house for about two months.

Every morning, she would jump out of bed, shower

and head off to work, leaving him asleep in bed and in the evening she would find him fast asleep, in the sitting room. In between, there had been some wild activity, involving the use of every glass, cup and plate in the house and, of course, all their food.

"Do you think this is acceptable behaviour?" She asked her husband, as she filled a second tray full of dirty dishes and carried it to the kitchen.

"Yes, I do, if there's no suitable job out there and I'm forced to stay at home. Please stop nagging, Abby, it's so unattractive."

"Watching my husband's brain atrophy at an alarming rate is more unattractive, I would say."

"You could take some time off and hang out here with me and some friends. Nobody's stopping you." Alfie thought it was very magnanimous of him to offer.

"The mortgage and the bills are stopping me, but you know what, you're right. I am working too hard and I think I will take some time off." Alfie had stopped listening.

She wasn't sure exactly when the idea came into her head, but the more she thought about it, the more it appealed to her. It wasn't difficult to make the arrangements as she was fortunate enough to have a wonderful team to manage the office in her absence. She finished work early and rushed back to an empty house. She would have liked to think that Alfie was out scouring the job market, but she wasn't that naïve.

She ran upstairs and changed into a pair of jeans and a loose shirt, popping a sports cap on to top off the casual look and packed a large suitcase. She checked she had her passport and left a note explaining to Alfie that she had decided to visit a school friend in Devon and would be back in a few days. The break would do them both good, after all, as he had correctly pointed out, they weren't joined at the hip.

For the first time in ages, her spirits were lifted as she drove down the motorway in the sunshine. In no time at all, she pulled into the designated carpark, showed her pass and excitedly boarded the *Holland Silhouette*.

The ship wasn't sailing until late afternoon which gave Abby loads of time to have lunch and explore. The buffet was open to guests immediately they boarded, serving an array of delicacies a five-star restaurant would struggle to provide and Abby helped herself. She found a table near the window and surveyed the room, wondering whether her parents had arrived. They would normally go to one of the restaurants with waiter service, but on the day of embarkation, the roof terrace buffet was the only restaurant providing lunch.

It was a vast floating city and she quickly saw how easy it would be to avoid her and her parent's paths crossing. If you were looking for somewhere impersonal, this was definitely the right place to be.

Abby knew she had done the right thing choosing to come along. From here, she could attempt to keep her eye on her father from a safe distance and make sure her mother's holiday wasn't spoiled by a silly indiscretion.

She thought the ship was a magnificent floating palace with beautiful décor and several bars and restaurants, some of them family friendly and others more intimate. Going from floor to floor, she noticed the carpet was plush throughout the ship, except for the areas with Italian marble flooring. When she reached the upper deck, she noticed the pool area and sundeck, surrounded by comfortably padded chairs and loungers.

As she walked around the deck, she came upon what she could only describe as a blot on the landscape. In a designated area, under a canopy providing shade from the hot sun, there was a taped off area meant to be used for a game of crazy golf, but not yet in service. The camera monitoring the area was turned to face the swimming pool. Abby thought the closure of this popular facility was definitely an oversight and wondered if she should mention it to the Entertainment Director.

She slowly walked back along the endless corridors, settling down in her cabin and began to unpack her suitcase. Standing on her balcony, she could see below people hurrying on board. Some had taken long flights to get to the ship before its departure and, judging by their raised voices and body language, they looked very stressed and in need of a break.

She was looking forward to the ship leaving Southampton and staring at an expanse of blue sea with no interruptions, just her thoughts to keep her company and a chance to think about her future and whether she wanted to spend it with the man she married.

She opened her well-stocked fridge and peered inside, rubbing her hands at the prospect of a drink fest at the same time as she received a text message from her mother, telling her that her father was unavoidably delayed and would catch the ship up further down the line.

Abby started to panic. Watching the ship pull away from the harbour, leaving the one person crucial in the planning of this trip behind, made her wonder if this hare-brained scheme of hers wasn't a complete waste of time.

———

For the first couple of days, she watched from a safe distance, as Nick Lombardo set up the room for the seriously competitive game. The scores were calculated and displayed on the open laptop at the end of the session and the players would congregate around it, jostling for first place.

She noticed that after four rounds, people would change tables and play with different opponents, until all the hands had been played.

Jacqueline had no trouble finding a partner and was thoroughly enjoying herself, despite Roger's temporary absence. At no time did her mother look lonely or pensive. Instead, Jacqueline's day was full of lively chit-chat, smutty banter and adventure.

Another person who seemed completely unphased by Roger's absence was his bridge partner, Cynthia. Abby could hear her dulcet tones long before she reached the card room. The little clique of four remained at the same table, preferring to stay together for every game they played.

Once she established the group's routine, which rarely veered off its course, she was able to move around the ship at her leisure. The eclectic mix of passengers on board respected each other's space, happy to spend time out from their busy lives and grateful to be anonymous.

Looking out at the endless view of blue from her balcony, she shook her head in wonderment as to why anyone would want to be cooped up for hours, rather than spending time breathing in the wonderful sea air.

Calm and relaxed, little snippets of her happy childhood kept popping into her head. So many scenes of fun and laughter with very few arguments or harsh words spoken. Other families she knew would argue and fall out, sometimes severing contact for years, but she always thought that could never happen. They were a tight little unit – Mummy, Daddy and baby.

It was while waiting to disembark the ship to go sightseeing around one of the pretty Italian ports that

Abby hatched the start of her plan.

She played a couple of different scenarios out in her head. Should she have a chat with Cynthia in front of her group of friends and shame her, show her up as a predator and destroyer of a long and happy marriage or, would a quiet chat in her stateroom be a better idea? Either way, Abby had to remember this was not a holiday, it was business that had to be dealt with once and for all.

She had wisely taken certain precautions, including in her luggage some cheap wigs as a form of disguise, whether she would need them or not. She assumed that on a security camera and amongst hundreds of people, it might prove to be a successful disguise. Nobody looks that closely at an unattractive person's appearance on holiday.

The simple task of arranging for the wheelchair to be delivered to the laundry room presented her with the greatest difficulty. She chose the laundry room as the drop-off point for the simple reason that emerging from such a place, at any time of the day or night, would be perfectly feasible should they be seen on camera. She had to admit that it was a stroke of genius to think of using one, for the sole purpose of giving herself and Cynthia more time to come to their mutual understanding that Roger was untouchable by any other woman other than his wife. This way, Cynthia couldn't just flounce off, walk away and not listen. Abby would be in complete control.

Using an emergency phone on the recreation deck and giving Cynthia's stateroom number as authorisation, it took all her considerable powers of persuasion to convince the stores department that the chair would not be in the laundry room long enough to cause any danger or obstruction and would be employed almost immediately, therefore not becoming a health and safety issue.

She was standing a few steps behind her mother, Cynthia and a couple of others and felt invisible – blending into the scene. The ease in which she was able to follow the group around, unnoticed, surprised and delighted her – she was just part of an array of colour around her, without taking on any form.

Once the security arrangements on board ship were understood and the precious key card kept on one's person at all times, that was pretty much it. She felt it was like having her own personal yacht, an extremely large one, ferrying her from place to place while providing incredible food and sumptuous comfort.

Of course, there was always a chance Cynthia would fight back – not physically, but verbally – making excuses for her behaviour and trying to justify it. Abby was tall and imposing, like her mother. Most people wouldn't want to take her on, but she knew that if Cynthia did that, she would see red and completely lose control. It wasn't easy to think this through and be sure of the outcome.

———

The steak was grilled to perfection – just as Abby liked it. She felt quite hungry. Her day had started with an organic breakfast, brought early to her stateroom and eaten on the balcony, followed by a mini workout in the gym. An hour's march, sticking to the walking trail around the viewing deck and then a light buffet lunch. The rest of the afternoon was spent in contemplation.

Later, her dinner was only slightly spoiled by watching Jacqueline enjoying her meal at a window table, basked in the setting sunlight. Her companions were amusing her and without Roger's extrovert personality and often juvenile jokes, her subtle wit came to the surface and was appreciated. Under normal circumstances, she would be joining that table, in her mother's delightful company, laughing at her mother's clever sense of humour.

After her meal, she decided not to avail herself of the evening's entertainment. Instead, she chose to go back to her cabin and wait.

———

The corridor was deserted and it was now or never.

Abby dressed for the occasion, deciding to don everything she thought she might need, fully aware that she would only get one shot at this and set off for a cosy chat with Cynthia.

Several corridors and two floors later she had barely seen another person, spurring her on to complete the task in hand. She juggled the bottle of champagne and glasses around, freeing one hand to knock loudly on the stateroom door. Panic set in as there was some delay before the door was thrown open. She was greeted by Cynthia's smiling face and invited in.

It was obvious that Cynthia was getting ready to turn in, a moment later and it may have been too late. Abby took this as a good omen. It was at that very moment that she had a change of heart.

The blonde, glamorous bimbo lying on the bed was cocky and arrogant, contemptuous of anyone who criticised or questioned her actions. Abby thought it strange that, rather than showing any interest in why her visitor was on the cruise, enquiring how she was spending her time or maybe even inviting Abby to join her little group, Cynthia launched straight into a tirade about herself, her and more about her. How very typical. Was it really going to be possible to reason with this woman? – To explain that her actions could do irreparable damage and expect a sensible or sympathetic response?

Fortunately, she had prepared for the likelihood that a

relaxed and chilled Cynthia would be easier to deal with and had grabbed some of Alfie's Diazepam tablets on her way out of the house. He said he needed them for his anxiety and to calm him down.

Once Cynthia was settled comfortably in the wheelchair and had fallen asleep, Abby felt that she had no choice. Everything she had meticulously planned was no longer relevant. From here on she was going to have to improvise.

Her heart was racing and she was close to tears. Up until this moment, it had seemed a sort of game. What was the worst that could happen, she asked herself a million times. Cynthia would laugh in her face, possibly even scoff and say, "Don't be ridiculous, your father wouldn't dream of changing the way we do things?" No! she couldn't take a chance that this would have been all for nothing.

The first obstacle was the amount of blood spurting forth after the first onslaught. She couldn't take the chance of any more bursting forth. There was only so much blood a person could pass off as a nose bleed. Fortunately, the cord from the iron provided a safe and cleaner alternative. She had thought of bludgeoning Cynthia over the bath in her stateroom, allowing for a quick hose down of the bathroom, but extricating the body from that position would have required two people.

The plan to wheel Cynthia around the recreation deck of the ship was still useable only now she would not be returning to her stateroom. Abby continued with the scenario with renewed vigour – a huge sense of relief caused her to forget that there was a dead person in the wheelchair, somehow believing that two friends were indeed having a late-night stroll, chatting companionably and breathing in the fresh sea air that smelled so good.

Arriving at the crazy golf pitch, she checked that the CCTV was still facing away from the area and braced herself for the difficult task of unloading and concealing Cynthia's body. She would have liked to have made a better job of hiding the body under the AstroTurf, but time was not on her side, nevertheless, she was satisfied with her handiwork. Nobody would look at lumpy AstroTurf and immediately be suspicious.

The journey to Cynthia's stateroom with an empty, blood-stained wheelchair and a pile of towels, wrapped in a dressing gown, topped with a stupid sports cap was the only part of the plan that Abby thought would be her undoing, convinced that at any moment a team of security guards would descend upon her and drag her away into the depths of the ship. She had obviously thought all along that at any stage this was a distinct possibility but decided that it was worth it. Either way, the problem would have been eradicated.

Safely back in Cynthia's stateroom, Abby was ready to execute part of the incriminating evidence disposal plan. Earlier on, she had asked which steward was responsible for cleaning, making sure to mention that Cynthia wished to tip, generously, the one responsible for keeping her stateroom immaculate.

Adopting Cynthia's fawning manner when she wanted her own way, Abby picked up the phone and called Freddy. He came immediately and she thanked him, hoping he wouldn't spot the imposter lying in Cynthia's bed. She felt euphoric as she watched the wheelchair and bloodied towels disappear from the room.

Making sure she left the room in the right persona, Abby waved and blew kisses to the empty stateroom for the benefit of the camera and legged it as fast as was safely possible to her own cabin, via the back stairs and staff exit. Finally, back in her room exhausted, she poured herself a brandy, threw herself onto the bed and closed her eyes.

In the early hours of the morning, she put a call through to the ship's Doctor and reported feeling very unwell. Her symptoms were a high temperature and loss of smell and taste, as had been reported by BBC World News on her TV. The Doctor proceeded to make arrangements for Abby's departure from the ship, without visiting her stateroom or checking her temperature. He wanted this guest to have as little contact with him, his medical team and other guests on the ship as possible. Abby suspected that this would be the stance he would take and had her suitcase packed ready.

Before she had time to finish her breakfast on her balcony, which she had sensibly ordered before she made her escape call, there was an urgent knock on her door. Standing before her was a medical team, covered from head to foot in protective clothing, ready to escort her off the ship and onto a tender to shore. She had never been so pleased to see a group of people in her whole life.

Lying in her comfortable bed in hospital, she had ample time to analyse the events of the past few days. She had to accept that murdering that woman was her only option.

Her original plan of laying her cards on the table, patiently explaining that she would not – could not – allow her family to break up, proved not to be viable. It was as simple as that. What other course of action was there? Looking around her spacious room, she felt a sense of achievement that she had turned what could have been a terrible failure into a great success.

The ship's medical team had been wonderful if you

wanted to be treated like a pariah. They couldn't wait to offload her onto a tender. They hastily scribbled something on some paperwork and thrust it into her hand and it all went brilliantly – better than she could have ever imagined. Safely in the ambulance waiting for her at the dock, she watched the ship and any incriminating evidence vanish into the horizon.

After a couple of nights and many negative tests, Abby was discharged. The fact that she had been in rude health all along didn't seem to bother anyone, in fact the medical staff seemed to be relieved. The only comment on the medical report handed to her before she left the hospital was some concern about her slightly raised blood pressure and a recommendation that she visit her regular doctor as soon as she returned home. Hardly surprising under the circumstances.

She made her way to the airport, bought a ticket at an exorbitant price and flew to London where she would hire a car and drive to Southampton to pick up her own. She was in no hurry.

Abby recalled the moment that she discovered her father was not on-board ship. She had been relying on both parents being there to support her, even though they would have been unaware of her presence. She may well have decided to confide in her father and let him in on her plan, still in its embryonic stage. Only he would have had the power to ensure that the events which unfolded might have taken a less violent turn but thinking on her feet was Abby's speciality.

Her life with Alfie needed to be re-assessed and she would be counting on the support of her parents more than ever. None of that would have mattered to Cynthia. As long as that woman could preen and boast that she had men sprawling at her feet, that was all that mattered to her.

She had called Alfie on several occasions, but their conversations were brief and cold. He always seemed to have company whatever time of day or night.

"You wouldn't want me to be here all by myself, would you?" Not waiting for Abby to answer, he chirped "I'm having a great time, I hope you are too, darling. When will you be home?"

Abby was vague, "In a day or two. I think I've had enough chilling. I'm looking forward to seeing you. How's the work situation?"

"Oh for fuck sake, Abby. You've been on the phone two minutes and you're already hassling me?"

Abby wanted to cry. Nothing had changed. "Alfie, I just asked. Stop biting my head off all the time." She could hear him flicking something on the coffee table with irritation.

"You just don't let up. I'm dealing with it, Okay?"

Abby could feel uncontrollable anger welling up but tried to stay calm. "You haven't said anything about or mentioned your plans, so I assumed you had given up. Not an unreasonable assumption, I would say."

"It is really, because I have actually been in touch with all the recruitment agents on a regular basis. I have been on loads of interviews and I'm really trying hard, Abby. I wanted to surprise you when you got home by securing a great job and taking you out to celebrate, but as hard as I've tried, that's just not going to happen."

There was silence on the phone and Alfie thought she had hung up on him. "Abby? Are you still there?"

"Yes, I'm still here. I'll be home soon. We can talk then."

———

What are we going to do?" Jacqueline was hysterical.

Roger had never seen her so agitated. She was usually calm and composed with her mind whirring, thinking of ways to solve whatever problems came their way and vanquishing them.

"We don't know for sure that it's her now, do we?"

Jacqueline was pacing around the stateroom. Their suitcases were packed and waiting to be collected and taken off the ship. Both she and Roger had just returned from yet another interview, only this time it was with the big guns – a whole team of murder investigators from the Hampshire Police Force descended, interviewed them again, separately, politely asking to take their fingerprints, a DNA swap and photograph. They both had a strong feeling that any minute they would be hauled off to prison, for life.

"Yes, Roger, we do know that for sure," Jacqueline's voice was raised, but she tried not to shout. "I would know my own daughter, even if she were dressed in a gorilla suit. It's a pity you wouldn't. It was only after several viewings of the tape that I spotted her – I nearly missed it. Did you say anything to the Assistant Superintendent when he interviewed you? Did you show any recognition at all?"

"Of course not, because I wasn't sure whether I recognised her. At first, I was just looking at a tall, badly dressed stranger running around the ship with Cynthia and right now, I'm still convinced that's what I saw."

"I've been trying to call Abby for a couple of days with no joy. I spoke to Alfie and he hasn't heard from her either. He said she's gone to a see a friend in Devon – at least I think that's where he said – he couldn't wait to get me off the phone. Something's not right there and I wish I knew what it is." Jacqueline took a last, long look over her balcony, forgetting that her sea view had now been replaced by the dock.

Roger was pacing up and down the cabin and went to join Jacqueline outside. "Let's look at this logically for a moment. Why would Abby be on the ship and not come to see us? Why wouldn't she tell us she was coming on board? It doesn't make sense. Apart from anything, I've left her to run things at home. I don't have to tell you how conscientious she is."

"Not come and see *me*, don't you mean?" Jacqueline was close to tears. "You boarded the ship *after* Cynthia was murdered. Even if she wanted to talk it through with you she couldn't, could she?" Jacqueline's mind was racing.

"That might have made all the difference, Roger. She wouldn't have known that you were caught up with your own police investigation elsewhere. She must have come on board to try and catch you in the act with stupid Cynthia, or maybe even to have a quiet word with you and warn her off. She didn't take me into her confidence, so I'm really not sure exactly what she had in mind, but that's what I would do if it were *my* father."

Roger looked aghast and stumbled to sit down.

"That's right, you may well look incredulous, but as usual, Roger, you underestimated me. I've known all about your sordid little affair, but guess what? Watch my lips – I DON'T CARE. It's all a lot of nonsense and I wasn't prepared to feed your ego."

"It wasn't an affair, darling, I would never, ever cheat on you," Roger insisted, "but you *are* right about one thing. It was a whole lot of nonsense."

Jacqueline wasn't listening to his blustering. "I do care, however, that it's upset Abby and I tried very hard to make nothing of it when I could see she was piecing it all together. I still don't think she murdered Cynthia, that's just ridiculous. My beautiful, clever, resourceful daughter isn't a murderer, but if she did, it will be down to you for not being there when she needed you most. I hope you can live with that."

Roger's face had turned a horrible shade of grey. "She was just my bridge partner and you know me; I like to flirt a bit. I love you, Jacqueline. I gave all that up when we got married, as you well know. There isn't another woman out there that can compare to you, that fascinates and excites me the way you do."

Jacqueline wasn't really listening – her mind was taken up thinking about her darling daughter. "I will just say that if Cynthia's brain was larger than a blue tit, I might have been worried, just a bit. As it stands, she was all tits, fake nails and bleached blonde hair and the affair hasn't kept me awake for a moment. We've been married for a long time, Roger, lasting much longer than my parents thought it would and by and large it's been a good life – very entertaining."

"What do you mean by that, darling? '...We've been married for a long time...'" Roger's voice was full of panic. "You're not going to do divorce me, are you? Please don't leave me – It will destroy me – I'll kill myself."

"Of course not, you silly thing. It would be crazy to divorce you now that she's dead. I've earned my comfortable retirement and shares in your business. All we have to do now is prove that Abby had nothing to do with it and things can go back to normal."

Roger was relieved to see that Jacqueline was back to her old self, busy planning a comeback from all of this.

———

The flight landed at Heathrow on time and Abby stared at the assortment of suitcases, folded buggies and the odd set of golf clubs going around the carousel. It was very important that she didn't engage in any conversation. Usually at this point, an elderly person would ask her to help them lift a heavy bag off the conveyor belt and onto a waiting trolley. She had that sort of face and it would be followed by profusive thanks and possibly even a hug, but not today. Today, her face was like stone.

She took her luggage and went to sit down so she could answer dozens of text messages from her parents without further delay. They were beside themselves with worry. She needed to reassure them that the person they thought they saw on camera, running around the decks of the ship, couldn't possibly be her. How could it be? She explained that she was driving up from Devon and would be home in a few hours.

She thought long and hard about what to say next, without it sounding disingenuous and decided to just mention how sorry she was to hear about Cynthia's brutal murder and what a horrible holiday it had turned out to be. However, she was very grateful that they had come to no harm and the three of them should plan another break away soon, in order to recover from this one.

Her mobile rang and it was her father – she immediately cancelled the call. She was still in a state of high tension and wasn't ready to chat to them on the phone and be put through the third degree.

There was a message from Alfie asking her exactly when she was coming home – he had missed her and was looking forward to seeing her. Abby stared at the message for some time before answering. She decided to reply that her friends had asked her to say just one more night and that she would be home tomorrow.

She soon had the keys to a nice little Mini Cooper and was negotiating her way out of the airport and on to

Southampton. The car was a bit smaller than she had hoped for – her suitcase filled the whole of the back seat, but it was all part of her plan not to draw attention to herself by making her usual fuss over something that wasn't perfect for her needs.

She pulled into the car pool belonging to the hire company and handed over the keys, making her way to the cruise terminal car park.

Once in her own car, she started to feel more relaxed. She was mentally and physically exhausted. This was the last leg of a very long journey, but she was battling with very mixed emotions. She thought she would feel euphoria, satisfaction at the completion of a plan beautifully executed, but now that it was all over, she just wanted to cry in her mother's arms.

She decided to stop at her favourite café and have something to eat, but not before popping into a small supermarket to pick up a few groceries for herself and her parents. She hadn't eaten anything since breakfast and she didn't want to spend a loving reunion with Alfie in the kitchen making a meal.

She ordered a veal Milanese with spaghetti and a glass of chilled white wine and ate slowly, taking in the familiar décor, but seeing it differently. She would be seeing everything differently now.

After dropping in a few things for her parents return, her car pulled into her own driveway. She jumped out excitedly and let herself into the house.

The door wasn't locked so Alfie must be home pottering about somewhere. She went into the kitchen and looked out the window at the overgrown garden. As she proceeded towards the stairs, she could hear a loud thud coming from upstairs, but before she could go and investigate, Alfie appeared in a tracksuit, followed by a woman wearing Abby's bathrobe.

Alfie walked unhurriedly down the stairs. "Hello! You're back earlier than you said. Didn't you have a nice time?"

Abby smiled at her husband. "I had a lovely time, but I decided to come home a little earlier and surprise you. I can see I've certainly done that."

"This is my friend, Isabelle. I met her at the job centre. She's also feeling a bit low about not finding the right job so I asked her to stay in the spare room."

"Hello Isabelle. Why are you wearing my bathrobe?" Abby was going to stay very calm. Turning to Alfie, she asked, conversationally.

"It's late afternoon, does Isabelle not have any clothes to wear? I have some in my wardrobe in the spare room that you're welcome to borrow – let me show you."

Abby pushed passed the pair still standing on the stairs and walked into the spare room. It was as she had left it – a perfectly made bed with her favourite teddy bear propped up by two pillows. She then pushed open her bedroom door and looked inside.

"We have either been burgled or you and Isabelle have had a wild time while I've been away." Abby wasn't in the least surprised at her discovery. She supposed that deep down she was expecting it. Showing consideration for her feelings had been relegated to the bottom of his priority list.

"I suspect it's the latter. Would you mind leaving now, Isabelle, I'd like to speak to my husband if that's alright with you." It wasn't a question.

Alfie waved a finger towards his shell-shocked friend. "You don't have to leave. Abby's just throwing her toys out of the pram."

Isabelle looked very embarrassed. Abby could see the

girl didn't have the courage to do battle and wisely bowed out.

"I think I do. Thank you for having me, Alfie. See you around." Isabelle hastily gathered her clothes. Alfie was a great host and a fun weekend, with unlimited free food and alcohol, is always appreciated. Isabelle had already established that he really wasn't the most interesting person in the world and certainly not worth getting into a brawl with his wife.

Abby noticed the expression on Isabelle's face. "Keep the bathrobe, Isabelle. I shan't be wearing it again."

—

"I've been going through Mrs. Manning's phone records, sir and I've found a message that's been overlooked. It goes way back, long before the cruise. It's been sent anonymously, but I've found the phone number. It belongs to an Abby Castleford and there is no doubt that it's a hands-off warning message. Quite sinister, I would say. Whatever Mrs. Manning was up to, she was definitely treading on someone's toes.

Edward took the print-out and read it again. "Well done, DS Long. Anything else?"

"We've got a partial palm print on the iron and a lip imprint on the glass."

"Run it through the national DNA database. This is always the problem with evidence. Anyone can drink out of a glass and use an iron on board ship."

CHAPTER TWELVE

"I want you to pack your bags and get out. We're finished. To be absolutely honest, we never really started."

Abby roared with laughter. "Shouldn't that be *my* line? I think you'll find that it's you who will be slithering off into the night."

Alfie had been pacing around the house most of the night, finally falling into a troubled sleep. He called his mother, whispering down the telephone putting her in the picture. She explained in her usual cold, calculating manner to sit tight and not be hasty. He was quite a catch, now.

He really believed he was the injured party. Abby's parents had created a monster. Spoiled and aloof, she had never really taken him or his needs seriously. He knew she loved him – no, she adored him and he could make her do whatever he wanted, if he tried. He just wasn't sure whether he wanted to bother. It was just too much effort.

He wanted to call off the wedding right up until the final moment, but his parents talked him out of it. Where else would he find such a girl? They were determined he overcome his misgivings and go ahead and marry her. They said he could make it work. He shouldn't have listened.

"Why should I leave my house? It's my home."

"It's *my* home. My parents bought it and I have paid all the bills and the upkeep. That makes it mine – all mine."

Abby was infuriatingly cool and Alfie wanted to slap her.

"Let's see what a solicitor has to say about that."

Abby had left it until the following day to confront her husband about his antics while she was away. She had resolutely refused to argue with him after Isabelle had left. The man was deluded enough to think he had right on his side, whining on about how neglected he felt and how unsupportive she had been towards his lack of employment. A better wife would find a job for him in her business after all, he was clever, handsome and charming – what more could her clients ask for.

She had, obviously, slept in the spare room – she would never be sleeping in her marital bed again. The very thought was too repulsive.

During the drive back from Southampton, she had naively thought that now the thorn was well removed from her side, she could concentrate on making her marriage work. Alfie wasn't career minded – he was never going to be a grafter, but with his support and a small contribution towards the household expenses, she would be happy to be the main breadwinner. When they started a family, she may well be pleased for him to be at home.

Now, without her rose tinted spectacles, she could see he was a selfish, feckless individual - completely irresponsible. It would be impossible to leave him in charge of their children. Goodness knows what would happen to them in his care.

Abby poured some muesli into a bowl. The doorbell had woken her up early. It was a delivery from a shop in the local High Street and she asked the driver if he would put it at the side of the house out of the way.

Alfie's words echoed in her head. "A better wife would find a job for him in her business..." That's what this has all been about. Having an easy life with a woman who would take care of all his needs, leaving him free to piss his life away. He couldn't love her or any woman – not really. He was too busy loving himself. He wasn't smart enough to think up this scheme of taking her and her parents for a ride, but his mother was and between them they cooked up their nasty little plan to exploit her.

Alfie came into the kitchen and leant up against the work top with his arms folded. "I see you haven't lost your appetite then."

"Do you want some tea?" Abby asked pleasantly.

"Go on then," Alfie stared at her. He knew there was more to come – a lot more, but maybe she had forgiven him and things could go back to normal – Abby working all hours with him pretending to look for employment.

"Go and sit at the breakfast bar and I'll bring it to you."

Alfie sat on the stool. He glanced at the front page of the morning newspaper and didn't see Abby take the Diazepam out of her pocket.

———

Roger and Jacqueline finally pulled into the driveway. It had taken several hours to get back from Southampton to the bridge club where their car was parked and another long stretch to get home. Roger and Jacqueline couldn't remember feeling so miserable.

The whole group had piled onto the coach in Southampton, chattering loudly about the trip and the unexpected events which had taken place. Everyone had crossed paths with Cynthia, you couldn't help it – she was one of those people you remembered meeting, however briefly.

The Sylvesters sat quietly at the back, each pretending to read the morning paper, but neither taking in one word of it. All efforts to strike up a conversation with them were ignored.

Once the coach stopped in the car-park of the bridge club, they hurriedly pushed to the front to get off, mumbling about feeling slightly travel sick and waving away any offers of assistance.

"My wife is feeling rather nauseous," Roger said to the driver, pushing a tenner into his hand. "I wonder if you could help me retrieve our cases first and we can be on our way, without further delay."

The driver looked at Roger and Jacqueline, making his own assessment of the situation. He remembered this man from the outward-bound journey and felt instantly irritated. Some people didn't give a damn how much inconvenience they cause to others. He pocketed the money and slowly got up from behind the wheel, taking a few minutes to have a stretch. He opened the doors and got off the coach, spending a further five minutes shaking his arms and legs, limbering up.

Roger watched him reach into his pocket and take out some paraphernalia to start rolling up a cigarette. He knew what this was all about but decided to say nothing. By this time, most of the other people had alighted and were standing around chatting quietly to Nick Lombardo.

Finally, the driver flicked his cigarette into the air and opened the luggage compartment, indicating for Roger to point to his luggage.

"I won't be able to find it under all of those bags, you might as well just unload it all and we'll help ourselves." Roger turned and walked away, deciding not to give the driver any more satisfaction.

———

The first thing Jacqueline noticed was that the heating had been switched on and the house was comfortably warm. A lovely 'Welcome home – I've missed you' note was on the kitchen table. Abby had also put some milk, butter, eggs and cheese in the fridge. A fresh crusty loaf and some croissant were in the bread bin. Jacqueline also noticed that the fruit bowl had been replenished and some ready meals placed in the freezer.

Over two cups of tea and a plate of chocolate digestives, Jacqueline and Roger stared at each other.

"I don't think we should go over to Abby's uninvited," Roger stated.

"I do. I think we should go as soon as we've finished our tea. There's no time to lose, as far as I'm concerned."

"If she wanted to see us, she would call, as she always does. Things might not be going so well; she and Alfie may be arguing. Now may not be a good time and you don't want to feel you're interfering, do you?" Roger was determined not to rush head on into anything.

"I couldn't care less whether or not I'm interfering. There are more pressing problems than that, wouldn't you say? Like keeping our daughter out of prison."

"Don't you think you're over-reacting?"

"Let me see now!" Jacqueline stood up and loomed menacingly over Roger. "My husband gets arrested; my daughter is running around pushing a dead body in a wheelchair which has been captured on CCTV and I want to go straight over to Abby's house and find out what it's all about. No, I don't think I'm over-reacting, Roger. I think you're in denial, as always."

"Well then we had better get ourselves ready to go - no time to lose. Shall we unpack first?"

———

Sandra grabbed the seat nearest to the front, just behind the driver. She didn't want to sit among people. She didn't want to talk or even argue with anyone. She wanted to be left completely alone. As far as she was concerned, the journey ended far too quickly. She would have been happy to sit on that coach for a week, rather than get home and decide what to do next.

She had spent so many years hating Cynthia, keeping a watchful eye on her to make sure her friend wasn't taking advantage that, right now, her life felt very empty. She had to admit Cynthia kept her very busy. How was she going to fill her?

While Cynthia was the butt of her insults, she was right in the middle of everything – she had a voice. It may have been a voice some people didn't want to hear, but she was vocal and insisted on being heard. She wasn't invisible like she feared she would be now. Feeding off her friend's huge personality would no longer sustain her.

She saw the Sylvester's were keeping themselves to themselves, and quite frankly she was pleased of it. If Roger had started a conversation with her, in the mood she was in, she would probably have been had up for assault. How did Jacqueline put up with him and his silly jokes? Sandra stared out of the window and sniggered to herself. One could look at the situation in two ways. Maybe the murderer had done Jacqueline a favour and her husband would now be fully returned, unscathed. Alternatively, he would get on her nerves full time, with no distraction.

Sandra saw Miranda about to get into Henry's car. She was such a lovely, understanding girl and quite mature for her age. Luckily, their relationship hadn't been damaged by all the drama. Sandra didn't know what she would have done without her. Things would have been so much worse if that were possible, without Miranda's calm, reassuring presence.

Lost in her own thoughts, she drifted off to sleep, only

to be woken by Roger trying to curry favour from the coach driver. The expression on the driver's face said it all. Sandra would normally take this as an opportunity to compound Roger's humiliation. Unusually for her, she decided to say nothing and let it all happen around her - she wasn't in a hurry.

She was the last person to get off the coach and walked, unnoticed, alone to her car. She noticed that Cynthia' sports car had been driven away from the car-park and that brought a lump in her throat. In happier times, they would have been bickering all the way to their respective vehicles. Mainly about the damage Cynthia's errant behaviour had caused and how it may or may not have impacted on Sandra's holiday.

Afterwards, she most likely would have driven to Cynthia's house and joined her in a simple snack of cheese on toast and the cycle would begin again.

She pulled into her driveway just as it started to rain, getting a bit soggy dragging her suitcase out of the boot and rushed to open the front door. The house felt cold and damp. She turned all the lights on and tried to make it feel homely.

She opened the fridge and suddenly remembered she should have stopped to buy some milk and a few provisions. There were two choices to make - either to go out again or make herself a black coffee. She found a tin of tomato soup in the cupboard and a packet of crackers to accompany the coffee – a veritable feast.

There was a message from her son and daughter-in-law on the answering machine and she called them straight away.

"Hello, Stephen, I'm back.".

"Oh good, Mum. We were so sorry to hear about Cynthia."

"Yes, it was rather shocking. I am, as you can imagine, distraught. How have you all been? It seems ages since I've seen my family."

Stephen hesitated, unused to his mother enquiring after all the family and it certainly *had* been ages since she had seen them. "We're all fine, thank you. I'm sure you had better weather than we did." He always struggled to make conversation with her.

"Would you like to come over on Sunday for lunch. I would love to see you all. I haven't made Sunday lunch for such a long time and you used to enjoy it. We have so much catching up to do. Just tell me how many of you are coming and I'll go shopping tomorrow."

The line was so quiet, Sandra thought they must have been disconnected. "Hello! Are you still there?"

Her son tried not to show that he was lost for words. He couldn't believe this pleasant person on the end of the phone, issuing an invitation for Sunday lunch was his mother. He was tempted to say something sarcastic but restrained himself.

"That would be great, Mum, thank you. We're looking forward to coming."

"Oh I'm so pleased. Shall we say one o'clock?"

He nearly fell off his sofa. On the rare occasions they were invited for lunch to his mother - and he couldn't remember the last time, they were summoned to attend at a certain time whether it was convenient or not. He was obviously going to have to persuade the family to go, but whatever happened on the ship to make his mother more approachable, he was determined to make the most of it.

"Yes, we'll see you then."

———

John Wood had always been clever. He was good in

business and particularly good at moving forward – knowing when one chapter had come to an end and a new one beginning.

He had plenty of time, sitting on his stateroom balcony, to analyse his feelings about this whole episode. He really needed to take stock of his priorities and he hadn't done much of that lately. After the years of hard slog at work with little respite, having fun was high on the agenda.

There wouldn't be a repeat of the larks he and Cynthia got up to with anyone else. He had firmly got it out of his system. How fortunate was he that his mid-life crisis, for that must have been what all this was about, had not caused the end of his happy marriage.

He had been dazzled by the bright lights of singledom and found them to be dim. Nothing was as lovely and rewarding as being in the bosom of his family - whyever did he think otherwise?

As he boarded the coach in Southampton and prepared for the journey back to the bridge club, he felt calm. He was ready to concentrate on his lovely wife and children and inject some excitement into their lives, rather than continue to pursue separate activities to fill the time. No! He definitely didn't want the sort of drama that he had just experienced, far from it. Something more humdrum would do, as long as they were all together.

He chatted a little to the other passengers. A considerable number had been briefly asked about their connection with Cynthia and had statements taken, but it had come to nothing. They were far more interested in discussing their own holiday stories.

He noticed the Sylvesters sitting at the back, whispering. There was no doubt in his mind that Roger had much to hide. He was a slippery, odious fellow and no amount of joking around and being the life and soul of the party would change that. He was rather glad he wouldn't have to see *him* again.

He would have driven straight onto the driveway, but a car was already parked on it and there were a few parked outside, too. He had to find a space further up the street and wheel his suitcase back towards the house.

He had left his door keys at home – one less thing to worry about - and rang the bell. He waited for some time, but nobody answered. He rang again, this time more urgently, but there still was no reply.

This was most unusual and rather depressing, he thought. It would have been nice if his wife had thrown open the front door and greeted him lovingly, immediately. He had, after all, kept her informed of his time of arrival.

He started to feel alarmed, wheeled his suitcase towards the side gate and turned the handle. Fortunately, it was open and he walked through into the garden.

He heard shrieks of laughter before he saw anyone. A long table, covered in a white cloth, was laden with food - beautifully prepared and presented. A young waitress was offering glasses of champagne to a small crowd milling about on the lawn.

She hurried up to him, smiling. "Hello darling, come and meet my friends. Everyone! This is my husband, John. He's just come back from a rather eventful cruise." There was a low rumble of laughter.

"Did you have a good journey back?" She didn't wait for John to answer. "You must be starving – I've made all your favourite things. It's lovely to see you."

She walked off to mingle with her friends and John reached for a glass of champagne and went to examine the delicious food on display. He imagined it would be more of an intimate homecoming. She hadn't mentioned the party to him on the phone and it really was the last thing he wanted.

Lavinia Wood was laughing at a joke one of her guests cracked and stole a glance at her husband. She would be watching him very closely from now on. She would not tolerate another strange, silly woman calling the house on a regular basis again.

———

Miranda's heart soared when she saw Henry waiting at the pick-up point outside the cruise terminal. She waved at everyone sitting on the coach, without looking at anyone in particular and threw herself into her beloved's arms.

He held her tightly and then his practical side kicked in and he started putting her suitcase into the boot, moving it around so it didn't hit the side and had plenty of space. She wished he would just get in the car and drive out of there.

"I know we've kept in touch and everything, but the enormity of what's been happening to you on the ship hasn't escaped me." Henry finally got in the car and put one arm around her shoulder as he skilfully manoeuvred it out of the car-park.

Miranda had fought it for so long, mindful that she had tried to be strong for everyone else around her who were dangerously close to losing the plot, that she immediately burst into floods of tears. "I'm sorry, Henry. I wanted to be upbeat and smiling for you, but it really has been awful. We all tried very hard to carry on. Nick Lombardo was brilliantly professional, running the bridge tournament as best he could. People kept being called away or felt a bit queasy at the thought of a murder."

"What about Sandra and the Sylvesters?" Henry asked.

"Roger and Jacqueline were very subdued. I suppose it probably hit Roger the hardest as he was Cynthia's preferred bridge partner. Jacqueline may well make him give up the game after this." Miranda almost felt sorry for him.

"I'm not surprised. His bubble was well and truly burst by Cynthia's death. It was very unlucky for him really."

"What do you mean 'unlucky'?"

Henry stopped smirking. "This is a lesson for anyone who thinks they can get away with deceit."

"We don't know that for sure, do we?" Miranda suddenly felt a bit guilty betraying Cynthia's secrets and making her sound so awful.

"I'm just going on the information you gave me. Anyway, it's not our place to second guess what happened to Cynthia. I'm sure the police will get to the bottom of it and make an arrest quite soon and what about the other philanderer?" Henry was being irritating by finding it all quite amusing.

"I'm not sure about John. I didn't see much of anyone once the ship docked. I wanted to get all the paperwork sorted out and jump off the ship as quickly as possible." Miranda snuggled up closer to Henry.

"You do know this is your fault, don't you?" Miranda looked at Henry accusingly.

"Yes, of course it is, but just remind me why?"

"If we had been on the ship together, such a horrible thing would never have happened."

"You're quite right, darling. I would have nabbed the assailant just before the murder had been committed and alerted security, already having tied them up with gaffer tape to await arrest."

"It wouldn't surprise me. I love you, Henry."

"It's very flattering that you think I'm so brave. Let's

get married."

"Yes, Let's."

———

"I just want to know why you don't love me?" Abby sat opposite Alfie at the breakfast bar and watched him drink his tea.

"I do love you, Abby, but you're a control freak."

"Why? Because I want to make a success of my life, both our lives and progress?"

"No, that's understandable, but you have to control everything and everyone, particularly me." Alfie's mobile rang and he took it out of his pocket to see the identity of the caller.

"Who is that?" Abby enquired pleasantly.

"Nobody important. Anyway, we're having a serious discussion about the future and that comes first."

That will make a change, Abby thought. "You could have taken control of your life, Alfie, but you seem to have chosen not to." She tried to make eye contact with him, but he wasn't looking at her.

"You see, that's exactly what I mean. *You* say I have chosen not to. That doesn't mean it's true."

"I would have done everything I could to make you happy, don't you know that?" Abby's eyes welled up with tears."

"I do know that Abby, but it's not working. I'm not happy. I feel suffocated. I think it's best we split up."

"What will you do? I would just like to know if you've already made plans."

Alfie felt relaxed. It was good that he could finally talk openly about his feelings. He had been bottling it up for ages.

"I've talked it over with my parents..."

"I thought you might have." Abby couldn't help interrupting.

"...And they have suggested that we split everything down the middle."

"Sorry, what do you mean by everything?"

Alfie was feeling a bit weary. "You know, the house and that."

"What exactly is 'that'?"

"I'll be able to buy something small, hopefully, with my share of this house, but I can't support myself, Abbs. You might have to set up a standing order to help me with expenses? Just until I get on my feet. The company can afford to pay for that, surely. You've really made a success of it. You're so clever."

"I'm sure we can sort something out. I've brought you something. I'm just going to get it. You stay right there."

"I'm not going anywhere. I'm going to stay right here." Alfie could feel himself drifting off, it must be the central heating was on too high and making him feel sleepy. He noticed Abby walking towards him pushing a wheelchair. How very strange.

"Where on earth did you get that? Who is it for? What are you up to now?"

Abby placed a towel on the seat and wrapped a black binbag across the back of the chair and handles. "It's for a project I'm doing at work. I just want to try something new. You sit in it for a minute and let me know if it's comfortable.

Alfie got off the stool. He was surprised at how wobbly he felt. "I think I'm coming down with something, I don't feel well at all."

"Then it's just as well I've procured something comfy for you to sit in."

He sat down heavily. "Very funny, Abbs." He hadn't

called her Abbs for ages and yet this was the second time in a few minutes. She wrapped her arms around him and hugged and kissed him. Tears started to trickle down her cheeks. She really had loved him and they could have been perfect together had things been different.

He looked up and smiled woozily at Abby, just as the iron came down hard and hit him in the face.

It was such a relief not to have to worry about the mess. She would have all the time in the world to clear it up. After bringing the iron down again and again with all her strength and probably unnecessarily, she wound the cord around Alfie's neck and pulled, putting on the wheelchair breaks to hold it steady.

Once again, the nylon wig, topped off with a sports cap, did its job in concealing her handiwork. She stripped off her clothes and put them all in a black bag, changing into something more suitable for walking across a field. The hard part was lowering the wheelchair out of the side door of the kitchen and along the path towards the front of the house.

———

Roger and Jacqueline pulled up outside the cottage, turned off the engine and waited.

"The house looks deserted."

"What did you expect - a brass band? A welcoming committee?" Roger felt nervous. How was he going to broach the subject to his daughter.

"Hello, sweetheart. Are you the shipboard murderer that the police are looking for?" He supposed he could pretend he was joking and take it from there. It had worked for the last forty odd years.

"Actually yes, I am waiting for a welcoming committee because that's what we usually have, Roger. The lights are on, the house looks cosy and Abby hears the car and rushes out to see us. That's always been the routine and I'm scared."

"Don't be scared, darling. I'm sure it will be fine. They're obviously home. Maybe we should go. If they're having a row, they won't want to be putting the kettle on now, will they?"

"I just don't think they're happy, Roger." Jacqueline sobbed, fumbling in her handbag for a tissue.

"No, Jacqueline, I don't think they are, but they won't be the first couple to be miserable. Why don't we wait until we all get together and see what she wants to do about it, instead of sweeping it under the carpet?"

Roger was about to start the engine when they both noticed activity at the side gate. Before their eyes, a scene unfolded they thought they would never see.

———

DI Edward Springer hoped he had all the evidence he needed. He was sure that even the best criminal lawyer in the land couldn't defend this client from prosecution.

He had to admit Abby Castleford had been either very clever or pretty desperate. It was clear, watching the CCTV footage and reading the forensic report, that she had just made it up as she went along and hoped for the best because it was such a simply executed plan and it nearly worked.

He had the feeling that Abby wasn't really bothered whether she got caught or not. If it hadn't been that her fingerprints and partial palm print had been on record for a little bit of criminal shoplifting that she had been involved in at school, he might have found it much harder to make the evidence stick. Evidence on board ship is easily missed, cleaned away or compromised. Abby was relying on that.

Abby Castleford had no reason to kill Cynthia Manning, but Abby Sylvester thought she had a very good reason. The phone calls and messages leading directly to Abby's mobile, a broken finger nail sticking on the iron for dear life, prints and blood on the iron and cord that should have been washed away by the Mediterranean - too many leads to be circumstantial. It was certainly a good start and hopefully the addition of Roger and Jacqueline Sylvester's evidence that they had recognised the woman pushing Cynthia around the ship's deck late at night.

Assistant Superintendent Samuel James had a very good instinct about the people he interviewed and had left copious notes that Edward could follow up. Samuel had been adamant that the Sylvesters had both recognised the strangely dressed woman in the footage, although Mr. Sylvester, during his interview, had been very keen to conceal this fact by blustering his way through.

It's always sad when a case unfolds and the motive is a drastic attempt to safeguard a family. Often, the perpetrator is a member struggling to keep it all together, however, cynically Edward thought it was more the desire to have their cake and eat it.

After so many years and thousands of cases, Edward Springer could understand how a person would do anything to save the one thing or person they loved most in the world from being stolen or destroyed by an interloper, particularly from someone who would do damage just for the thrill of it.

However, the law is the law and thank God for that. Edward Springer would be sending a team to arrest Abby Castleford for murder as soon as possible.

———

Roger leapt out of the car, shouting his daughter's

name. When Abby saw him sprinting towards her, she burst into tears.

"What's going on, what do you think you're doing?" Roger bent down to have a closer look at the person in the wheelchair.

"I had to do it, Daddy, he was going to ruin everything we had worked so hard for. That was what he was after all along, you know. He wasn't in love with me at all. They told him to do it." Abby blurted it all out.

"Is that Alfie? Who told him to do it?" Roger wrapped his arms around her. They were both sobbing. "We have to call an ambulance right now."

"His parents. They cooked this up between them."

"I don't understand, Abby."

"He's been hanging around doing nothing for months. I caught him with another woman and I'm sure there have been others. I had to stop it, Daddy, you do see that don't you?"

"Put the phone down, Roger. Let's think about what we're going to do." Jacqueline was trying to buy some time.

Roger stared at Alfie, almost folded in half sitting in the wheelchair. Blood was trickling down his face and the incongruous head covering had slipped to one side.

"What do you mean 'think about what to do.' Isn't it obvious? We have to call an ambulance."

Roger put his arms around his daughter, but not before she saw the tears roll down his cheeks. "You killed Cynthia, didn't you? I prayed to God I was wrong, but you did it. I can see that now." Roger was staring disbelievingly at Alfie, willing him to moan, move, twitch, do something – anything to show some sign of life.

"I wasn't going to kill her. I was going to talk to her. *We* were going to talk to her – all of us, like we always do.

That's how we've always sorted things out, haven't we Mummy? Daddy?"

"Why didn't you speak to me? Tell me how you were feeling? I would have done anything."

"Anything not to get caught, Daddy. That's part of who you are."

Abby ignored the horrified look on her parents' faces. "I tried to talk to Cynthia, but in my heart I knew it would be a waste of time – just like it would have been to talk it through with you. I knew there was only one thing to be done."

"No, Abby, not if I knew how desperate you were feeling. Cynthia meant nothing to me."

"She didn't think so. She thought she meant everything. She was so arrogant, so sure that you would sacrifice us both for her. I couldn't take the risk. Mummy, you understand, don't you? I love you both with all my heart, you're my whole world."

Roger had never seen his darling wife so broken. Jacqueline's face was white and there were beads of sweat on her forehead. She couldn't take her eyes off her son-in-law in the wheelchair.

Roger and Jacqueline looked at each other and then at their daughter. This time, there was nothing they could do to save her.

In the distance, they heard a police siren and people started to appear from neighbouring properties.

"Give me that."

Roger grabbed the handles of the wheelchair. The pains in his chest that had started on the way over to his daughter were getting worse. He started to push it hurriedly away from the house towards the fields. He had to cover as much distance as possible.

"It's okay, we're all fine." Jacqueline shouted, trying to

shoo people back into their houses. "Everything's under control – we're just waiting for an ambulance."

"We have to say Daddy did it." Jacqueline took her daughter's face in both hands. "We have to get our story straight."

"No, that's crazy." Abby couldn't believe her ears.

"He did this to us, Abby. He knows that he's responsible. He intends to tell the police that he murdered Alfie. You have to let me do the talking."

Abby nodded and smiled weakly. She had no intention of allowing her father to take the blame. Putting her arms around her mother's waist, they both waited for the police to arrive.

Printed in Great Britain
by Amazon